Her Wolf's Guarded Heart

Weres & Witches of Silver Lake
Book 10

Vella Day

Her Wolf's Guarded Heart
Copyright © 2017 by Vella Day
Print Edition
www.velladay.com
velladayauthor@gmail.com

Cover Art by Jaycee DeLorenzo
Edited by Rebecca Cartee and Carol Adcock-Bezzo

Published in the United States of America

E-book ISBN: 978-1-941835-46-3
Print book ISBN: 978-1-941835-48-7

A deadly secret and an over-the-top curiosity is a dangerous thing.

Protecting beautiful women is one of the perks of being a security expert. But when your wolf insists she's your mate, it can be pure hell. Mate or not, Connor McKinnon is here to do a job, and he means to see it through. His wolf can just go chase his own tail for all he cares.

EmmaLee Donovan's bodyguard might be hotter than sin, but he's stubborn, guarded, and doesn't share her passion for all things paranormal. How ironic is that? He's a shifter for heaven's sake! Not only is he nothing like her abusive ex-boyfriend, the man is absolutely mouthwateringly irresistible.

After she and Connor stumble across the path of a larger-than-life killer, she ends up on a passionate journey of self-discovery that she may not survive. Murder and mayhem ensue, and no matter how much she believes in gods and goddesses, the only way out of this mess is to trust Connor—and the instincts that say he's the one.

Beneath the calm and shimmering surface lie intrigue, power, magic, and danger.
Welcome to Silver Lake—where appearances can be deceiving, and what you see isn't truly what lies below.

Chapter One

To learn about Vella Day's other new releases, contests, and find new authors, subscribe to her newsletter and get three free books!

An Unexpected Diversion (book 1 of Hidden Hills Shifters)
Bare Instincts (book 2 of Hidden Hills Shifters)
Montana Desire (book 1 of Rock Hard, Montana)

"I'M NOT LEAVING town." EmmaLee Donovan planted a hand on her hip as she spun around to face her bodyguard, Connor McKinnon—a bodyguard her best friend, Vinea Summers, had insisted she use.

As much as EmmaLee appreciated his help in keeping her safe, now that her injuries had fully healed, it was time to take back control of her life. It didn't matter that her ex-boyfriend had beaten her up in this very apartment; she had to remain in town in order to continue her important research. She hadn't worked all these years for a master's degree only to leave right before she finished her thesis.

Connor ground his teeth together. "Slater Coghill is still out there. Do you want him to come after you again? The next time he might kill you."

"You're exaggerating." Slater was too scared to attack her again—or so she wanted to believe. "With the cops looking for him, he won't come near me. The idea of being penned up in a jail cell frightens him."

Connor quirked an eyebrow and continued. "I'm glad to know

he has one redeeming quality, but if you're dead, you won't be around to testify."

Now he was being ridiculous. "Slater's not a killer. He just has a bad temper."

"Bad temper, huh? He ruptured your spleen." He inhaled deeply then glanced to the side as if trying to come up with a good argument as to why she should move to another state. "Are you still in love with him? Is that it? Do you secretly want him to come back?" His voice escalated as his Adam's apple bobbed.

She had to blink, to make sure she had seen hair sprout on his face and not just imagined it. EmmaLee should be angry over his ridiculous comment, but he had some basis for his opinion. She had let Slater back into her life, time and time again, since her ex was an expert at apologizing. The last beating, however, had taught her a lesson: at all costs, avoid slick talking men who seem to have a good heart, but who are tortured by unseen demons.

Connor stepped even closer, and her pulse sped up just like it always did whenever he was near. It was similar to the visceral reaction she had with Slater, except that with Connor, the sensation was more intense and far more enjoyable. Perhaps she reacted so strongly to him because his eyes were more startling than Slater's. Right now, Connor's were hazel streaked with amber, but she doubted it meant this werewolf was interested in her—merely furious.

All he'd done in the last few weeks was grunt and growl when she came too close or if she suggested leaving her tiny apartment. "No, I'm over Slater. He can burn in hell for all I care."

The muscles in Connor's face softened. "Then what's the attraction of living in Billard?"

EmmaLee lifted her chin. "I've already told you. Not only do I make my living here, I need to finish my thesis."

"You can finish it in Silver Lake. We do have Internet there."

"You don't understand. There is a world-renowned professor coming for one semester to shed some light on dinosaurs and their possible link to dragons. I've already paid the tuition. I believe that what he's recently uncovered while doing an archaeological dig in Africa will be the final piece to my thesis." She held her breath, waiting for the ridicule that was sure to come.

"Are you saying you want to learn if dragons exist? Or rather existed? Is that where your stubbornness stems from?" Connor huffed then turned his back, but she refused to address the ache in her heart.

The only person aside from her thesis advisor she'd confided in about her research had been Slater. The strange part was that her former boyfriend never mocked her belief in werewolves or werebears, but he did when she spoke of dragons—just like Connor was doing now.

"I'm not saying dragons per se exist, but that dragon shifters do. A real dragon couldn't hide for long."

When he finally faced her again, one side of his mouth lifted upward. He was obviously fighting a smile. Heaven forbid if that look was one of disgust. "What makes you think a dragon shifter exists?"

EmmaLee didn't know why she bothered explaining anything to this pigheaded man, but he claimed he was a shifter—the first one she'd met—and her curiosity about him and others of his kind was still off the charts.

"I've seen a picture of one. While I couldn't pinpoint the location, the background has the same type of hills and tall pines found around here. It's possible one might be lurking nearby." She'd only told the cops what she'd seen that fateful day when she was twelve, and their response convinced her to never mention it again.

"And you're willing to put your life in jeopardy because of a photograph you saw on the Internet?" He stabbed a hand through his hair.

Sarcasm didn't suit him. "As I said, it's for my thesis."

"What are you getting your degree in?"

"History, with a specialty in Lore and Legends."

He chuckled. "Do you hear yourself, Lore and Legends? The

words imply that it's all make-believe."

"To you maybe, but I want to prove that werewolves, werebears, and weredragons exist. Don't worry—I won't reveal that I know a real life goddess or that my bodyguard is a shifter."

"Anyone can claim to be one. Can you really be sure I am a werewolf?" Connor asked with a challenging tone.

"Yes. I've seen your eyes change color and your facial hair grow. But don't worry, I won't tell anyone."

He held up a hand. "Thank you. We really don't need the world to know we exist. The panic alone could have dire consequences."

So she'd been told. "I will be discreet. As for whether dragon shifters exist, I'll show you why I believe they are here with us."

EmmaLee was taking a big chance in revealing what she'd found, but given he was a werewolf, Connor couldn't deny that paranormal beings existed. In her heart, she hoped he might provide her with some insight. Even if he could show her why the picture was a fake, she'd be closer to the truth. She wasn't ready to show him her real proof just yet.

EmmaLee ducked into her bedroom, knelt by her bed, and pulled out the box from underneath. Her fingers hovered over the tangible evidence for a moment then lifted the photo she had printed off the Internet and returned to the living room. "Here it is."

Connor studied it. "I only see part of a dragon, or rather what someone might say looks like one."

"I'm guessing the photographer had to hide and as a result didn't have a good angle for the shot."

"I can buy that. The head might have the right shape, and the scales are quite realistic, but the part of the wing we can see looks a tad oversized."

How would he know? Unless.... Her pulse sped up. "So you believe me? You told me you've never seen one before, or were you holding back?"

He handed her the photo. "No. In all seriousness, it's too blurry to tell much. If I had to guess, I'd say it's someone in a costume."

EmmaLee tried not to let her shoulders slump. After all, she had expected him to claim it was a fake. "I take it no one in your Clan has ever mentioned anything about dragon shifters?"

"No."

"What if I said I believed in giraffe shifters or even otter shifters? Would you still be so skeptical?"

She thought he'd say no right away, but he did seem to think about it. "I suppose if the animal exists in the real world, it's possible a shifter could exist too."

"If you met a dragon shifter in human form, would you be able to tell he was one?"

"I would know he was a shifter, but I can't tell what kind he is—whether it be a werebear or a werewolf," Connor said, his confidence deflating. "You've not met her, but the mate of one of the men who works in my office can tell the difference."

But not him. "So when you run into a person who is a shifter, you assume it is one of the more common varieties, right?" She rushed on. "Which means you might have met a dragon shifter and not even known it?"

He held up his palms in surrender. "Okay, fine. A dragon shifter could exist."

From the flash of black shooting through those amber-brown eyes, he clearly thought she was just some kooky waitress and part time student who lived in the world of make believe. Oh, well. She had to ask to know for sure.

No matter what she said or did, he'd never change his mind. And if he didn't believe in her passion, she saw no reason to ask him to stay any longer. After all, he wasn't here to date her, merely to protect her. While it was wonderful to have him around, it wasn't fair to ask him to put his life on hold forever. He did have a company to run in another state.

It was also possible Slater would never show his face again since he had a bounty on his head. As Connor pointed out, Slater might want to make sure she couldn't testify against him—assuming he was caught. The uncertainty was driving her crazy.

One reason why he should leave was that after that last attack, the goddess Vinea claimed she'd given EmmaLee the ability to ward off Slater, but unfortunately she had no way of testing that theory. EmmaLee debated letting Connor in on that little secret, but to be honest she liked having him around. He intrigued her. His eyes were pools of mystery, and while his nose was strong and straight, his full lips were slightly uneven, making him look like he had a permanent scowl—something she found sexy as hell.

She'd fallen for Slater because he was charming and way too good-looking for his own good, and it was the same with Connor. Her friends were right to claim she was a sucker for a pretty face.

Okay that settled it. Because she understood her own weakness, Connor needed to leave, and she needed to get back to finishing her research and then polishing her thesis.

"If you'll excuse me," she said. "I need to make a call."

"Who are you calling?" Connor's body tensed.

"Not Slater, if that's what you're thinking." She didn't want to keep secrets. "I need to discuss something with Vinea."

His shoulders relaxed. "About?"

The man would never stop. "Girl stuff."

"Oh. Well, tell her and Devon I said hello."

"Can do."

Once in her bedroom, she closed the door. Because shifters had good hearing, she walked to the far end of the room and pulled up a chair before dialing her friend.

The cell rang only once before she picked up. "EmmaLee? How are you?" Vinea sounded genuinely excited to hear from her.

"Good. Hey, I need your advice."

"Sure. Is Connor driving you crazy or something?"

She almost chuckled. "No, but I can't ask him to stay here any longer when I know he has a business to run. Physically, I'm good as new, and Slater hasn't been seen anywhere."

"I'm glad to hear it. How are you holding up emotionally

though? Sitting on pins and needles waiting for him to return?"

How well her friend knew her. "Kind of, but I know Connor can take care of him if he does show up."

"I'm getting the sense that while you feel guilty keeping Connor there, you want him to stay."

EmmaLee did love Vinea. She always cut to the chase. "Yes. I know that once he leaves I'll miss his protective presence, but that isn't a good enough reason to ask him to put his life on hold."

She wouldn't mention that Connor starred in her nightly dreams. The man was this sleek animal, full of hot muscles, tightly wound, and ready for action. He moved with such grace it constantly made her fantasize about what he'd be like in bed. That unleashed power of emotion, if tapped, could be amazing, and she had no doubt he could wake up every cell in her body if he ever touched her intimately.

"What does Connor want to do?" Vinea asked.

"Go back to Silver Lake and take me with him."

"Ooh, that sounds promising."

EmmaLee stood and then paced. "Remember, I'm almost finished with my thesis, so I don't want to leave."

"Let me ask you this. Do you like Connor?"

This wasn't about her feelings for him. It was about what she'd worked so hard for. "Of course I do, but just because he is hotter than sin doesn't mean he's someone I should drop everything for. It's not like he's Mr. Perfect; he's far from it." She leaned her head back and glanced to the ceiling, hoping it would provide her with answers. "Fact of the matter is that he and Slater have a lot of traits in common besides their handsome faces and sophisticated ways."

"You're comparing them now? Trust me. Connor is absolutely nothing like Slater."

"For the most part that might be true, but both men are skeptics when it comes to dragon shifters, and they both keep too many secrets. I need to tell him to go."

EmmaLee admitted that she would fall for him if he stayed

much longer. She also recognized that even though Connor wasn't the violent type toward women, he'd move on and she'd be hurt once more. No, it was time to break that cycle.

"Think of the bright side," Vinea said. "Silver Lake is full of shifters. You could get firsthand knowledge about how they live and what their secret talents are. It could be a huge boon to your research."

She dropped down onto the bed. The temptation to take Connor up on his offer tantalized her. "I've thought about that."

"Connor might be a skeptic, but one of the men who works for him, Jackson Murdoch, is not. You could learn a lot from him."

Vinea was only making this harder. "I'll think about it. Thanks. How are you feeling?"

"I'm still having morning sickness." She chuckled. "You'd think that since I'm a goddess, I'd be immune to those usual human issues."

That made EmmaLee laugh. "You'd think. Otherwise, you're happy?"

"Happier than I thought I could ever be."

They talked a little bit longer and then Vinea had to go. Once they hung up, EmmaLee stayed in her bedroom, trying to decide what she should do. After much thought, she stepped back into the living room.

"Everything go okay?" Connor asked. "Is Vinea doing well?"

"Yes, she still has a bit of morning sickness, but she's good otherwise. Listen, we need to talk." Connor moved closer, disrupting her thoughts. *Focus.* "I appreciate all you've done for me, but since I'm healed, there's no reason for you to hang around," she said with as much compassion as she could muster. Unfortunately, her stupid lips wouldn't stop trembling. "I know you have a company to run back in Silver Lake."

He crossed his arms and widened his feet. All he needed were dark sunglasses and an earpiece and he could pass for an FBI agent. "I'm not leaving you."

The force with which he delivered that statement surprised and delighted her, but EmmaLee didn't dare hope it was because he liked her.

He doesn't—not really. In the few weeks he'd been babysitting her, he hadn't as much as tried to steal a kiss or rub up against her accidentally on purpose. The opposite in fact had happened. He seemed to avoid her whenever possible, though he rarely succeeded. Her postage stamp size apartment was just too damn small. She didn't want him to like her, as that would complicate things. If he told her he cared, she'd be a goner faster than he could shift.

"EmmaLee? Are you okay?" His sympathetic tone snapped her out of her daydreaming.

What had he just said? Oh, yes—he wasn't leaving. "Why won't you go?"

"The reason doesn't matter." Connor looked conflicted as he stabbed a hand over his short dark hair.

He had a hidden agenda, and she wanted to know what it was. "This is my life, and I think I have a right to know why you won't let me live it!"

Connor got right in her face and growled. "I won't be responsible for another death!"

Chapter Two

"WHAT ARE YOU talking about?" EmmaLee asked.

Breathing heavily, Connor stepped back, putting some space between them. "A few years ago someone died under my watch, and it was my fault. I never want a repeat of that experience for as long as I live."

The pain in his voice nearly sliced her heart in two. "How was it your fault?"

He scrubbed a hand down his jaw. "My first job in the security business was to protect a woman who had a restraining order against her abusive ex-husband."

The abusive part resembled her situation, making her inwardly wince. "I take it that piece of paper didn't stop him?"

"No."

"What did he do?"

"He killed her."

Her heart snapped. "How? Weren't you there?" She hadn't meant to blurt that out.

"No. I'd received a tip about his location, and because he'd already tried to speak with my client twice, I needed to find him and drag his ass to jail. I told Mrs. Andrews I'd be gone less than an hour. Mind you, I insisted that she lock her doors and not let anyone in, no matter who it was. When I didn't locate him, I rushed back to her house, but Caroline was already dead."

EmmaLee sucked in a breath. "I'm so sorry."

"So am I. The lead detective claimed rumor had it that someone had purposefully lured me away. The saddest part was that there was no sign of forced entry."

"Which means that she let him in, right?" EmmaLee stepped over to the small living room sofa and sat down.

"Yes." He moved next to her, short-circuiting her thoughts once more.

This Caroline woman probably couldn't say no to her ex-husband any more than EmmaLee had been able to turn down Slater. "It wasn't your fault."

She reached out and stroked Connor's arm to comfort him, but he pulled away. That hurt. His touch affected her more than she thought possible.

Connor huffed out a breath. "I should have asked for backup or not left her in the first place. Hopefully, you can see why I am not going to have another beating or death on my conscience."

So Connor was here out of guilt, and not because he'd grown fond of her. That was just as well. Regardless, she couldn't ask him to put his life on hold for her. Damn. What was she to do?

EMMALEE GLANCED AWAY, probably trying to decide if she trusted him enough to truly protect her. A moment later, she returned her gaze to his face.

"I've been selfish," she said.

That wasn't what he thought she'd say. "What do you mean?"

"I can see you're determined to stay if I don't leave town with you, so I'm going to ask my boss if he can handle losing another waitress. He's been struggling to keep his staff, and I didn't want to be the one to add more pressure to his life, but it can't be helped."

He hadn't expected that concession either, but he was pleased. "Thank you. I don't understand your change of heart, but I'm glad for it. When do you think you could speak with him?"

She chuckled. "I hadn't realized you were in such a hurry."

"I'm not. It's just that—"

EmmaLee held up a hand. "I get it. You're in charge of a lot of cases. I appreciate all the time you've spent with me already. I owe you."

He didn't need her sympathy, though he enjoyed her gratitude. "Just so I'm clear, this means you'll come back with me to Silver Lake, right?"

"Yes," EmmaLee said, lifting her chin.

His animal howled, rejoicing in the fact they could be together for a while longer. "That's great."

She pressed her lips together. "I doubt I'll need to be there for long though since I'm sure Slater will be caught soon."

She acted as if it would be unpleasant to have him watch her longer than necessary. Here he'd thought her reluctance to move had been because of her research and not because she didn't care for him. No one could blame him for thinking otherwise. She always seemed to watch him with hunger in her eyes.

His wolf harrumphed. *You actually believe that? You've been nothing but an ass to her.*

Connor did not respond to his horny animal. "I can't promise we'll catch Slater in a few days though. You might have to stay there for a while." *A long while.*

She lifted one shoulder. "I know, but I can hope, can't I? In case the cops are successful, I won't cancel my lease here right away."

"It might take months to bring him down." Connor was pleased he succeeded in hiding his disappointment. He wanted to spend more time with her and get to know her better, especially when they'd be in a place where she didn't have to look over her shoulder all the time, wondering if Slater would come back.

"You think?" She pulled her ponytail over her shoulder and pressed the ends against her lips. It made him lose focus, wanting it to be his lips that touched hers.

Then kiss her, his wolf begged. *She's our mate.*

Stop it, he warned his horny animal.

I didn't do anything. I just wanted to remind you how important she is to us.

Like he could forget?

"Tracking people who want to avoid being found takes time."

"So does finding a cheap apartment, especially one so close to the diner."

Her logic was sound. "You're probably right. Besides, if Slater does return and peeks inside, he'll believe you're coming back. Maybe he'll hang out in Billard and wait for you."

She wrapped her arms around her shoulders. "Thinking about him skulking around here gives me the creeps, but I have no reason to believe he will return."

"We can't chance that." As much as Connor yearned to give her comfort, he couldn't. His wolf would go wild if he pressed her against his chest.

"I know."

"I realize this is hard for you, but it's for the best." He cleared his throat. "Ready to see what your boss has to say?"

"Sure."

EmmaLee and Connor drove over to the diner to discuss her imminent departure. Halfway there, she twisted in her seat to face him. "Now that I'm feeling healthy again, do you think I could work a few days before we leave, so I can earn some money? If I don't have an income source, it'll be expensive to pay for this apartment and be on the run."

"No can do."

"Why not?" There went that challenging tone again.

"I can't watch you every second when you're at work. At some point you'll have to step into the kitchen to pick up an order. Slater could lure you away."

"I won't let him."

Of course she'd say that. "What if you have to empty the trash in the back alley and he jumps out at you, injects you with some drug, and then kidnaps you?"

She turned back around and stared out the window for the next two miles. "Fine. We can leave whenever you want."

"Thank you."

To his delight, her boss, Drew Nemlin, agreed with him that EmmaLee should leave town. Slater wasn't a good man, he'd said. "Take as long as you need, but I can't promise your job will be here when you return," her boss said. "I still remember that Vinea thought she'd only be gone a short time, and she left for good."

"I know. That's why I'm okay with you hiring someone else if you need to. I'll understand."

Connor could almost feel the disappointment pouring off her, but to her credit, she held her head high.

"Thank you," Drew said.

"I don't want the girls to have to take extra shifts just because I have to hide out for a while, anymore than you do."

They chatted a bit, and Connor finally had to place a hand on her back. "EmmaLee, it's time we get going."

She nodded. "Give me a sec, okay?" She rushed up to each of the waitresses and hugged them goodbye. Even he was moved when a few tears were exchanged. It was clear her kindness had affected so many people.

For a moment, he wanted to give in and let her stay a little longer, but common sense reminded him that they should have left last week. He'd only remained because his damn wolf had insisted on it. His animal claimed that being in such close proximity with his mate would help them bond.

That had been a big fail. All the delay had accomplished was make Connor grumpier. Her lilac scent and cheerful ways had caused him to want her even more. But damn it, he couldn't act as if she meant a lot to him when he had a job to do.

Bullshit, his wolf threw out.

What are you talking about? His wolf was growing more discontent by the day, and Connor was tired of his constant interference.

This isn't really about the job and you know it. You just suck at dealing with your emotions, his wolf chided. *You want to tell her she's our mate, but you're chicken.*

You're wrong. Not only is she not ready for another relationship, it's my job to protect her, not have sex with her. Once we take down Slater, I'll show her what she means to us. Assuming she wants us.

Be in denial, his wolf shot back.

Whatever. Connor would explain to EmmaLee at some point why he kept his distance and why it had been pure torture being so near and not touching her. Knowing her history with men, he couldn't just blurt it out. She'd run. Then he would be devastated.

After giving him the cold shoulder while EmmaLee packed, they piled into his SUV, ready for their three and a half hour drive to Tennessee. While he was thankful she'd only taken two suitcases and not half the apartment, he was concerned she believed she'd be returning shortly. Now wasn't the time to discuss their future however.

"Buckle up," he said.

Without a word, she did as he asked. Seeing her miffed made leaving all the harder, but it couldn't be helped.

EmmaLee stared out the window as he pulled down her drive. "Just so you know, I don't have enough money to pay for an apartment in Silver Lake," she said with a curt tone.

It wasn't as if she could move in with him. He'd never get any work done if she did.

"I've got it covered. My parents have a guesthouse you can stay in. It was where Vinea lived when she was there."

EmmaLee twisted toward him. "I thought she had rented a trailer."

"Only at first." His brother Devon had seen to her change in accommodations once he admitted they were mates.

"Then thank you. That would be wonderful."

At the sudden cheer in her voice, he glanced over at her, and EmmaLee's smile lit up his insides.

While she was usually a chatterbox, once they were on the road, she clammed up again. She seemed to be having second thoughts. He wanted to remind her again that if she had stayed behind, Slater might return and either beg her to take him back or make certain she wasn't around any longer to prosecute him.

Connor could only hope the man lacked the skills to find her. If Slater did locate her, Connor would make sure it was the last thing the man ever did.

Chapter Three

THE LONG DRIVE gave EmmaLee time to think about Slater, Connor, and her research. She had been harsh with Connor—or rather she'd been a bit too stubborn—regarding her desire to stay in Billard. The Internet was everywhere. Her research was important but not more important than her life.

Be honest, Em.

Okay, the real reason she'd been hesitant to spend more time with Connor was that there was something about her bodyguard that made her want to hug him, tell him everything would be okay, and then give him some love. Why he needed it, she wasn't sure. From what Vinea said, the McKinnon parents were loving and wonderful. The problem was if he rebuffed her, she'd be devastated.

Sure, Connor might have made a tactical error with that woman Caroline Andrews, but he seemed to be dealing with other issues too and had bottled them up. She was no psychologist, but all this turmoil couldn't be good for his health. As much as she would have enjoyed peeling back his hard exterior, it would only make her want him more. In the end, she decided to steel her heart against his bad boy charm. She just wasn't strong enough to resist him.

So why had she agreed to go with Connor to Silver Lake? Her sympathy for him had won out. Hopefully that hadn't been a critical error on her part.

EmmaLee glanced over at him, his eyes straight ahead and focused on the road. All through Georgia, his hands had a firm grasp on the wheel, as if he feared relaxing them, even for one second, would result in something bad happening.

Once they crossed the Tennessee border however, the deep etched lines around his eyes and mouth softened. It was as if he believed they'd finally be safe from Slater—at least for a while—and his improved attitude helped her anxiety levels too.

Three and a half hours after leaving Billard, they arrived in Silver Lake, and she was quite impressed with the little town. Compared to Billard, the sidewalks were cleaner, the shops had newer looking awnings, and the business signs appeared to have been freshly painted. Maybe staying here would be a nice change. Yes, it would be tough to lose her income for a few weeks, but EmmaLee had paid April's rent in advance, giving her some financial security.

Her coworkers always accused EmmaLee of finding the proverbial silver lining in everything, but right now she was struggling. All she could come up with was that this move would allow her to see Connor in a different light—as a leader of men, a controller of fate—and possibly learn more about shifters in general. She wasn't sure how she could make it happen, but she'd love to watch him interact with the men who worked for him to see if he was as distant with them as he often was with her.

The downside to being here was not only the loss of income, it was not being in Billard when the archaeologist, Wilmer Crenely, came to town. He had discovered some ancient bones in Africa that were believed to be flying dinosaurs, claiming they might be the precursors to dragons. Dragons!! She could only hope that in the coming week or two she might be able to video chat with him.

"EmmaLee?" Connor asked.

She jerked her attention back to him. "Yes?"

"This is Silver Lake's Main Street."

She'd figured as much. "I like it. It's very charming."

One side of his lips hitched upward. "I like it too."

They passed by some restaurants, a hardware store, and a rather brightly colored flower shop. Once through town, the area turned more rural. While the leaves had yet to sprout on the dormant trees, the many pines gave the roadside a welcome splash of green.

She'd never asked how far out of town his parents lived, but when he pulled through a gated entrance about two miles past the center, she couldn't be more pleased. "This is really beautiful."

"Thanks." Connor nodded toward a side street. "Down that road is my house."

Butterflies beat against her stomach. She'd be close to him, but she couldn't be sure if that would be a good or a bad thing. Close meant he could check up on her if she decided to go for a walk, making her feel as if she lived in a fishbowl. The good part was that she might see him interact with his friends and maybe even his family.

The road turned to hard packed dirt. One block later, a two-story brick home, surrounded by elegant landscaping appeared at the end of a paved drive. He turned in.

"Your parents live here?"

He chuckled. "Yes."

Wow! Without further explanation, he headed a hundred feet past the house where another home appeared. The one-story brick house matched the larger home in style, though not in size. "It's really cute," she said.

Connor pulled to a stop. "I'm glad you like it."

He slipped out of the SUV, and she waited for him to open her door. When they were in Billard, he'd insisted she not jump out and become a target. Even though she doubted that applied here, she waited for him, appreciating that he still wanted to keep her safe.

Slater never opened my door.

Stop comparing them that little voice in her head said.

Once inside the guesthouse, he led her through the living room to the bedroom. "It's small," he said, "but it should suit your needs."

"Small? You saw my place."

Connor had the decency to smile. "You have a point."

Deciding to unpack later, she followed him back through the

living room into the kitchen. The rooms were open-concept, making them look large in the quaint home. Connor stepped over to the refrigerator and pulled it open. "I see my mom has been here."

EmmaLee sidled next to him and peeked in. The fridge was stocked with eggs, milk, bread, cheese, and an assortment of fruit. "She bought all this? For me?"

Before he could comment, someone knocked on the door. When he didn't tense, she figured he knew who it was.

"Must be my mom. She probably saw me drive in." Connor opened the front door and once more EmmaLee followed him.

"Hey, Mom." He kissed the older woman on the cheek then lifted something from her hands. "Come on in."

As soon as his mother stepped in, Mrs. McKinnon's gaze shot to her. "You must be EmmaLee."

"I am." She ran a hand over her mussed blonde hair. This was not how she'd expected to meet the family—tired looking and without makeup.

His mother was tall and trim, making EmmaLee wonder if shifters resembled their animal counterpart. Would werebears be quite large and dragons enormous? If she had been a shifter, she wondered what she'd have been. A fox perhaps? Assuming there was a blonde fox breed.

When his mom hugged her, EmmaLee tensed, mostly because she wasn't used to affection. The aunt she lived with certainly never gave her much.

"Welcome to Silver Lake," Mrs. McKinnon said.

"Thank you."

"Is Dad home?" Connor asked, placing the casserole his mother had brought with her on the kitchen counter.

"He is."

"Would you mind chatting with EmmaLee while I speak to him about something? I'll only be a few minutes."

This was totally uncharacteristic of him. He never trusted anyone before to watch over her.

"I'd be happy to."

Since his mom was also a werewolf, she probably could defend both of them against Slater. As soon as Connor left, his mom faced her. "I'm so glad Connor was able to convince you to move here. I know how hard it must have been to leave your old life behind."

She sounded like she believed EmmaLee would be here permanently. "I merely took a leave of absence. As soon as the man who attacked me is caught, I will return home."

A dark shadow crossed her face but disappeared as quickly. "If Connor has anything to do with it, the man will be as good as gone. Have you two had lunch?" Her tone switched from proud yet serious to upbeat.

"No." After they spoke with Drew, Connor had made her pack then rush out.

"Then how about some now? I made a casserole."

EmmaLee was blown away by her kindness. "That would be great. What can I do to help?"

"Just rest. I'm not used to having Connor out of town for so long, and I miss doing nice things for him. My husband fusses too much to let me pamper him."

She almost choked. In the last few days, after she started to feel like her old self again, she'd tried to cook for Connor, but he rarely let her, saying he was capable of taking care of himself. "He's okay with that?"

His mom waved a hand. "No, but I try to do it anyway. If Finn—he's my youngest son—weren't so busy, I could dote on him. He and Connor are the last to find a mate, and I want to take advantage of them being single for as long as I can. I have Chelsea, who's Finn's twin, and she loves the attention. Even though my children are adults, and some are mated now, it fills my heart to take care of them in little ways."

"It sounds like you have a wonderful family." Vinea had mentioned how closely knit they were. Her friend had also commented how hard it had been for her to gain their acceptance. That wasn't surprising, given she had been a goddess from the dark realm.

His mom smiled. "We do, and you? Do you have family in Georgia?"

A knife-like ache stabbed her. "Not any longer. Both my parents died fourteen years ago." Or rather, they were murdered, but EmmaLee wasn't ready to talk about that. The case had never been solved and most likely never would be.

"I'm sorry. Losing both must have been so hard."

"It was."

"Did you live with relatives then?"

"Yes." At times, she'd believed it was worse than living on the streets and fending for herself.

"DO YOU HAVE any idea where this Coghill fellow is?" Connor's dad asked.

"No, and that worries me. The Billard police have no leads either. I doubt he's left town for good. His things are still in his apartment."

"As I told you before, we're happy to have EmmaLee stay at the guesthouse, but wouldn't you feel more comfortable if she stayed in the office safe room?"

"It's occupied at the moment."

His father padded over to the refrigerator. "I see. Will you join me for a beer?"

"Sure." It didn't matter it was only lunchtime.

His dad handed him a bottle and motioned they should sit at the table. "Tell me what's really going on. What are you hiding?"

Connor debated not telling his dad the truth, but he needed the guidance. "I never could hide anything from you, could I? Okay, here it is: EmmaLee is my mate."

His dad's grin nearly touched his ears. "That's fantastic, son. Then what's the problem?" His eyes darkened, and his smile disappeared. "Doesn't she want to mate with you?"

"I've not asked her. You must know how hard it is being around her now. Even if the safe room were unoccupied, if I put her there, I wouldn't be able to get any work done. My wolf would go berserk if she were that close. Plus, EmmaLee doesn't know she's my mate."

"Why not? When I first met your mom, I told her right away."

"There's a difference. Mom was a shifter; she would have already known she was your mate before you told her." Connor had heard the story of their meeting many times. "Though if I recall, Mom told you to take a hike."

Dad waved a hand. "She was playing hard to get."

"EmmaLee is not that way. She likes me, but she's cautious. It's almost as if she thinks I might harm her."

His father tipped back his beer. "She knows you're a shifter, right?"

"Yes. She's Vinea's friend. Devon's mate told her everything about our world and hers."

"I don't see the problem then."

He didn't need this pressure. Connor was under enough stress as it was. "Remember her ex-boyfriend beat her up, repeatedly. It's why I'm protecting her."

"Because of that you think she's not ready to commit to a relationship?"

"Wouldn't you be afraid?"

His father leaned back in his seat, twisting the beer bottle in his hands. "How well do you know her?"

"Just what I told you."

His dad shook his head. "Son, if you plan to mate with her, you need to understand her."

"I understand enough. She's intelligent, inquisitive, and determined to get her master's degree."

"I'll ask again. What's the problem?"

"She's obsessed with learning more about shifters—dragon shifters in particular." He held his breath waiting to see if his all-knowing dad would shed some light on whether they existed.

"Dragons. Are you kidding me?"

Damn. "Yes. She's convinced they are real."

"Maybe they are."

"Not you too!" Connor said. Was he the only skeptic?

"Listen. Figure out why she's obsessed, and you might learn to understand her better. Communication is the key to a good relationship. Without it, life can be hard. This applies to everyone. Remember, EmmaLee isn't a shifter, so she won't get the signs like you do regarding being your mate. Be patient with her, son."

His father's words resonated with him. "I'll try."

"Good, now what else can I do to help?"

"Make sure nothing happens to her while I'm at work."

"Fine. How much freedom are you willing to give her?"

JUST AS HIS mother pulled the casserole from the oven, Connor returned, and relief shot through her. For the last few weeks, Connor hadn't left her side, and EmmaLee hadn't realized how much she'd grown accustomed to him being close by.

His mom gave Connor a knowing look. "Have a good talk with Dad?"

"Yes."

She smiled. "Good. I'll leave you two alone then. The casserole is done. Let it cool a bit and then you both can have some lunch." Mrs. McKinnon squeezed EmmaLee's shoulder. "If you need anything else, please stop by. And feel free to make the place your own."

"Thank you."

As soon as she left, Connor motioned they sit at the table. "I hope she didn't grill you too much," he said.

"No, she was amazingly sweet. You're lucky to have a mom like that."

"I am. Sorry I left you, but I wanted to speak with my dad and ask if he could watch you while I'm a work."

Talk about bursting her bubble. Not that she expected Connor to stay with her, but—well, she hadn't thought he'd keep her jailed in the guesthouse with a babysitter. She had hoped he'd wanted her to stay at his office. He'd told her it contained a safe room. "Am I allowed to leave here?" It was one of the draws of being one state away from Slater.

"If you remain in the compound, you should be safe."

"You mean this gated community?"

"Yes. We call it a compound because everyone here is a shifter. You'll be safe. Dad and Rye will make certain everyone is aware of what's happened to you. I've asked my brother to circulate a photo of Slater so they can apprehend him if he shows up."

Having everyone know what a sap she'd been would make her uncomfortable, but that couldn't be helped. "Do you have to give them the sordid details?"

"They needed to know what they're up against, which is that Slater Coghill is dangerous. That's all."

"Okay." Having all those shifters look out for her did help calm her. "Who's Rye?"

"He's my older brother. He's also our Clan's Alpha."

"Oh. Does that make you the Beta?"

His eyes widened. "You have been doing your homework, but no, the Beta is Kalan Murdoch. His father was the Beta before him."

She needed to change a few things in her thesis. "Got it."

"I know this won't be easy for you, but give me a few days to figure out where it's safe for you to go outside of the compound."

That was all she could ask for. "Thanks."

He sniffed. "This casserole smells amazing. Let's eat. I've missed my mom's cooking."

She inhaled but couldn't smell much. Then she remembered about a shifter's acute sense of smell. Connor stepped over to the kitchen counter, picked up the potholders, and carried the dish to the table.

"What should I do?" she asked.

He returned to the kitchen and removed two plates from the cabinet. He handed her one. "Just help yourself."

What she'd really like to do was help herself to him.

Chapter Four

C ONNOR WAS IN a foul mood this morning. Not only had sleeping on a too-short sofa at the guesthouse put him in a foul mood, his wolf was panting, wanting to be near EmmaLee. Hell, he wanted to be near her too, but he had work to do. Knowing she would be safe should have helped him get back into the flow of things, but so far it hadn't. Nothing short of mating with her would, and neither of them was ready for that.

Although his wolf and his cock would argue that fact, Connor had to control those emotions. Everything about her drew him in. She was smart, caring, honest, and that damn body of hers called to him. Cripes, if he didn't get a grip, he would probably jump her at the first available opportunity. EmmaLee was torture on his libido.

He adjusted the hard-on in his jeans. *Fabulous. By the end of the day my dick will look like I had a zipper tattooed onto it.*

Before he'd even booted up his computer to begin work, a knock sounded on his office door, and Sam Pompley strolled in. "Hey, I heard you were back. How did things go?"

Connor looked up from his laptop. "We came back into town yesterday, and EmmaLee is settled in at my parents' guesthouse. Of course, she balked at first about leaving Billard, but eventually she saw things my way."

Sam laughed. "I'm anxious to meet her. She sounds a lot like Lexi—stubborn to a fault."

"EmmaLee's definitely an interesting woman, I'll hand you that.

I think she and Lexi will get along quite well."

Sam nodded and then frowned. "Any leads on this Slater ass-hole?"

"Not yet. To be honest, I really don't have the time or desire to chase all over the country looking for him. I'd say good riddance, but I couldn't live with myself if I let my guard down and he came after EmmaLee. I have to make sure she stays safe."

"Makes sense. What do you think of using Ronan?"

"Ronan?" Even though he was Sam's mate's brother, he lived in Vermont, not Tennessee.

"Why not? He's a shifter bounty hunter. Being an independent contractor, he chooses his own clients and works where and when he wants."

That made sense. "With Devon running the office in Pittsburg and not wanting to be away from Vinea for long stretches, Ronan would be a welcome addition. I'll speak with Lexi to see whether she thinks he might help. Hopefully, he has the time and desire to lend a hand."

Sam slipped down onto the chair across from him. "Do we know if Slater is a shifter? It might help us decide how to approach him."

"Devon told me Vinea recognized a shifter scent from Slater when he was with EmmaLee."

"EmmaLee doesn't know?"

"No, and I didn't let on. Strangely, Vinea didn't say whether he was a bear, wolf, or tiger."

"Didn't say or wouldn't say?"

Sam would always be leery of her. "I don't know." He stretched out his legs, looking like he had a lot to discuss. "I find it odd that Slater never revealed his shifter status to EmmaLee given she researches the paranormal."

"He might have known what she researched, but maybe he didn't trust her enough to let on he had an animal side. EmmaLee told me that she never told Slater that Vinea was a goddess either. Apparently, they both were good at keeping a secret."

"Listen, if you want me to look into this guy I will."

"I'll let you know how you can help once I figure it out myself," Connor said.

Sam nodded as he got up. "Sounds good. You know where to find me."

As soon as Sam left, Connor's dad's words came back to him about needing to know EmmaLee better. Not that she was close-mouthed, but the few times he'd asked about her parents, all she'd said was that they were dead.

While Jackson was the best researcher of the bunch and could probably learn everything about her youth in a few hours, Connor needed to do the digging himself. If he could keep her past just between the two of them, all the better.

He had two main questions he wanted answers to. One was why would a beautiful, smart, charming woman end up in an abusive relationship? From experience, he'd learned that it often occurred as a result of previous abuse or a troubled childhood, and the mere thought had acid burning in his gut. If her father or some authority figure beat her self-confidence down, she would be headed for heartache.

The second question, and perhaps the more important of the two was, why was she so intent on researching dragon shifters? This was more than just hanging on to some childhood fascination, and he didn't think it stemmed from her reading a lot of romance novels that glorified the mythical creatures. No, this came from something deeper. But what?

She had revealed that she'd grown up in a small rural town south of Athens, Georgia called Dunlap Gorge. There might be something in that town or in their newspaper archives that would give him a clue.

Starting with something easy, he pulled up the property appraiser's site and found the location of the Donovan's home on River Bend Road. It had been purchased in the eighties for fifty thousand dollars. After checking whether the taxes had been paid, he found out they had been in arrears. The property then went into foreclosure, and the land sold, implying the house was no longer standing. With her roots gone, it was no wonder EmmaLee had moved away.

Before he let his emotions get the best of him, he located the local newspaper and searched information from fourteen years ago. It took him nearly three hours before he found what he was looking for. The headlines showed the Donovan's home engulfed in flames. The article said the burn appeared to be arson. The parents, both of whom worked at the nearby university, were survived by their twelve-year old daughter EmmaLee, Mr. Donovan's brother Robert, and his wife Kathy. Had she gone into foster care or had her aunt and uncle taken her in? He definitely needed to find that out.

Closing the lid to his computer, Connor leaned back and closed his eyes, almost feeling the heat of the fire and the pain it had caused. Before the fire, he wondered if she'd had a happy childhood or had it been bleak?

He sighed. There would be records from the Department of Children and Family Services placing her in someone's care. While Connor had some talent when it came to research, he didn't like to break any laws since he was a *by-the-book* type of guy. Jackson, on the other hand, didn't seem to have a problem with it. That meant it was time to ask for his help.

Connor knocked then entered Jackson's office. "Got a minute?"

"Sure. Welcome back, by the way." Jackson dragged a gaze down Connor's face. "What happened to you? You look like shit. Didn't you sleep in the last couple of weeks?" He smiled. "It's EmmaLee, isn't it? She kept you up all night." Jackson wiggled his eyebrows at him.

Damn him. "No jackass. Get your mind out of the gutter. We drove here yesterday, and the traffic made it stressful." A total lie, but he wasn't going to explain that EmmaLee was his mate. It didn't matter that Jackson was his best friend.

"Uh, huh. What can I do for you?"

"I'm trying to find Slater Coghill, the man who attacked Emma-

Lee. I thought that if I learned a bit more about her, it might lead me to him."

Jackson grinned. "You do realize that you suck at lying."

His pulse sped up. Was nothing sacred in this world? He refused to give in. "Hey, I am merely curious about EmmaLee, that's all. I need to figure out what questions to ask her in regards to Slater."

"What do you need?'

"Can you find out who took care of her after her parents died?" Connor told him what little he knew.

"Sure, but why not just ask EmmaLee?"

"She clammed up when I tried to discuss her past. It makes sense since they died when she was twelve. I don't think anyone can get over something like that."

Jackson sobered. "That's tough. I'll dig deep and see what I come up with. You want to know the good and the bad?"

There would be no bad. "Yes. As long as you're investigating her, maybe you can see where Slater Coghill fits into her life."

"Tell me about him."

Connor filled him on what EmmaLee had said.

"I'll try. Could you ask her if she has one of Coghill's credit card receipts? If she does, I might be able to figure out where he's been recently."

"I can ask, but I'm not expecting she will. Why would she bring something like that from Georgia?" A few days ago, he'd thought about asking her to search Slater's apartment, but he didn't want to put her in that kind of danger or bring up bad memories.

"She could have shoved it into her purse and forgotten about it."

"It's possible," Connor said.

"If you need help with this case, why not ask Ronan to lend a hand? I heard he can track anyone. With Devon staying put in Pittsburgh, we could use another investigator." In the past, his brother dropped in at a moment's notice. Now that Vinea was pregnant, he'd requested that he stay put, and Connor couldn't deny him. His mate had to come first.

"Sam suggested that too."

"Let me know what he says."

Connor returned to his office. Wanting to be prepared if Ronan hesitated, he pulled up a fresh word document and then listed the reasons why Ronan should come down and help.

Next, he jotted down a few questions he had for Ronan. Connor was interested in knowing how Ronan believed he could help him capture Slater Coghill. Lexi always bragged a lot about her brother, but it would be nice to hear from the man himself about his accomplishments.

Lastly, Connor listed everything he knew about EmmaLee's attacker. The bounty hunter would need something to go on.

With that chore done, it was time to check in with the Billard police. He usually called every few days and spoke to Officer Terrance Waters, the man in charge of the case. He wanted to stay on top of any progress they might be making on their end in locating Coghill.

"Officer Waters, how may I help you?"

"This is Connor McKinnon."

"Oh, yes, Mr. McKinnon. Before you ask, we're doing everything we can to find this man Slater Coghill. Unfortunately, we've had no more leads than the last time we spoke."

As much as Connor wanted to rant and rave, it wouldn't do any good. "I appreciate your effort. You have my number if you do learn something."

"Rest assured, you'll be the first person we call."

Connor hung up, disgusted by the lack of progress. Clearly, he had to find EmmaLee's attacker on his own. Her face appeared in his mind's eye—not the beautiful one it was now, but the one with the split lip and black eye. He squeezed his eyes tight, willing away the horrible image. In its place, a picture of Caroline Andrews appeared. A tic formed around his eye. If only he hadn't left her that day, she might still be alive.

This is why you need to be near EmmaLee. Go see her, his wolf urged.

He understood what that horny animal wanted—sex with Emma-Lee.

Connor couldn't let his wolf distract him. Right now, Connor needed to tend to business. His two-week departure had put a strain on his short-handed team.

Before he could return to the task at hand, Jackson's dad, Daniel, stepped into his office. "Heard you were back and might need help with a case." Either Jackson had spoken with him, or Connor's father had filled him in.

At his age, Daniel didn't need to be out chasing down a bad shifter. Coghill was a dangerous man. "Thanks. Maybe you can give Jackson a hand. He's doing some research on EmmaLee's case."

"I'll ask my son what he needs help with then. Glad to have you back."

"Glad to be back." Daniel would be discrete if he found information on EmmaLee. Even though his dad and Jackson's father had turned over the running of the firm to him, they still owned the company. "Before you leave, let me ask you something." Connor explained his plan to ask Lexi's brother to help with the Slater Coghill case. "If he works out, what do you think of asking him to join the firm? Having a talented bounty hunter would be an asset."

Daniel asked a few questions, and Connor had to dig deep into his memory to recall what Lexi had said about Ronan.

If you mate with EmmaLee, the release will help you focus better, his wolf said.

No, it won't. Christ, his wolf needed to quit panting about mating and go lay down. Horny bastard.

"Sounds like a plan. Let me know what you think of him," Daniel said.

As soon as Daniel left, Connor went in search of Lexi. Head down, she was working away on her computer, filling in data in one of her color-coded spreadsheets.

She looked up and smiled. "Hey there. What can I do for you?"

"I was wondering if Ronan might be free to give us a hand on the case that involves EmmaLee, the woman I was protecting in Georgia."

"He's a bounty hunter, not a bodyguard."

Connor would never ask an unmated male to watch EmmaLee, mostly because she had no idea they were fated mates. He couldn't afford for her to fall for another man now. "I need him to look for the man who wants to harm her. There's a bounty on his head."

Her eyes brightened. "Oh. That's right up his alley, but my brother lives in Vermont. It might be hard to convince him to take a case down here."

"I'd like to give him a call anyway. I figure he might like the change in scenery. After all, it's warmer here than in Vermont this time of year."

"Don't I know it?" Lexi wrote down her brother's number. "Try to convince him to at least visit. I'd love to see him. It's been too long."

"I'll do my best." Once back in his office, Connor made the call.

"Yeah?" Ronan said with a hard edge to his voice.

Given the road noise in the background, he was in his vehicle. "Ronan Laramie?"

"Yup."

While Ronan didn't seem to be much for formalities, Connor liked him. "This is Connor McKinnon. Your sister works for my firm."

"Oh, sorry, man. I didn't look at the screen when I answered. I thought it was someone else."

"No problem." He told him about Slater Coghill and the woman this man might come after. "There's a bounty on his head."

"I'm listening."

"I'm not sure where he is right now, but I was wondering if you could lend us a hand. You can have the whole bounty. I just want the creep caught."

His horn blasted in the background. "Fuck you, man!" Ronan

VELLA DAY

shouted a split second after someone's tires squealed. "Sorry about that," he said. "Some asshole just pulled onto the road without looking."

"Nice to have those quick wolf reflexes, right?"

He chuckled. "Totally. Listen, I'm interested, but I'm in the middle of another case. As a matter of fact, I'm heading south now to locate this scum."

Connor wasn't sure what more to say since begging wasn't his style. However, if Connor could lend support at his end, Ronan might find him faster and then be able to help him out. "Can I help you in any way? I realize you work alone, but McKinnon and Associates has a lot of resources."

"You might be able to."

"Tell me about this guy," Connor said.

"Timothy Delahart is a real sleazebag. He's into drugs, prostitution, you name it. I'll send you all the info on this guy as soon as I stop. I really want to catch him. Once I do, I'm free to help. I'd love to catch up with Lexi too. I haven't seen her since all that shit went down with our father trying to sell her."

Connor still remembered that nightmare. The image of Lexi in her wolf form dumpster diving would forever be burned into his brain. "When do you think you could get here?"

"I'm halfway to Tennessee now. No promises, but if Delahart continues heading south, I'm thinking tomorrow afternoon at the latest. I should know more tonight."

He gave Ronan directions. "Looking forward to meeting you."

Once they disconnected, Connor leaned back in his seat, pleased he'd found help. A few seconds later, he realized that once they put Slater in jail, EmmaLee would want to go back to Georgia, and there was no way he could agree to that.

34

Chapter Five

EMMALEE WAS HAPPY with her new living quarters. While the kitchen wasn't any more updated than the one in her apartment in Georgia, the furniture was a lot nicer and more modern, not to mention the seat cushions weren't ripped like the ones she had. The only complaint was that the living room sofa sat in the middle of the room, taking up too much space. If it were up against the living room window, it would make the area seem bigger. It was how she had her furniture arranged back home.

Since the flooring was wood, it would be easy to slide a few things around and see whether she liked the change. When she returned to Billard, she'd be sure to put things back the way they were, even though Mrs. McKinnon implied EmmaLee could do what she wanted.

Because she had already unpacked her clothes, she set about redecorating. It would make her more comfortable to be in familiar surroundings. First, she moved the wooden coffee table off to the side and then slid the two heavy leather chairs out of the way. It looked better already.

Next came the sofa. Because it was the heaviest item, she leaned over and gave it a big shove, but it fell short by a foot. Using all her effort again, she pushed harder and immediately felt something snap in her back. She froze as the twinge raced up her spine. Taking a few short breaths, she pleaded with whoever would listen to not let this be a serious injury. She slowly rose and winced. Well, damn. This was not how she wanted her first full day in Silver Lake to end.

Determined to nip this strain in the bud, she eased her way to the kitchen and filled a kitchen towel with some ice then placed it on her back. For a split second, she considered calling Connor for some sympathy, but then she remembered he'd told her not to even turn on her cell phone. Slater might have figured out a way to trace it. So as not to be out of communication range, Connor had promised to bring her a burner phone in the next day or two. Bothering his mom was not an option either. EmmaLee owed the McKinnons enough as it was.

Well, damn. The best thing to do was rest.

After sitting with the ice on her back for twenty minutes, she returned the dripping mess to the kitchen and dumped the remains into the sink. Testing her back, she found she wasn't as bad off as she thought. Hurray!

Thinking some exercise would do her good, EmmaLee debated bundling up and going out for a walk but then thought better of it. She doubted Mr. McKinnon was sitting at his window waiting for Slater, and even if every shifter in the compound was aware her ex-boyfriend might come after her, she didn't think walking around alone was a good idea. In the end, she grabbed her e-reader and eased down onto the sofa, ready to get lost in her world of fantasy.

When four turned to five, and then five to six, she decided Connor wasn't stopping over. She might as well prepare dinner for one. Most likely, Connor reasoned that if everyone in the compound was watching out for her, why should he come by? The poor man hadn't left her side in a few weeks and was probably happy to have some time to himself.

EmmaLee tried to remember if he mentioned his plans for the evening, but she didn't think he'd told her anything. Not stopping by tonight was fine, but if he thought she'd be content to sit in this house all day long, everyday, and never leave, he had another thing coming. She wasn't built for being idle.

Before she reached the kitchen, someone knocked on her door.

She jumped, and her heart jackhammered in her chest. For a moment, she thought it was Slater, but then dismissed it. He couldn't have found her so soon. Or could he have? Because Connor sounded so confident that she'd be safe, the Clan must have a good system of surveillance.

"Coming," she called, knowing it might take her a minute to reach the door. Standing caused some pain, but once she was upright, she was pleased she was able to move a lot better. "Who is it?"

"It's Connor."

EmmaLee smiled. Anxious to see him, she pulled open the door and then just stared, ignoring the chilly air rushing in. It didn't matter it had only been a few hours since she'd seen him. He must have stopped home after work because when he'd left this morning, he had on a black T-shirt. His jeans and boots looked the same, but now he wore a crisp white button down shirt. He hadn't shaven, and the worry lines seemed to have deepened. "Come in."

Instead of looking at her, he studied the room. "Something's different."

"I thought I'd rearrange the furniture."

His brow rose. "So you did. I like it better this way. I'm surprised Vinea didn't do something like this. It makes the room seem bigger."

EmmaLee was pleased Connor liked what she'd done. "Can I get you something to drink? I have water, coffee, and orange juice."

He didn't make eye contact. "Water's fine, thanks."

Connor wasn't usually this uncomfortable around her. "Did something happen at work today?"

He finally looked at her. "No, why?"

She shrugged. Even if she said he seemed to be avoiding eye contact, he'd never admit it. "You seem preoccupied."

He stepped into the kitchen, snatched a glass from the cabinet, and filled it with tap water. Well, so much for her offering him something to drink. "I had a lot of catching up to do today."

All because of her. "I'm sorry."

As if he remembered who she was, he set down the glass and clasped her shoulders. "No, I'm the one who should apologize. This isn't your fault. I should have convinced you to come here right away. If I had, I could have had my team working on finding Slater sooner."

The urge to hug him was strong, until she remembered she was a sucker for an apology. At least this apology had nothing to do with someone hitting her.

EmmaLee moved out of his grasp, but the act of twisting caused an intense pain to race up her back. She grabbed the edge of the counter and gasped out loud.

"EmmaLee, are you okay?" he asked with such concern she almost didn't recognize his voice.

"I'm fine." She rubbed her back. "I pulled a muscle when I moved the furniture."

Connor stepped over to the dining room and dragged over a chair. He then came back and placed his hand on her elbow, gently guiding her to the seat. "Come sit down."

As much as she didn't like him waiting on her, she would be more comfortable sitting. "I'm okay, really. I just can't move quickly."

"I can see that. Remember I mentioned Kalan Murdoch, the Beta of our Clan?"

"Yes."

"His sister, Blair, is a physical therapist in town. I can give her a call to see what she suggests you do."

While she didn't need that much help, meeting people in the community would make her stay more enjoyable, especially if Connor remained at work all day. "Is she a wolf too?"

"No, a werebear."

Ooh, even better. "Then by all means contact her."

EMMALEE HADN'T SLEPT well last night in part because her back was giving her a fit, and because Connor remained distant when he'd stopped over. Sure, her injury concerned him, even suggesting Blair Murdoch stop by and help, but he was pre-occupied about something. Did he regret asking her to move to Silver Lake or had the build-up at work been the issue?

Foolishly, EmmaLee had thought if Slater wasn't an imminent risk that maybe Connor would let down his guard, but apparently, she'd been wrong.

Once Slater was brought to justice, she'd be on her way home, and the last thing she needed was to have her heart broken yet again. But damn, the enigmatic Connor McKinnon intrigued her. Too often she debated seducing him, but that little voice in her head told her it was too soon. She needed to study him more in order to decide if she wanted a fling to have something to remember him by.

A rapping sounded on her door and jarred her out of her day-dream. That must be Blair. With her hand on her lower back, EmmaLee walked carefully toward the door. After looking through the peephole, she opened up. A tall redhead with a folded table leaning against her leg stood there.

The beautiful woman smiled. "Hi, I'm Blair."

"Come in. Do you need help with that?"

Blair chuckled. "So you can hurt your back again? No thanks."

"I forgot. I'm not used to being hurt."

"I understand. It happens often." Blair carried the table inside and set it between the living room and dining room. "I'd be screwed if I hurt my back. I know I take too many chances lifting heavy things, but I have confidence my bear can heal anything minor."

"What I wouldn't give for some shifter blood in me." Heat instantly raced up her face at what it would take to accomplish that. "I mean, I wish I had been born a shifter."

Blair tossed her a knowing smile then looked around. "I haven't been in this guesthouse in a long time. I remember playing in here when we were kids, especially in the winter. The McKinnons didn't get many guests when it was cold."

"We?"

"The Murdochs and the McKinnons. My parents live next door in the two-story white house. Our two families are tight, in part because our fathers were the two Clan leaders."

"I remember Connor telling me that your brother Kalan is the Beta."

"Yes." Blair set up her table. "Let me take a look at your back. Tell me how you hurt it."

EmmaLee regaled her with her overzealous attempt to move the furniture. "I guess I was still too tired from the long drive here to try moving stuff around."

"You should have asked Connor to help."

Like he needed more work? "I wanted to give him a break. Poor guy has been doing everything for me for weeks, especially that first week when I was recovering."

"I heard what happened. I'm sorry."

"Thanks. It's in the past—or rather it will be as soon as Slater is caught and jailed."

Blair patted the table. "Hop on up and lay on your stomach. I want to feel around to find the sore spot."

With care, EmmaLee did as Blair instructed. Stretching out helped the achy pain. While she needed the physical therapy, EmmaLee also wanted to pick her brain. "Since you grew up here, what can you tell me about Connor?"

Blair chuckled as she pressed her fingers down EmmaLee's spine. "Even though I'm a year younger, we went to school together and goofed around when we were kids. That being said, once he reached high school, Connor kept to himself more than the others, so we didn't interact that much."

That didn't surprise her. "Would you say he was more the brooding, caring, or angry type?"

Blair pressed on a painful spot and EmmaLee winced. "I'm going to press here for a bit to get the nerve to release."

"Okay."

At the moment, her physical condition wasn't as important as learning about Connor.

"Connor is complicated. It had to be hard living in the shadow of the man destined to be the Clan's Alpha."

"Rye."

"Yes. Devon, the brother in between Rye and Connor, was more like Connor than their younger brother, Finn, who's the inquisitive and happy one. Now that he's managing McKinnon's Pub, he's become more serious."

"I'd like to meet him." Mostly to see the contrast between these two brothers. Blair released the spot, and EmmaLee could feel some relief. "So Connor didn't run around with a ton of different friends?" She wasn't sure why she asked, but it would help give her insight into the man.

"He did for a long time. When he reached high school, he became a more focused student. The girls were always after him, but he only went out with a few. He wasn't wild like some of the kids I knew. Connor had a few close friends he was very protective of."

EmmaLee liked that Connor was noble. If only she'd known Slater when he was young, she might not have made her mistake. "Is Connor still close with them?"

"Some. His best friend now is my brother Jackson, but when Connor was eighteen, he and Drew Balko were besties."

"But not now?" Had they fought?

"He died."

EmmaLee's heart broke. Poor Connor. She understood what loss could do to a person, especially at such a young age. "What happened?"

"I wasn't there, but apparently, a bunch of guys got together at a shifter's house, whose parents were out of town. Drew thought that because he was a werewolf he could hold his alcohol better than most. Apparently, he couldn't. Connor tried to stop him from driving home, but Drew refused to listen. They even got into a shoving and shouting match over it. In the end, Drew got behind the wheel. Halfway home he ran into a telephone pole. He was killed instantly."

EmmaLee sucked in a breath. "Knowing Connor, he felt a little responsible for not stopping him, didn't he?"

"Yes, and he was devastated for a long time." Blair patted her back. "Sit up. I need you to stretch a little."

EmmaLee did so and found the short massage had helped. "Has he always worked at McKinnon and Associates?"

"No. He worked for another company for nearly two years beforehand. Then when our dads started the investigative firm, he worked for them. When our parents retired, they asked him to take over. I was out of state going to school for most of that though. Sad to say, I didn't keep up with him much. Even now, we really don't run in the same circles. Over Sunday dinner, Jackson might make some comments about Connor, but mostly he talks about how the man is a workaholic."

That much she'd figured out. "So he's not dating anyone?"

Blair smiled and shook her head. "I think I'll let you ask him that."

When she had, he'd merely grunted his response. So far, she hadn't seen or heard anything to indicate that he was anything other than a protective man whose life was centered around his work. If he had a love life, it couldn't be much of one.

As much as EmmaLee believed it would be fun to crack his crusty veneer, she doubted she was the woman for him. Men who ran successful businesses were logical and focused. They'd never value a part-time student with crazy ass notions of dragons who lived long ago in some ancient realm.

CONNOR'S INTERCOM BUZZED. "Yes?"

"My brother is here to see you," Lexi announced.

"Good, send him back."

A moment later, Lexi knocked then stepped in with a big smile on her face. She motioned the large bearded man inside. "This is Ronan," she said with obvious pride.

Connor stood and walked around his desk, not expecting the man to be a good two inches taller than he was. "Hey, good to meet you."

Ronan had a coffee cup in one hand and a manila folder in the other. He slipped the packet under his arm and shook hands. "Likewise. Lexi has told me a lot about you."

"I hope it was all good?"

They both smiled.

"You need anything, Connor?" Lexi asked. "Coffee?"

"No, thanks." As soon as she left, Connor pulled up a second chair so that they were facing each other. "I really appreciate you coming down," Connor said.

"I've been meaning to visit Lexi for a while, but I've been busy." He set his cup on Connor's desk. "So what's going on with this Coghill fellow?"

Connor liked his cut-to-the-chase attitude. He gave him as much information as he could. "One of my team members, Jackson Murdoch, is trying to locate him via his cell phone. We're also trying to get access to his credit card number so we can trace him that way."

"I wish I had that kind of info on my man."

"Maybe we can help." Even if he hadn't asked Ronan to lend a hand, Connor would give assistance to any team member's relative.

"That would be great." Ronan handed him the file. "Everything I have on Timothy Delahart is in here, from police reports to the people he's associated with to where his family is located."

Connor was impressed with not only the depth of the information but with the clear way it was organized. "I see you and Lexi have something in common."

He raised an eyebrow. "What's that?"

"You both like spreadsheets."

Ronan laughed. "I do at that. You do know that Lexi and I are

Wendayans, right?" Ronan asked.

"I do. Do you have the same talents?"

"Yes and no. Lexi is extremely strong for a woman and quite coordinated, as am I, but I also have an acute sense of smell. In fact, I track my bounties by their scent."

Connor had never heard of anything like that. "Like a blood-hound?"

"More or less. A shifter's scent isn't unpleasant, but each person's is distinctive. It leaves a long trail if you know what to smell for."

"I'm curious. How far away can you be to detect his scent?"

"Depends on the shifter, the temperature, and how long he's lingered in one spot. I don't need much of a trace to track him."

"That's amazing." Connor crossed his ankle over his knee. What he wouldn't give to have this man's talent at his firm. "I want to work with you on your case, but I worry this Coghill guy might find EmmaLee if I'm not here. Unless I can line up someone to watch over her, I don't want to leave town."

"I understand." Ronan's voice held steady, but his eyes had changed color enough to indicate he was disappointed. "I totally get that your team likes to protect people. Sam helped Lexi when she had a stalker."

Sam had been extra diligent in part because Lexi was his mate. "I can offer you the services of our extensive databases. The brother of one of the men in my employee works at the sheriff's department. He often provides us with excellent intel."

Ronan smiled. "That would be terrific."

Connor's cell rang. Fearing something might have happened to EmmaLee, he checked the screen. It was his dad. He held up a finger to indicate he'd only be a minute. "Hey, Dad. What's up?"

"I totally forgot that your mom and I were invited out to dinner tonight. It's Patsy O'Neill's sixtieth birthday and your mom can't miss that."

She and Patsy were best friends. "Of course not. Go."

"What about EmmaLee? Can you come home right now? We're

44

leaving in a few minutes."

"I'll call EmmaLee and let her know to keep the doors lock. And yes, I'll make sure someone watches her. Have a good time." He disconnected and pocketed the phone.

"Problem?" Ronan asked.

"Kind of." He explained that his father would not be able to keep an eye on EmmaLee after all. "I'm hoping Lexi can do me a favor." He pressed the intercom button. "Can you step in here?"

"Sure." A minute later, Lexi popped her head in. "What's up?"

"Ronan and I aren't quite done here, and I need you to do me a favor if you can."

"What is it?"

"Would you mind keeping an eye on EmmaLee until I can get there? She's staying at my parents' guesthouse. Dad was supposed to watch her until I finished work, but he and Mom have a dinner engagement they have to go to. I want to pick Ronan's brain some more."

"I'd be happy to. Sam's out on assignment tonight, so my only plans were to chat with Ronan, but if you're with him, I might as well meet your new lady."

She wasn't his new lady, but to deny it now would only cause more speculation on Lexi's part. "Tell her I'll be there when I can."

She faced her brother. "Where are you staying? We have a couch you can crash on if you want, though I can't vouch it'll be all that comfortable given your size."

He glanced at Connor and then back at his sister. "I saw a hotel on the drive in. I'll check it out when Connor and I finish up."

Ronan had come down here to help out, so the least Connor could do was offer him the safe room. "Nonsense. We have a room downstairs you can stay in. The couple that was there left this morning." He'd thought of asking EmmaLee to move into the room, but he didn't want to uproot her again. Besides, she really seemed to like the guesthouse.

Lexi smiled. "Ah, the safe room." She faced her brother. "You'll love it. It's a suite."

"Sounds great."

Lexi gave Ronan a hug. EmmaLee would be safe with her. "Don't tell her too many bad things about me," Connor said with as much cheer as he could muster.

"There's nothing bad to say." She winked.

"You're a diplomat. I like that."

Once Lexi left, he called EmmaLee to let her know his change of his plans, and that he'd get there when he could.

"Is this necessary?" she asked, sounding somewhat upset.

"Possibly not, but I'd feel more comfortable if someone stayed with you."

"I can take care of myself. I promise to lock the door."

That last part was in reference to Caroline Andrews, the woman who died under his watch. "I'm sure you can, but Lexi can fill you in on the comings and goings of the town." EmmaLee loved gossip.

"Really?"

Her sudden cheerful tone worried him. "Yes. Do you have enough food for dinner?" he asked wanting to change the subject.

"You saw how much food your mom left. Don't worry about me. I'll be fine. See you later."

He should be happy that she didn't whine. There was a lot more to EmmaLee Donovan than met the eye.

Yes, like the fact she's your mate, his wolf reminded him for the umpteenth time.

Once Connor said goodbye, he disconnected. Needing to take his mind off of the alluring EmmaLee, he opened the Timothy Delahart folder, noting the banking information. "Let me ask Jackson to step in here. I'm betting he can find where Delahart has been just by his spending habits."

Ronan grinned. "Don't make my life too easy. I might never leave."

That was what Connor was hoping for.

Chapter Six

"WHAT'S IT LIKE working for Connor?" EmmaLee asked as she handed Lexi a glass of Merlot. She then sat on the sofa across from her.

"It's... good."

That wasn't a resounding endorsement. "Is he tough on his employees or something?"

Lexi lifted her wine and smiled. "Not tough, just intense. Connor takes every case seriously. You just have to be around him for a while, and then you'll know that he is fair and protective of his people. Sam sure adores him." She sipped her drink. "But didn't you spend a few weeks with him? What's your take?"

EmmaLee didn't like to be put on the spot. Connor would probably hear about everything she said. "He's definitely the protective type—almost too much so. He never let me leave the house alone."

"That makes sense. Someone did harm you."

"Yes, but I could have handled Slater if he'd returned."

Her eyebrows rose. "Handle him? Like you did the last time?"

She deserved that. "All I meant is that after one of his *outbursts*, he was always sorry. I never saw him after the last beating though. If he shows up again, it will probably be to apologize." She held up a hand. "Forget I said that. I'm being naïve, I know."

Lexi smiled but quickly sobered. "Do you have a concealed weapon permit?"

EmmaLee's heart nearly dropped to her stomach. "No! I could never shoot anyone."

"Not even if he were attacking you?"

She sipped on her drink. "I don't know if I could. Ugh, I understand why Connor worries about me. I'm a wimp."

"No, you aren't." Lexi set down her glass. "Connor is like Sam. When I had a stalker after me, Sam never let me out of his sight, and I felt as if I was in jail—albeit a really nice one."

She liked that she and Lexi had that in common. "Are all shifters like that?"

"Oh, Sam wasn't a shifter until we mated. He's a Wendayan. For the most part, shifters are highly protective, but honestly I think most guys have that trait—at least the good ones do. It's a man thing, whether shifter, Wendayan, or just plain human." Lexi laughed. "Then again, Sam and I were fated to be mates, so he was extra careful to make sure nothing happened to me."

EmmaLee stilled. For a split second she let herself think she and Connor might be destined for one another, but then dismissed it. "Do you know of anyone who has been mated to a human?"

Lexi looked to the ceiling. "Yes. Kalan Murdoch, Jackson's brother, is mated to Elana. She was a human."

"Really?" Her pulse shot up.

"Yes, after her parents were murdered, the thieves came after her, so the sheriff's department assigned Kalan to protect her."

It kind of sounded like her situation. "This mating thing sounds like the luck of the draw."

Lexi smiled. "Was it? Or did Naliana have her hand in who was chosen?"

"Ah, yes, Vinea's sister, the goddess of mating. Has it worked out between her and Kalan?"

"Yes, and they are very much in love. They even have an adorable toddler named Aiden."

EmmaLee sighed. "That sounds wonderful."

"And you? Tell me about yourself."

Ugh. Her life was boring. "I'm a friend of Vinea's."

Lexi's lips firmed, almost as if she wasn't sure how to react to that statement. "I remember now. It was because Devon and Vinea were on their honeymoon that they asked Connor to watch you."

EmmaLee wasn't quite sure how to take her comment. "Were you one of the ones she did something bad to when she was a goddess of the dark realm?" Vinea had harmed a lot of people. After a while, the names became jumbled.

Lexi's eyes widened. "You were aware of her evil ways—or should I say her former evil ways?"

"Yes. She told me everything—from how she'd tried to kill Missy's mate to how she had stolen cars. After one of the cars she'd taken was stolen from her, Vinea ended up at the diner where I worked. The first time I saw her, I felt a connection. She had a sad aura encompassing her."

"Vinea, sad?"

"Yes. I'm sure you know she had been born in the light realm and was then kicked out. For hundreds of years, she had to live as a bad person, hurting a lot of them."

"That may be, but the first time I met her, Vinea was trying to steal my mate's powers." Her lips pinched and her respiration increased.

"Oh, shit. I just put the names to the crime. She tried to steal Sam's magic." Lexi nodded. "It was then that Naliana shot her with the light." EmmaLee didn't want to spend the night discussing Vinea's dark days, but she would if it helped Lexi get some closure.

"Yes. If it hadn't been for Naliana, Vinea would have succeeded." Lexi's breathing slowed. "Thankfully, Devon dunked her in Silver Lake, which seemed to be the turning point." A wistful smile crossed her lips. "When she came back to Silver Lake the next time, she ended up saving my life."

It was all coming back. "Ah, yes. Vinea mentioned how she'd raced to find the EpiPen in time."

"Bad memories." Lexi polished off the rest of her wine. "So tell me what you do for a living, and what you like to do."

Clearly, Vinea was not Lexi's favorite topic. "I'm working on my master's degree. To make ends meet, I waitress on the side."

"Cool. What are you studying?" Lexi asked.

"The official title is Lore and Legends of the Ancient World, but much of what I study is more than a legend, it's real—especially when the tales are about men who can shift into animals. Vinea was a goddess, and you certainly can attest that shifters exist."

"What do you hope to accomplish with your research? Are you planning on exposing us?" While she kept her tone even, it was tinged with fear.

"No! I'll only discuss what is already written in the literature about shifters. I'd never state that my bodyguard is one or that my best friend was a goddess. Not only would they boot me out for being a kook, leaking firsthand information would scare people."

Her shoulders relaxed. "Then what will you do with it?"

"Defend my thesis, which focuses on dragon shifters." She held up a hand. "Before you tell me they don't exist, let me say you might be right. I just like learning what research has been done on them. If they don't exist, then I can't harm anyone by writing about them."

Lexi smiled. "Thank you for not giving the world proof we exist, but it must be so frustrating to know the truth but not tell people."

EmmaLee shrugged. "It is."

"How did you get interested in the topic?"

As much as EmmaLee wanted to tell someone the real reason for her passion, she wasn't ready to dredge up the memory. "Growing up, I was fascinated by witches, fairies, and stuff like that. I was a very curious child. Hell, I still am."

"Fairies? Do you think they are real?"

EmmaLee almost laughed at the look of surprise on her face. "Witches, or rather Wendayans are real, so why not other types of beings?"

Lexi held up her hands. "You're right. Who am I to say they don't exist? If I weren't a werewolf and a Wendayan, I probably wouldn't believe in any of it."

Excitement raced through her. "Exactly. I'm glad you're open-minded, unlike your boss."

"Connor doesn't believe too much in heresay."

"So I've found out." EmmaLee leaned forward to rest her elbows on her knees, then winced and sat up straight. How quickly she'd forgotten about her sore back. "I'm really close to learning whether dragon shifters exist, but Connor thinks I'm quite the eccentric." Lexi's mouth curled downward. "You haven't met one, have you?" Her pulse hammered.

"No, but my brother Ronan is a bounty hunter—a shifter bounty hunter—and he's made mention of them a time or two."

"For real?" This was too good to be true.

"Yes. He's talking with Connor right now. You should meet him. I bet he'd share what information he's found."

She grinned. "I'd love that." Assuming Connor would let her. Her cheer then evaporated. "Connor would have to drive me to the office, and I doubt he'd want me to bother your brother."

Lexi tapped her foot then snapped her fingers. "I got it. Tell Connor that you need to do research, and that I told you how McKinnon and Associates has access to a lot of databases. If Jackson is free, he could help you. He's into the existence of other realms and things like that."

EmmaLee's throat almost closed up. "Other realms? Are you kidding me? Okay, I know there's the dark and the light realms, but are you saying other ones exist?"

Lexi planted a hand on her chest. "You need to speak with him."

There was something she wasn't saying, but that was okay. EmmaLee would find out from Jackson. All of this was too good to be true. "How far away is your office?"

"Maybe two miles." Her eyes widened. "You don't have a car?"

"No. Connor didn't want me to have a lot of freedom. Given the circumstances I can understand why."

She nodded. "He lives only a few streets away. Ask him to drive you to work."

EmmaLee almost laughed. "I think Connor is trying to avoid me."

She shook her head. "He's too professional."

"I still don't think he wants me around."

"I doubt that, but what if I pick you up tomorrow morning? It would have to be early since I would have to hook you up with a computer before I start my day. You can do your research there. When Connor comes in and sees you, I doubt he'll insist you leave."

EmmaLee wanted to hug her. "That would be fantastic. If I run into Ronan or Jackson that would be even better."

"I'll see what I can do."

Someone knocked on the door, and Lexi jumped up. "That must be Connor. Remember, what was said here, stays here," her new friend announced.

She liked Lexi. "You don't have to worry about me!"

When Lexi let Connor in, it was as if the air evaporated from the room. His facial hair had thickened from not having shaven today, but she liked the rugged look. EmmaLee also appreciated how his tight jeans hugged his ass.

Stop staring. "Hi." EmmaLee stood, not knowing what else to say.

He looked straight at her—or rather straight through her. "EmmaLee, everything go okay today?"

Given Slater hadn't shown up, why wouldn't it have? "Great. Thanks for sending over Lexi."

Her friend placed a hand on Connor's arm. "I need to get home." She turned back around. "Nice meeting you. Hope to see you soon!"

"You too."

Once the door closed, Connor moved closer. "What did you do today?" His voice sounded forced as if he felt obligated to ask.

"I read. I tried doing some research, but the Internet is spotty here. I got frustrated."

"The signal doesn't always reach from the main house. I'll see if we can hook you up with something better."

"I appreciate it. As long as you're here, we should talk."

"About what?" She couldn't tell if he sounded afraid or concerned.

"I know it's only been a day, but I'd really like to be able to get out. I'm a people person. I need to talk to others."

"You talked to Lexi."

"That was for maybe an hour. What should I do for the rest of the time? Do you expect me to stay holed up here forever? What if Slater is never caught?" EmmaLee moved closer to drive home her point, and she swore his eyes lightened. "Do you have any evidence he knows where I am?"

He had the courtesy to look away. "No."

"So why not let me loose? It can't be fun for your parents to have to watch me all the time, or you for that matter. Besides, I'm not the same person I was before. I am smarter and can protect myself against Slater." She gave him a finalizing poke in the chest. There. She told him.

A small smile lifted his lips but only for a moment. "Is that right?" He strode over to the refrigerator and retrieved a beer. She hadn't even noticed his mom had brought any over.

"Yes. Vinea gave me the power to wrap myself in some kind of force field thing that will repel Slater or anyone else who attacks me."

He thumbed off the lid and tossed back a good portion of the drink. "Interesting. Show me."

Damn, she figured he'd say that. "I have to be frightened for it to work. Vinea said if I'm threatened this bubble of protection will appear around me."

One eyebrow rose. "Hmmm. So this bubble wrap is merely speculative? You can't be certain it will work, can you?"

"Why are you always such a skeptic?" She hadn't meant her words to come out so sharp, but she was tired of being doubted all the time. It didn't matter she'd wondered the same thing.

He set down his bottle on the counter and strode toward her. With each step, her pulse rose. She really wished she could get a spell to make her immune to his...his...charms. Not that he was charming in any way. There was just something about him that made her want him. Damn. *Heartbreak, here I come.*

"I don't want you hurt again. Is that so difficult to understand?" This time his voice had softened.

"No, but I'll go crazy if I can't leave this place."

He held up his hands. "Fine. You can be free."

She didn't believe him. "Free as in I can go where I want?"

"Yes."

Something was up. "Will you lend me a bike or something?" She couldn't afford to rent a car. While it would be chilly being outside, she'd deal. If nothing else, EmmaLee was used to adversity.

"I can do that." He sat down on the sofa and clicked on the television, acting as if they hadn't had the conversation.

She crossed her arms. "You don't have to stay, you know."

He placed the remote on the coffee table and jumped up. "Are you sure?"

From his tone, he was challenging her. "Yes."

"Then have a good night. Don't forget to lock your door."

With that he left.

It took her a few minutes to believe he'd actually walked out on her. Why the sudden change of heart, especially since he didn't believe she possessed this extra talent? What wasn't he telling her?

She'd thought about asking him to pretend to attack her to see if this bubble thing would appear, but since she could never be afraid of Connor, it would only prove to him that she was making it up.

EmmaLee paced her tiny living room, trying to figure out why he had caved. For the first time in a long while, she needed a drink.

Chapter Seven

BECAUSE EMMALEE SEEMED to be at her wits end, Connor had decided to let her believe she could have free run of the town. Little did she know that either he'd be watching her or someone else would be if he had to attend to business. He'd slipped a tracking device into her purse tonight, but he understood that wouldn't be enough to keep her safe. It was merely a precaution in case Slater nabbed her.

That thought almost made him turn around and insist she move in with him. He wouldn't because he wanted EmmaLee to get to know his better side and not think he had no control around her.

Then tell her she is your mate, his wolf urged. *She'll understand why you're so protective.*

Connor couldn't do that yet. It was why he always acted so standoffish around her and worked hard to put some emotional distance between them. He feared that with one touch, he'd combust. Making love with her was totally out of the question. His wolf would insist on biting her, and he couldn't let that happen yet—at least not until this Slater business was settled. He'd die if anything happened to his mate.

Because she'd never met his father, his dad could follow her for a day or two while Connor figured things out.

Connor reached his house and headed inside. Needing to stop thinking about her, he grabbed a beer and settled in front of his television. She'd be safe for the night.

Or would she?

He lasted about an hour before he admitted he wouldn't get much sleep tonight if he didn't make sure EmmaLee was figuratively tucked in for the night. Connor would check up on her while giving his horny wolf a chance to let loose. After undressing, he stepped out of his house and then shifted. Once in his animal form, he ran toward EmmaLee's house, enjoying the strain on his muscles and letting the endorphins build. He had no intention of changing back into his human form when he reached his destination. If he did, he'd be naked, and that would really freak her out. She'd stare at his erection, and if she came too close, he would have to claim her. No, this was all about keeping her safe, which meant once he was certain she was okay, he'd leave.

As he neared her home, he didn't detect any other shifter signature looming nearby and his muscles relaxed. Connor should probably turn around and sprint home, but it wouldn't hurt to edge a bit closer—just to have visual confirmation she was okay.

Light lit the living room and all seemed calm. Not that he could smell her alluring scent from outside, but he could sense her essence. After circling her property a few times, his wolf began to whine.

One look is all I need, his wolf said.

You can't see inside from this close to the ground. The problem was that Connor wanted to look inside too.

Then shift.

Even though it was cold, he moved to the side of the living room window and did as his wolf suggested. One peek was all he required.

Oh, shit. Big mistake. She was on the sofa with an e-reader in her hand. That part was all well and good. The problem was that she was wearing a camisole, and her nipples were protruding. If that wasn't bad enough, her tiny panties made his mouth salivate and his cock harden.

Knock on the door, his wolf urged.

Are you crazy? I'm naked. No, you got your peep show. Now it's time to go back.

Let's watch a little longer.

Before he gave into his horny wolf, Connor shifted, and then high-tailed it out of there.

THE NEXT MORNING, Connor was slow to rise. Sleep had been a long time coming. It didn't seem to matter that he'd taken care of his sexual urges before hitting the hay. The moment he fell asleep, he dreamed of EmmaLee—and the desire and need for her returned with a vengeance. This constant edginess wasn't good for his health or for those he worked with. Something had to give—and soon.

The only antidote was to delve into work and try to forget about EmmaLee Donovan for a bit—assuming that was even possible. There was certainly enough to do at the office, especially since he needed to show Ronan the ropes, but concentrating would take all of his control.

Connor showered, shaved, and dressed. After he ate breakfast, he touched base with his dad to make sure he had an eye on EmmaLee.

"Don't worry. I'll be extra aware for any shifter signatures," his father said. "Are you certain this Coghill guy will come after her?"

"No, but I'm not taking any chances."

"That's good. Don't worry; she'll stay safe. Your mom's calling me to breakfast. I need to go."

Once at work, Connor parked in front with the rest of the crew, and then headed inside. Lexi barely glanced up as he walked by, which wasn't her usual style. Just as he was about to ask if something was wrong, a heavenly scent invaded his body—the same scent he'd tried to forget all last night in his dreams.

Connor spun around and faced Lexi. "EmmaLee is here?"

She lifted her chin. "Yes."

"Why?" He'd never be able to concentrate with her around. It was one of the reasons why he hadn't suggested she remain at the office in the first place. That and the fact the safe room was occupied at the time.

"When I told her that McKinnon and Associates had these amazing databases, she asked if she could come in and access them. I figured that since you want her protected, what better way than to have her here?"

Connor couldn't argue with her logic or admit why he didn't need EmmaLee there. "Good thinking."

As soon as he entered the large break room, he spotted Emma-Lee's back, her blonde head bent over a computer. He wanted to walk on by, but he couldn't ignore her.

We want her, so be nice, his wolf whined.

I'm always nice.

His wolf chuffed at him. *You can be a jerk. Please don't piss off our mate.*

His wolf said the last part on a growl and Connor pictured him baring his teeth. As hard as it was to admit, his wolf was right for a change.

"EmmaLee!" Connor said with as much cheer as he could muster, trying not to let his eyes betray him.

She spun around and smiled, and not merely a friendly type of smile, but one that looked like she wanted to eat him. And here, he thought he was the wolf.

"Connor, I was beginning to worry that you weren't coming in today."

"I slept in." He wasn't about to say her face kept invading his dreams and prevented a restful night. He moved closer and instantly realized his mistake. "What are you doing here?" Thankfully, he didn't sound too accusatory.

It didn't matter that Lexi had already explained it to him. He wanted to hear what EmmaLee had to say. He also needed to ask his dad why he hadn't let him know EmmaLee had left the compound.

"Lexi offered me a ride in this morning. She thought I'd be safer being surrounded by you all. Besides, you have much better Internet service."

His father must have spotted Lexi's car and figured it out. "I thought you wanted your freedom."

If he'd suggested she come here—which he never would have—she would have balked, believing he wanted to imprison her.

"This is freedom to me. I like being around people."

"Great. Let me know if you need anything."

He spun on his heels and strode off, hoping she didn't call his name. Her scent was swirling inside him, causing all sorts of things to happen to his body. He didn't need her seeing his teeth sharpen or the hair on his arms sprout. If she made a comment about his reaction, he hoped he could tell her it was because he just wanted to protect her and not because he wanted to ravish her until she became his.

WHEN CONNOR WALKED off without any further discussion, EmmaLee's heart turned heavy. What had she said to make him run away this time? Yes, he needed to get to work. She got that, but he could have asked what she was working on. EmmaLee mentally shrugged. Maybe it was for the best. He probably would have scoffed at her anyway. It wouldn't matter that Jackson, his best friend, had shown her some research he'd uncovered. It addressed a realm called Cargonia that mimicked the Earth. She had to say it was a little out there even for her, but Jackson assured her this place really existed.

Pushing Connor's less than welcoming response aside, she continued reading the article Jackson had shown her. If she thought the first half was hard to swallow, the rest was really strange. But if dragons did exist, why couldn't this other realm? Cargonia had demons, witches, shifters, gods, goddesses, and a portal connecting it to earth.

"Enjoying the article?"

EmmaLee nearly leapt off her chair at the intrusion. It was Jackson. She swiveled around to face him. "It's unbelievable." Literally.

"I thought so at first too, but a man by the name of Zane Barons is from Cargonia. He works over at the firehouse, or at least he will for the next few months."

The only way she would have been more stunned would be if Jackson had told her that a dragon shifter lived nearby. "You've met him?"

"Yes. In fact, he's mated to the sister of our Clan leader's mate."

EmmaLee was overwhelmed. "Do you think I could talk to him?"

"I'll see what I can do." He nodded to the computer. "Do you have any questions so far?"

She chuckled. "Questions? Only like a million, but I don't want to take up any more of your time. I'm sure you have plenty to do without babysitting me." She wanted to ask if Connor had told him to be nice to her, but she didn't really want to know the answer.

"I have a few minutes." Jackson dragged a chair over. "What would you like to know?"

"Naturally, this new realm has me curious, but let's start with the basics. What can you tell me about fated mates?"

He leaned back in his chair and stretched out his legs. "Interesting topic. I don't recall the article mentioning that."

Oh, crap. She had hoped he wouldn't have noticed. Now he'd think she was referring to Connor. Okay, she was a little bit, but she would be leaving soon. "I want my research to be complete. Start with how shifters are mated on Earth." Then she'd compare it to the sketchy information Vinea had provided.

Jackson's eyes sparkled with amusement. "I thought Vinea would have filled you in."

"It was a sore topic. To be honest, I don't think she had much expertise in that area. It wasn't as if she and her sister compared notes." That was mostly true.

Jackson chuckled. "I'm sure you're right. Devon has assured me that the two have recently made amends though."

Her pulse soared. "I'm so happy to hear it. I can see we have a lot to discuss the next time I call."

"I'll tell you what I know. Supposedly, Naliana decides who will be paired or mated with whom, though how she makes that decision, nobody knows. One of the two persons involved must be a shifter or a Wendayan, though I've never asked two humans if they think they've been paired."

This was all so exciting. She'd heard bits and pieces about how Naliana had been chosen over Vinea for the job of mating the shifters. "Go on."

"What I do know from experience is that when a shifter gets near his mate, his body, or maybe it's his inner animal, goes wild."

"Wild, as in he shifts?"

Jackson leaned forward. "That can happen, but usually we can control it. For example, the first time I met Ainsley, my mate, my body betrayed me totally. I could barely catch my breath, nor could I stop the hair from sprouting on my arms. The damnedest part was that I hated Ainsley. You see, she was a Changeling."

"A Changeling?"

"Yes. It's a long story. Suffice it to say that even though I didn't want to be attracted to her, I couldn't help it. I was in denial for quite some time that Ainsley was my mate."

EmmaLee tried to think back to whether Connor ever had such a strange reaction. His facial hair had grown, and his eyes turned amber on occasion, but she didn't know if that counted. "Did it get better? I can't imagine going through life like that."

"Thankfully yes. The need to be with Ainsley kept growing until we mated, and then it became worse."

"Worse?"

He smiled. "Yes, but over time, it has leveled out to where it is tolerable. At least now, I can focus on my job, in part because I can sense if she's in danger or if she's upset. All high level emotions are shared between us."

EmmaLee couldn't imagine being able to feel what Connor was thinking—assuming he was turned on or afraid. "If you're in a fight and are hurt, would Ainsley know?"

"Absolutely. The hard part is that she'd want to help. Fortunately, she can become invisible when she wants. Her adversaries don't stand a chance." He smiled.

"Vinea could do that."

"Very true, but Ainsley isn't a goddess—at least the world doesn't consider her one."

Aw, that was so sweet. "This really helps clear up a few things. Thank you."

"Any time. Anything else?"

"Not at the moment. I need to finish reading the article first."

Jackson stood and then headed back down the corridor. Emma-Lee's mind reeled. Had she known how much she would have learned about shifters and their habits by coming to Silver Lake, she might have agreed to take Connor up on his offer sooner.

A minute later, different voices sounded down the hallway, and butterflies attacked her again. It was Connor talking with someone, and she looked over her shoulder to see who it was. A huge bearded man, matching the description of Lexi's brother, walked alongside him.

"Let me introduce you to the woman I'm watching over," Connor said as he led this man over to her.

Was that all she was to him? Of course, it was. His older brother had asked that he make sure Slater didn't bother her again, and Connor had done just that.

"EmmaLee, this is Ronan Laramie, Lexi's brother."

"Nice to meet you." While this might not be the time or place to ask him questions, she didn't want to lose her opportunity to find out what he knew about dragon shifters. "Your sister said you might have seen a dragon shifter during your bounty hunting days."

"Ah." He glanced over at Connor whose brow had risen. "I thought I did, once, but I couldn't swear to it."

Connor clamped a hand over Ronan's shoulder. "Let me pour that coffee I promised you, and then I want to show you our technological headquarters."

"Sure." He turned toward her. "Nice meeting you, EmmaLee."

"You too."

Really? Connor had to drag away her most important source just when things were getting good? What was up with that? Because Lexi believed Ronan would be in Silver Lake for a while, EmmaLee would surely have other opportunities to speak with him.

Once Connor made the two coffees, they returned down the hallway again. She turned back to her computer, wanting to reread the story Jackson had shared, after which she'd search for other information about this new realm. Unfortunately, her mind refused to stop spinning. Connor wasn't indifferent to her, but he was uneasy around her. Why? Did he think her crazy ideas would rub off on him? Or did he know something and didn't want to chance spilling the beans?

She now had a new goal. To find out which it was.

Chapter Eight

"I 'VE LOOKED OVER what you have on this Slater Coghill man," Ronan said. "He's intriguing."

Connor hadn't expected that description. "Why do you say that?"

"He seems to be rather elusive. Says here there is no known address before he showed up in Billard, Georgia. In fact, I don't even see a social security number for him."

"I'm thinking he's using an alias."

"I thought the same thing. It makes it harder to trace him though. He probably has assumed another new alias by now."

"I agree." It was all the more reason to have Ronan on board.

Lexi's brother flipped over the page and tapped it. "For some reason, this guy looks familiar."

That was the first bit of good news he'd heard. "Do you think there are warrants out in other states on him? Is that where you've seen him?"

Ronan scratched his head. "I can't say. It will come to me eventually. What would you like me to do first?"

"Had I known about your ability to track with your nose, I would have gone to his house and *borrowed* something of his."

Ronan smiled. "I'm better when I meet the shifter in person first, but an object of his can work. Do you think EmmaLee has anything of Coghill's with her?"

Connor's stomach twisted. He hoped the hell not. She'd said she wanted nothing to do with him. "I can ask her."

"Good."

Connor's cell rang. It was Kalan. "This might be good news." He pressed the cell to his ear. "Hey, Kalan."

"I called in a favor and found Timothy Delahart's credit card number."

"That's great." He picked up a pen off the desk. "Tell me."

Kalan gave him the information. "I hope it helps."

"I'm sure it will."

"How's EmmaLee?" Kalan asked.

"Good. In fact, she hitched a ride in this morning with Lexi, and she's working away on one of the computers here at the office."

"Perfect. Let me know if you need help with anything else."

Kalan was such a stand up guy. "I will, and thanks."

Connor disconnected and slid the paper across the desk. "We have the credit card number for your man. If you'd like, I can have Jackson check to see if any activity shows up on it."

Ronan smiled. "Like I said; don't make my job too easy."

Connor laughed. "Trust me, knowing the man's location at one point in time doesn't mean you can catch him."

"I know. Now it's just a waiting game with Delahart. Do you mind if I question EmmaLee about Coghill?"

Connor was more than happy to turn that task over to him. Even being in the same building with her was enough to make his wolf ready to pounce. "Be my guest."

EMMALEE WAS SURPRISED when Ronan pulled up a chair. "So what are you working on?" he asked.

She'd read and reread the article that Jackson had given her and had just moved on to finding any more sightings of dragon shifters when he arrived.

"Dragon shifters."

His eyes widened. "Did you find any?" he asked with total sincerity.

"I found an article that claims a dragon descended on Hickory, Florida and set a warehouse on fire after being confronted. I was in the middle of reading it when you arrived."

"Any pictures?" Ronan asked, leaning forward.

"This one, but it's just of the torched building."

He leaned closer. "Click that link."

She did and a very blurry photo of what looked like a dragon appeared. EmmaLee nearly lost her breath. The problem was that the animal was backlit by flames, casting him in a shadow, but the outline of his wing was clear. "What do you think?"

Ronan studied it. "Looks like a fake to me."

Damn. She looked a little closer and noticed a small gap between the animal and the background. "I agree, but what tipped you off?"

"Not the photo per se, but a warehouse? Smells like arson to me. Sure seems like someone wants to point a finger at something else."

She chuckled. "I think I would have picked an animal less obvious than a fire-breathing dragon." Now was the time to find out what he knew. "You said you might have seen one?"

He chuckled. "Like I said before, I thought I had, but I'm convinced it was another ruse."

That was disappointing. "Too bad. If you had the chance, would you want to meet one?"

"Yes and no. I have no idea if they really do shoot fire, but if they do, I wouldn't want anything to do with them. A wolf would be fried to a crisp in seconds."

She shivered at that thought. "I want to see one but only from afar."

"I hear ya."

"Thanks for not laughing at me."

Ronan's mouth curled downward. "Not me. Who around here makes fun of you?"

"Connor. He thinks the whole idea is ridiculous."

Ronan leaned back in his chair and crossed his arms over his chest. "I say that's shortsighted of him. Since there are wolf and bear shifters, why wouldn't there be dragon shifters?"

She liked this man. "Exactly. Connor says it's because wolves and bears exist in the real world, and dragons don't."

"Can he prove dragons don't exist?"

She chuckled. "Even I don't believe they do. Their eating habits alone would make them too conspicuous."

"Maybe you're right. Change of subject. Do you mind if I ask you a few questions regarding the man who harmed you?"

Acid dripped into her stomach at the mere thought of Slater. "Are you working with Connor on the case?"

"Yes."

She'd told Connor everything, but if Ronan needed to hear it again, that was okay. "What would you like to know?"

"Where did Slater Coghill live before he moved to Billard?"

She stilled. "I asked him, but he said he lived in a lot of different places. He was a rather restless soul and liked to move around."

"I see. When he lived in Billard, did he have any special place he liked to go?"

She thought his questions rather odd. "You mean by himself?"

"Or with you. Billard is in the mountains. I'm wondering if he had a cabin that he owned or liked to rent."

"Yes! One of his good friends had a place in Darnell, Georgia."

Ronan lifted his cell from his shirt pocket and made a note. "You don't happen to have an address or the name of this friend, do you?"

She shook his head. "Slater called him Bubba. I know that doesn't help."

"It might."

"You think he's holed up there?"

Ronan smiled. "I guess I'll have to find out. Last question. I know this is a long shot, but did you bring anything of his with you—like a shirt or something he held a lot?"

That was the strangest question to date. "No. I want nothing more to do with that man." Her mind spun. "Do you work with a bloodhound?"

"No." He stood. "Thanks for your time, and keep looking for those dragon shifters. I'd love to learn one exists, but I don't want to get tangled up with one."

"I totally agree."

Ronan returned the way he came. She liked Lexi's brother. He was open-minded, quite different from the way his sister had described him. Then again, siblings didn't always share everything.

A short while later, Lexi entered the room. "I'm on my break. Do you want me to drop you off at home, or do you want to stay here until I leave at five?"

Since Connor didn't seem to be too pleased that she'd stopped by, EmmaLee might be better off heading back to the house and not upsetting him further. "I'll catch a ride back with you now, thanks."

"Do you want to tell Connor you're leaving?" Lexi asked.

She shrugged. "I don't think he cares one way or the other."

"You know that's not true." Lexi asked. "He must care if he watched over you for a few weeks."

"It was a request from his brother. Remember, Vinea is my best friend."

Lexi nodded. "What if I let him know that I'm driving you back?"

In a way, she wanted him to worry, but if he took the time to drive over to the guesthouse just to check, she would feel guilty. "Sure, if you want to."

"Be right back."

Lexi strode toward the hallway where the offices were located. As much as she had wanted to see where Connor worked, it was best not to dwell on the reserved man. She'd be better off to lay low until Slater was caught and then return home to her friends.

AROUND FIVE, CONNOR had mentioned to Ronan that he was swamped with work, and the newcomer immediately volunteered to stand watch over EmmaLee. While Connor wasn't really sure why Ronan agreed to the bodyguard job, he wasn't going to turn down the offer. After meeting the man, he had full confidence that Ronan was too dedicated to his job to put the moves on her.

Almost three hours later, his wolf interrupted him. *You should have told Ronan you and EmmaLee were mates.*

Maybe, but I didn't want to chance that piece of information getting back to her.

You are a chicken shit.

He was beginning to think that was true. Pushing his unwarranted concern aside, he believed Ronan enjoyed what McKinnon and Associates had to offer. Most likely, Ronan just wanted to prove he could be a team player, despite having worked on his own his whole life.

His wolf grunted. *Did you forget that Ronan believes in dragon shifters? That alone could cause a bond to form.*

Shit. If you think I'd tell anyone that EmmaLee is ours—other than Dad—you're crazy.

What if Ronan asks her out? You act like you don't like her, his wolf shot back. *There's no reason for him not to pursue her—or for EmmaLee not to accept.*

Ronan won't. He's not that kind of guy.

Can you be positive? his wolf asked.

Fuck. Maybe he had screwed up. Showing up at her house right now would only make things more awkward between them. He had to trust that EmmaLee would not show any interest in the newcomer.

It's almost eight. Why not take a break and get your head on straight? his wolf said. *I don't need you to mess things up for us permanently.*

That was true. Connor was more convinced than ever that his thoughts were in the wrong place right now and that he was incapable of making rational decisions when it came to EmmaLee.

Heeding his wolf's warning, he shut down his computer, slipped on his coat, and left.

Once in his car, he needed to decide where he wanted to go. If he went home, he'd want to go over to EmmaLee's and check on her. Ronan had checked in once to say she'd provided him with some useful intel on Coghill. Hopefully, she hadn't been holding back information, though she had no reason to do that.

Damn, this whole mate thing was clouding his mind, and he couldn't allow it to make him miss asking important questions. He was always so thorough. The only solution was to put some space between them.

Instead of going home, he headed east, and ended up in the parking lot of McKinnon Pub and Pool. Connor could have spoken to Rye about his problem, but knowing his older brother, he'd suggest telling EmmaLee the truth about them being mates, and Connor was sure that would lead to disaster.

Because Finn wasn't mated, he might have a better solution. And being a bartender, he was used to listening to a lot of people's problems. Hoping his younger brother could help him make some sense out of everything, he went inside.

The bar had a fair number of people in it for eight o'clock on a Thursday night. As usual, his brother was at the bar pouring a beer for a customer. Connor slid on the end stool, not wanting to engage in conversation.

When his brother was free, he came over. "Haven't seen you in ages—what's the occasion?"

Finn always complained that Connor worked too hard. "Thought I'd enjoy some R&R. After a few weeks of bodyguard duty, I'm ready for a break. Lexi's brother is watching her." He smiled, hoping to convince Finn he was glad he didn't have to be by EmmaLee's side.

"Mom said EmmaLee is really nice. I take it you didn't think so?"

"She's nice if not a little out there." He couldn't say that the woman had already invaded his soul or that his wolf wanted her something fierce.

Finn laughed. "Out there? Too much to handle, huh?"

Finn clearly saw through his lie. Connor leaned forward. "Actually, yes. I'm really confused. She's my client, but I'm highly attracted to her."

"Ah, I see the problem. Maybe you should bring her by, and I can study how she reacts to you."

Then Finn would know for sure they were mates. "She'd like that I'm sure."

"Great."

You came here to get his opinion, his wolf asked. *Ask him.*

He'll say to tell her the truth. Fuck. So why didn't he? He would just as soon as the moment was right.

"Can I just get a beer?" Connor asked.

Chicken, his wolf growled, but Connor didn't respond.

"Coming right up."

Finn turned away to reach for a bottle and popped off the cap. As he returned to place it in front of Connor, he noticed the dark circles under his brother's eyes. So, Connor wasn't the only one who hadn't been sleeping well either.

Finn slid the beer across the bar. "Jackson and Ainsley were just in here, by the way. He was chatting up a storm about how sweet EmmaLee was. I have to say, her interests are quite intriguing."

Dear goddess. He didn't need the town to know what she was working on. "They are indeed. Tell me, have you been sleeping?" Connor asked, wanting to change the subject.

His brother glanced off to the side. "It's on and off."

The sudden seriousness of his tone caught Connor off guard. "Are you having nightmares or something?"

"Nightmares? No. It's more like I hear this amazing and sensual voice in my head, and then I see this gorgeous auburn haired beauty floating above me. She beckons me, and my wolf wants her really badly." He waved a hand. "I figure it has to be the stress of being the manager here that is causing it. I've never dreamt anything like that before."

Finn never let stress get to him. "Have you ever met this woman before?"

"No, never, but I swear I can smell her scent, and trust me, she's not in my room." Finn leaned closer. "I get so excited I have to do something about it, and that's not like me."

Finn never lacked female companionship. "I'm sure there are a lot of women who would be willing to ease your pain." Connor probably should take his own advice, but no one other than EmmaLee would satisfy him.

Finn shook his head. "That's the thing. I don't think it would help. I was thinking of seeing a shrink, but what could he do other than prescribe some meds, claiming I'm anxious, but I'm not. This woman seems so real."

"Does she have a name?"

"Kaleena."

That was spooky. Connor dreamed of people, but if he hadn't met them, he didn't name them. "What else does she say or do?"

His face reddened. "She says we're meant for each other."

Connor leaned forward in order not to be overheard. "Meant for each other? As in she's your fated mate?"

Finn looked off to the side before answering. "I think so. I know this sounds crazy, but I asked if we could meet."

"What did she say?" Connor dreamed about EmmaLee, and each time, she answered him. Finn might not be overworked but rather in need of a mate.

His brother pressed his lips together, clearly debating how much to tell. "That the time would come when we would no longer be apart."

Maybe Finn was losing it. "What are you going to do?"

"Do? It's not like I can ask you or Jackson to search for her. She's not real."

"Maybe she is. I'm thinking you've met her but don't remember. Was there some hot woman who you saw in here who caught your wolf's attention?"

Finn slipped the white bar cloth off his shoulder and polished the already clean bar. "Not that I can think of. Besides, this woman is different than a normal woman."

Now Finn was beginning to scare him. "What do you mean?"

His brother lifted one shoulder. "She'll be fully human one minute and then almost transparent the next." A small smile appeared. "Once I thought she even had wings! Yes, I know I've lost it."

EmmaLee never changed forms in his dreams. Connor finished half of his glass. "How about seeing if Ophelia will meet with you? Dev said she was amazing with Vinea, revealing all sorts of things."

"I might have to do that. Not that I'm really big into spells and shit, but hell, I can't go on like this."

Here Connor thought he had problems being around EmmaLee. Finn just might have it worse.

Chapter Nine

"SO TELL ME what Slater was like," Ronan said after he explained why he'd suddenly shown up at her door instead of Connor.

Not that EmmaLee was surprised that Connor hadn't come, but she was disappointed. She'd wanted to see him. If nothing else, she needed to discuss what Jackson had shown her regarding this other realm. That should make Connor more open-minded about the existence of dragon shifters.

She mentally shrugged. All she could think of was that Connor must be growing tired of her. If that were the case, maybe it was for the best that he kept his distance. Every time she was around him, her heart went on a rollercoaster ride. Stupid, really, since he consistently shut her out.

Ronan placed a hand on her arm. "EmmaLee? Are you okay?"

She jerked her attention back to him. "Yes, sorry."

She'd never tell him Connor had been on her mind, nor would she admit that she wasn't really in the mood to discuss Slater since she'd made a fool of herself over him. Slater needed to be caught, and if Ronan were willing to help, she'd do whatever it took.

"I get it. You've been through a lot."

"I have. For the most part, Slater was a nice guy. He just had a bad temper, that's all."

"What was his trigger?" He pulled out his cell phone.

"Do you mean what set him off?" she asked. She'd already told

Connor, but he must not have mentioned it.

"Yes. If, for example, a guy from work was hitting on you, did Slater become enraged?"

She chuckled. "No, Slater wasn't the jealous type." She sipped her coffee, trying to think if there was one thing that bothered him. "My research troubled him—at least it did at times."

His eyebrows knit together. "What was it that made him mad?"

EmmaLee clasped her coffee cup with both hands and lifted it to her lips again. "Like Connor, he thought I was a bit crazy to be researching dragon shifters."

"Dragon shifters upset him that much?"

She almost chuckled at his look of surprise. "Yes. I have to admit I can be a bit obsessive on the topic. I always assumed his anger stemmed from the fact he was jealous that I wasn't paying him much mind, but there were a lot of times I had to study or work an extra shift and he was okay with that."

"Did anything else bother him?"

She had to think back. "The first time he hit me, I'd just received a phone call from someone I used to date."

"So he was the jealous type," Ronan said.

Now, she was confused. "I don't know. Maybe. Slater was like Dr. Jekyll and Mr. Hyde. That was what made it hard to walk away. After each angry episode, he'd say he was sorry, and I believed him. I always believed he'd change."

"I've heard most men don't."

"You're probably right," she said. "But Slater oozed sincerity. I swear the man could charm a snake. He was definitely a slick one. I guess I was taken with him because he was more sophisticated than the usual Billard, Georgia man. Why he picked me to date, I don't know."

Ronan smiled. "Oh, come on now. You're easy on the eyes, and your curiosity is contagious. You're a smart girl. How many women in Billard are working on a master's degree while having a full time job?"

What she wouldn't give if Connor saw her that way. "Not many, I guess."

Ronan made some notes. "What did he do for a living?"

"He managed a local department store."

His forehead rose. "Would you say his main characteristic was that he was sophisticated?"

EmmaLee blew out a breath. She didn't know what he was implying. She tried to find a better way to describe Slater. "Eerily smart might be a better word. Slater seemed to know things, like how things worked, better than the average man. I always told him he should open up his own store instead of working for someone else, but he said he didn't want to be tied down."

"What was the name of this store?"

"Hanson's."

Ronan leaned back in his seat and tapped his screen. "Is it a chain?"

"Yes. It's mostly in the southern part of the US." Ronan added that piece of information, but she didn't see why it was relevant. "Do you think he will try to get hired at one of the other sites to be closer to me, assuming he knows where I am?" Connor thought that if Slater figured out where she was living, he might ask for a transfer.

"It's possible, but he knows he's a wanted man. Let me ask you this. I believe you mentioned that Slater liked to travel?" Ronan said.

She didn't know how any of this would help find him. "Yes. He said he wasn't good with staying in one place."

"Who was his best friend in town?"

"He worked a lot and liked his alone time when he wasn't with me, but he did hang out with Bubba a bit—the guy who owned the cabin in the woods."

He typed in a note. "Okay. How did you meet Slater?" Ronan asked.

"At a bar. I was with a group of my girlfriends, and he offered to buy me a drink. The rest just happened."

"I see."

While Ronan might believe her answers could lead him to Slater, his questions had dredged up bad memories. EmmaLee yawned. "Do you think we can continue this at another time? All of a sudden, I'm exhausted. Maybe it was reading all those articles that did it."

From the look in Ronan's eyes, he didn't buy her story, but he stood anyway. "I'll give Connor a call to let him know I'm heading out."

He was such a nice man, though she wished he wouldn't tell Connor she'd be by herself. Then he might stop by and she wasn't ready for more rejection. "Thank you."

"Keep looking for that dragon shifter. If anyone can find him, you can." With that he left.

EmmaLee sat there for a minute, trying to figure out what he meant? Why would he think she'd be successful when no one else had? She liked Ronan, but he was a strange one.

IT WAS PAST nine by the time Connor rolled into his driveway. Finn asked more questions about EmmaLee, and even asked outright, if they were mates. Tired of lying, he told him the truth. Once he explained her situation, Finn agreed that Connor should wait a bit before they mated, but that he should let her know he wanted her. Whether he could express his emotions without making love with her was anyone's guess.

As soon as Connor shut off the engine, his cell rang. From the area code, it was Ronan. "Hey there."

"I'm sitting down the street from EmmaLee's house now. She wanted to go to bed, so I left."

"Everything go okay?"

"Yes. We spent quite a lot of time discussing Slater."

"Learn anything useful?"

"I'm not sure. When I get back to the safe room, I'll do a little research. I have a few ideas rattling around in my head."

"I appreciate you watching her," Connor said. More than he

could know. From his tone, the two of them got along well. "I'll call my dad to make sure he remains vigilant." Unlike this morning.

"I'll wait here five more minutes then take off."

"Thanks." Connor appreciated that Ronan didn't want to take any chances with her life. As much as it made sense for EmmaLee to move in with him, Connor didn't trust his wolf—or himself for that matter.

Try it, you'll like it, his wolf urged.

Not bothering to answer, he called his dad who assured him he'd make sure to keep an eye out.

Knowing that his mate was in good hands, he dragged himself out of the car and went inside his house. While he was pleased EmmaLee seemed to be doing okay, Finn was not. He'd never seen his brother so upset in his life. Now that he'd told someone about the dreams, maybe they'd lesson in their frequency. Or so he hoped.

Connor grabbed a beer and drank it, though he didn't enjoy it as much as usual. Guilt at not stopping by to see EmmaLee tugged at him. Since he had a few hours before he hit the hay, he decided to drive by the house just to check that she'd gone to bed, and then he'd return home and relax.

As he entered his parents' drive, he decided to stop in. His dad might have some insight as to the best way to make sure Slater didn't slip by unnoticed. Connor rang the bell to let them know they had company then tested the doorknob. To his surprise, it was locked.

His dad answered a moment later. "Hey, I thought I heard your car. Come on in."

Connor looked around. "Where's mom?"

"She had a headache and went to bed."

While he was sorry to hear that, it was his father he wanted to speak with. "Are you still okay watching EmmaLee?"

His father smiled then walked into the den where he sat on his lounge chair. "Haven't had to do much. Lexi picked her up this morning, and she wasn't home for too long before Ronan showed. I appreciated the heads up that he was coming. At least he and Coghill look nothing alike."

His dad was a good watchdog. "Thanks, but if any one comes by to take her someplace, please let me know."

"Sure, son. Oh, I have good news."

Connor hadn't expected that, but most likely it was to change the subject. "What's that?"

"I have a friend in the airline business who I asked to do a little snooping."

"Dad." Connor didn't want the firm to get into legal trouble.

"She's cool. Christine is a wolf shifter and knows how to keep her mouth shut."

His father always did push the boundaries. "What did you learn?"

"Let me back up. Actually, Daniel and I called in some favors with our fellow shifters around the country. I sent them the photo of Coghill and asked them to be on the lookout for him."

His father's contacts were extensive. It would take Connor at least twenty years to have so many. "Don't tell me they found him?"

"As a matter of fact, yes. He was spotted in New Orleans."

His pulse soared. "That's fantastic. Where exactly?"

His dad held up a hand. "Just hold your horses. Something strange is going on with this young man."

Connor leaned forward. "What do you mean?"

"My airline friend said Coghill bought a ticket for a nonstop flight leaving Atlanta at eleven p.m. last night for New Orleans."

"So?"

"He never got on the plane, yet he was seen at one in the morning at a bar in New Orleans. Apparently, there was a slight altercation that involved Slater Coghill. No one was hurt so there were no charges. When the cop returned to the station and ran both names, he found that Coghill was wanted. When he returned to arrest him, he was gone."

"He has been elusive, but it's not strange that he bought a ticket but then didn't use it. He could have purchased a non-refundable ticket a few days ago, and then decided to drive to New Orleans."

"I thought of that, but Coghill checked in at nine at the ticket counter but never boarded the plane."

That made no sense. "Are you sure it was him?"

"Yes."

Connor tried to come up with a logical explanation. "He might have purchased a different airline ticket, especially if he thought someone was following him."

"It's possible. Jackson might be able to get a hold of the surveillance footage in New Orleans and check to see if he got off on different flight."

Connor didn't even want to know how many laws that would break. "This is good information. I might have to pay a visit to New Orleans. If I do, can I ask you to take care of EmmaLee?"

"You know I will."

The tension in his body almost disappeared as soon as he learned Slater wasn't in Tennessee. EmmaLee would be safe for a while unless Slater was headed in their direction.

Once Connor left his dad's, he glanced at the guesthouse through the trees. The lights were on once more. Instead of driving to her place, he decided he could use the short walk to clear his head. Besides, his headlights might scare her if she was still up. He'd only meant to peek through the window to see if she was fine, but somehow his finger found the doorbell instead.

"Who is it?" she called.

Just hearing her voice had his wolf jumping up and down. "It's Connor."

The door opened, and all she was wearing was a thin nightgown underneath an open terrycloth robe. His heart pounded and his wolf clawed. This wasn't good. "I have some news about Slater."

"Really? Come in."

As he stepped past her, her scent caused his teeth to sharpen. *Stand down wolf,* he commanded.

She wants you, came the response. *I can sense her rapid heart rate, and her pheromones are pumping.*

Connor refused to listen. "I didn't mean to disturb you. I saw the lights, and I hadn't realized you'd dressed for bed. We can talk tomorrow."

Her mouth opened slightly, and her pink tongue nearly peeked out. "I won't sleep until I hear what you have to say. Please sit down. Can I get you anything to drink?"

"No, thanks." He wouldn't be staying long. "My father called in a few favors and learned that Coghill was spotted in New Orleans." He took the chair while she slid down on the sofa across from him. The furniture was too damn close to each other for his comfort.

"New Orleans? What's he doing there?"

"I have no idea. I was hoping you'd know."

She shook her head. "I have no idea."

"There is one thing that Dad and I found a bit odd." Connor detailed what his father told him.

"Could he have taken a private plane down there instead?"

Connor straightened. "I hadn't thought of that." He wouldn't mention that he'd ask Jackson to hack into the surveillance footage since it might make her more anxious.

The resulting smile had his cock hardening even more. He leaned forward with his elbows resting on his knees and clasped his hands together to block her view. It was damn uncomfortable and made his dick feel like it would snap in half, but he was willing to deal with it just to be able to gain a bit of control while he spoke with her.

"A commercial airline ticket and a seat on a private plane would cost a pretty penny. Does he have that kind of money?" he asked.

"No. He was a manager of a store, but he didn't make that much. His car was about seven years old, and when we went out, it was often to fast food places."

"Interesting. Let's hope he stays in Louisiana for a while."

"That would be nice."

Now that he'd told her the news, he was curious how her evening went. "How did it go with Ronan?" Connor worked to keep his tone light.

Between the shrug of her shoulder and the lack of tension on her face, he'd acted appropriately. "He asked a lot of questions about Slater, which as you know is not my favorite topic, but I understand he was only trying to help."

"When I compare what I've learned to what Ronan thinks, we'll get him."

"I doubt I told him anything new." She leaned closer, and he swore he could see her breasts through the top, forcing Connor to look away. "Are you going to go after him, or will you send someone else?"

From the tension in her voice and the way it wobbled, she wanted him to stay close. "Sam volunteered to help, as did Ronan. Someone needs to stay here to protect you."

"I'll be fine if you want to go. You said your dad is here to make sure nothing happens."

"He is. As the former Alpha, he's still a powerful man." Connor stood, not sure how much longer he could handle being near his mate without pulling that lush body against him and kissing her into oblivion.

EmmaLee jumped up from the sofa. "Thank you for everything."

He watched her come closer, but he was unable to move a muscle to step out of the way. Even when she wrapped her arms around his neck, he remained frozen. It was as if she was a Wendayan with a power to stun him.

It's her mate appeal, his wolf said with way too much glee in his voice.

EmmaLee stood on her tiptoes and tilted up her chin. As if his wolf forced his head to dip down, their lips met, and hormones flooded his body. Holy hell. After being cooped up with her for those few weeks, his needs had escalated to the point of being painful. His wolf clawed at his gut for release. Connor groaned as their lips melted together and their breaths became one.

He finally gave in and ramped up the heat of the kiss. Just as the tips of their tongues touched, EmmaLee stepped back. Connor wasn't sure what he would have done if she hadn't. He pressed his forehead against hers and looked at her through hooded eyes.

"EmmaLee." His voice cracked along with his bones.

Chapter Ten

C ONNOR'S LOOK WAS lustful and predatory, almost as if he wanted to devour her. It reminded EmmaLee of the wolf from the fairytale that exclaimed: *All the better to eat you with, my dear.* A small nervous giggle escaped and she tried to cover her tracks. "What? It was only a thank you kiss."

She watched Connor blink a few times, his body stiffening as he stepped away from her. "I know. And you're welcome. I should go."

She'd had enough of his distant attitude. It was obvious he was attracted to her, but he kept putting up a concrete wall between them. "I've been thinking," she said. "Since I can't pay you for watching over me, now that Slater is gone, maybe I should just catch a bus back to Billard."

"No!"

Okay, she hadn't expected the response to be quite that strong, though his vehemence pleased her. "Why? I feel as if I'm inconveniencing you. I understood your need to get back to work when we were in Georgia, but now that you're here, would it be so hard to smile once in a while?"

She probably shouldn't have been so direct, but her heart and ego could only take so much coldness, or should she say hot and coldness. One minute he acted as if he wanted to ravage her, and the next it was as if she was distasteful to be around—like now.

Connor stabbed a hand over his head and glanced away. "I'm sorry."

He sounded like Slater. "Saying you're sorry won't cut it."

"Shit. I'm sorry… I mean I'll try to do better." He smiled, but it didn't reach his eyes.

Now she was the one who felt bad for forcing the issue—kind of. "It's okay."

"Listen. How about tomorrow night I take you out to dinner?"

Her pulse sped up. "Like a date?"

"Like a date." This time his smile turned genuine.

At first, she thought it was a pity date, but he almost sounded happy about the way things had turned out. "Okay then."

She placed a hand on his arm to escort him to the door, and he stiffened for a moment. She was about to ask him what was his problem when she noticed his five o'clock shadow had thickened and his eyes had turned almost amber. Her pulse soared. As much as she wanted to think it was because he was attracted to her, she didn't want to get her hopes up.

The biggest question she needed to ask herself right now was whether she was ready to be with Connor and chance being hurt emotionally.

Baby steps, EmmaLee, she thought to herself happily, as she ran her fingertips over her lips remembering their kiss. *Baby steps.*

CONNOR ROSE EARLY the next day and was in the office before EmmaLee had the chance to arrive. He needed to get in a few hours of work before her presence distracted him. Last night, he'd managed very little sleep, mostly because he kept reliving that kiss. It had been stupid on his part to check up on her, as being around her always caused his wolf to go wild, but he hadn't been able to stay away.

Freezing her out like he had hadn't been wise either. He'd hurt her feelings, and for that he was sorry. If he'd stayed however, he might have given into his wolf urges, and that could have led to something he might regret later.

He just hoped she didn't decide he wasn't worth being around and demand he drive her to the bus station—instead of merely hinting she should go back to Billard.

Connor didn't blame her for wanting to go. Every time they shared a nice moment, his body would react, and he'd run off. Letting his wolf rule him was not an option right now nor was making love with her. She wasn't ready.

She's ready. She kissed you! his wolf growled. *It's you who aren't ready.*

Connor ignored the slam. *That doesn't mean she wants to mate with me. She was thanking me.*

His wolf huffed, and he would have sworn he heard his wolf calling him *idiot*.

Well shit, he knew he was being a jerk, but it was easier to convince himself she wasn't attracted to him than face his true emotions. The day was fast approaching, however, when it would be too late to make amends. Tonight's date might be his last chance. He'd wine and dine her and enjoy being with her. When he took EmmaLee home, he'd kiss her goodnight and tell how good they were together. Then he'd leave—with a smile on his face.

As long as he didn't expose his sharpened teeth or elongated nails, he would be okay.

Wishful thinking, his wolf said. *I won't let you just stop at one kiss the next time.*

You have to behave. Our goal is for EmmaLee to really want us.

This time, his wolf didn't respond.

He was worried she would be more interested in his wolf because he was a shifter than in him as a man, and he wanted her feelings to be true to both sides and not just for shifter research.

Connor checked his watch, antsy for Ronan to arrive. He needed to ask if her rants about dragon shifters had merit. Had Connor been too narrow minded about such things? If only dragons existed in the real world, he'd believe there could be shifters who were.

Dinosaurs were real at one point, his wolf chimed in. *Some could even fly! Dragons aren't far off the evolutionary chain, you know.*

Perhaps he should do some research on that topic. It would give them something to discuss at dinner tonight. Connor opened his laptop to check it out when he spotted an email from Jackson labeled, *About EmmaLee*. His pulse soared. Why hadn't Jackson called him with his findings instead of emailing them?

He had asked Jackson to do a background check on her, but did he really want to find out more? If she grew up under terrible circumstances he'd feel horrible.

The only way to know would be to open the damn thing. So he did. Connor had to read it a few times in order to make sure he was getting the facts right. While he'd thought he understood her, he wouldn't have guessed that both of EmmaLee's parents had been college professors teaching medieval lore and legends no less. At least one piece of the puzzle fell into place as to why she was so focused on the paranormal.

Next, he opened the attachment. It was from Social Services stating that after her parents died in a horrific fire when she was twelve, her father's oldest brother and his wife, who were childless, adopted her. Uncle Robert was a doctor and Aunt Kathy worked in his office as his nurse.

There was no mention of whether they were still alive, but that would be easy to find out. Connor typed in the man's name and location, and sure enough, his medical office, along with his picture, appeared.

Before he could read up on them, someone knocked on his door. "Come in."

It was Ronan. Good. He could use a sounding board.

"I have some information on Mr. Coghill," Ronan stated.

"So do I," he said and motioned that he take a seat.

Ronan pulled up a chair. "You first."

Connor told him that the cops spotted Coghill in New Orleans. "I'm thinking he might have bought two airline tickets as a decoy."

"I'm not sure why he would do that unless he expected the cops to arrest him when he got off the plane. If that were the case, why get on a plane in the first place? Or pick that town?"

"You're right. Surely, police have better things to do than waste their manpower on a man only accused of assault."

Ronan shrugged. "Agreed." He stroked his beard. "Nothing is making sense."

Jackson tapped on the opened door and then stepped in. "Good. You're both here. I have news."

This was a record day. "I was just bringing Ronan up to speed," Connor said. "Dad said he asked you to look at the surveillance cameras at the airport. Did you find something?"

"I did. Coghill didn't get off any plane that landed in New Orleans around midnight. I did see him in the airport checking in, but then he walked out."

"He must have flown." Ronan said.

"Then it had to have been on a private flight," Connor said.

"That's just it," Jackson said. "I thought that too so I checked all of the local airfields around Atlanta. No one fitting Slater's description was on any of them."

"What time did you see him exiting the Atlanta airport?" Ronan asked.

Jackson scrolled through his phone where he always kept his notes. "Around ten, ninety minutes before departure."

"Then how did he get to New Orleans in less than two hours?" he asked.

Jackson held up his hands. "Beats me."

They threw out a few more possibilities, but in the end they decided it didn't matter. Bottom line was that Slater Coghill had been in New Orleans yesterday. Whether he was still there, they didn't know. "If we knew his reason for going there, we might figure out what his future plans are," Connor said. "I really want to know if he has any intention of returning to Billard to pick up his things or come after EmmaLee."

Ronan leaned forward. "Can you think of a reason why he'd want to harm her again?"

"No. From what she told me, sometimes she'd say something that made him mad. I didn't get the sense that he was targeting her," Connor said.

"That's what I sensed from our conversation. I'm happy to fly down there to check him out," Ronan said. "If I see him and get his scent, he's as good as mine."

"Don't bother," Jackson said.

They both faced him. "Why?" Ronan asked.

"That's what I came to tell you. My father, who seems to have resources I can only dream of, said that Coghill was spotted in New York City this afternoon."

Connor shook his head. "That person has to be wrong."

"They swear it was him."

"Could Coghill have a doppelganger?" Ronan asked.

"If that's true, we're really screwed. We'll never find him," Connor said.

EMMALEE WAS NERVOUS yet excited to go out on a date with Connor. A date! As in, they'd make eye contact, talk, and enjoy themselves. Lexi had called this morning to see if EmmaLee wanted a ride into work, but she told her no because she didn't want to jinx anything. Just her luck, she'd find something on the Internet to tell Connor about, and then he'd cancel their dinner. No, it was better to keep out of his hair for at least one day; that whole absence makes the heart grow fonder thing.

Deciding what to wear was her biggest challenge. It never occurred to her when she was leaving Billard to pack something dressy. Even though Connor hadn't told her where they were going, she wanted to look as nice as she could. The days were warming up, but the nights still had a chill to them.

After trying on and then eliminating half her wardrobe, she chose dark jeans and ankle-high boots, along with a black sweater to accentuate her blonde hair. The first time she'd let it hang loose,

Connor had commented that he liked it that way.

When the doorbell finally rang, she jumped, not even aware she'd been standing there thinking. Inhaling, she rushed to open the door. While it had only been a day, seeing Connor jacked up her libido something fierce. He too was dressed in dark jeans and boots, but his blue button-down shirt and sports jacket had her hormones dancing. She was about to tell him how handsome he looked, but she wasn't sure he'd appreciate hearing it from her. Connor was touchy when it came to personal things—or feelings.

"Come in. I'll get my coat."

Before he could step in, EmmaLee rushed over to the dining room table and grabbed it. Connor followed her and helped her on with it. Thrilled he really thought of this as a date, EmmaLee relaxed.

"Ready?" he asked.

"Yes." As she headed out the door, she grabbed her purse then locked up. EmmaLee didn't need Slater returning from New Orleans, sneaking into her place, and then lying in wait when she returned.

As always, Connor opened and held the car door for her then motioned she slip inside. When he started the engine, she debated asking him if he'd learned anything more about Slater, but then decided it would be best if she concentrated on Connor the man, not Connor the bodyguard.

The problem now was what to talk to him about? Too many topics seemed to be off limits. "So what's there to do around here for fun?" she asked, pretending as if she were free of Slater for good.

"What do you like to do?"

She chuckled. "I've mostly spent my life working. I've never really had time for fun, and the few free hours I've had, I usually read romance novels. You?"

He pressed his lips together as if he needed to think. "Well, when I was younger, I loved to hike, ride horses, fish, and stuff like that."

"But now that you're the owner of your company all you do is work, work, work, right?"

He glanced over at her and smiled. "Maybe I should hire a publicist to polish my image, but yes, I do work a lot."

"You don't go to parties?" she asked. While she didn't attend many, when she was invited, it was the highlight of her month.

"I mostly attend family get-togethers—Sunday dinners and all. Not that we shifters don't mix with humans, we do, but it makes for a more relaxed atmosphere when we don't have to watch what we say."

She'd never considered what it would be like to have to conceal her identity. "I'm lucky I don't have to worry about those things."

For the last mile to town, she studied the countryside instead of engaging in conversation. Toward the end of town, Connor pulled in front of an upscale looking restaurant. The building was covered in weathered wooden siding, and the windows and doors were decorated with rope lighting, making it rather festive.

"This is the Lake Steakhouse. Best food in town," Connor said as he cut the engine.

The best, huh? Her heart warmed. He opened her door and escorted her toward the entrance, all the while looking around.

"You don't think Slater's here, do you?" she asked, trying not to sound worried.

Connor glanced down at her and smiled. "No. It's an old habit. Jackson told me Coghill was spotted in New York City today."

"I thought he was in New Orleans."

"I thought so too. It's possible the new intel is flawed. It would take some cash to fly from city to city like that. Furthermore, if he's trying to avoid the law, flying isn't the way to do it."

He would know. "Are you sure it was him? I wouldn't be surprised if Slater hired someone to go in his place."

"Our person recognized his face. Or does he have a twin?"

"No. He's an only child. But I've heard a ton of times that I look like someone else."

Connor seemed to look right through her. "I find that hard to believe."

What did that mean? Before she could ask, the hostess showed them to a table near the back. EmmaLee liked the lit candle decorations, the rolled white napkins, and the soft music. Several people were at the bar, but most of the tables in the main room were empty. Perhaps it was still too early for the dinner crowd.

Connor helped her off with her coat and then slipped in the booth across from her after she sat down. She had to give him credit. He was acting as if this were a real date.

A waiter rushed over and asked what they'd like to drink before either of them had the chance to start a conversation. Connor looked over at her. "White or red?"

"Red, please."

"A bottle of your best Malbec," he instructed the waiter.

EmmaLee almost became giddy. "What's the occasion?"

"Occasion? I want to show you that I can be a civilized man instead of a bodyguard goon."

"You're not a goon. You're a little distant at times, that's all."

He reached out, and when he placed his hand on hers for a moment, her body almost melted. "I'm trying to change."

"I can see that, and I like it."

Once the waiter delivered their bottle and poured the glasses of wine, Connor held his up in a toast. "May Slater Coghill be apprehended soon and your troubles be over for good."

She touched his glass and smiled, but she struggled with the whole concept that this nightmare might be over soon. Once Slater was in jail, she'd have no reason to stay in Silver Lake. For the longest time, that was what she had wanted. Now, she wasn't so sure.

Chapter Eleven

"TELL ME ABOUT your parents," Connor said as he cut into his steak.

Because the topic of their death was painful, EmmaLee shunned discussing them, but it was time for Connor to understand why she was so focused on dragons. "I told you my parents died when I was twelve, right?"

He winced. "Yes. They couldn't have been very old."

"They weren't. They died in a house fire."

He set down his glass of wine. "I'm sorry. Don't tell me you were in the house at the time?"

"No."

He blew out a breath. "Where were you then?"

"I was on my way home from having dinner at my best friend's house." She sipped her drink. "As I got close, I smelled the smoke. All week I'd had this eerie feeling that something bad was going to happen—and then it did. In retrospect, I think my parents must have been anxious, and it rubbed off on me."

"Do you know what caused their anxiety?"

"No. Something to do with their research most likely, but it wasn't like they discussed a lot with me."

"Research?"

"Yes." She told him that both of her parents were professors of Lore and Legends, like her.

"So that's why you are so interested in the paranormal."

Something seemed off. He wasn't as surprised as she thought he would be, but EmmaLee didn't want to get into a heavy discussion when this was supposed to be a fun date. "Yes."

"Maybe they said nothing because they were trying to shield you from their world. They just wanted you to grow up happy and innocent."

"I suppose." She appreciated that he didn't think she was imagining things. "Anyway, fearing the worst, I took a short cut home through the woods, praying it wasn't my house that was on fire. As I neared our property, I heard this really loud squawk overhead. Actually, it sounded more like a cry of pain. I looked up and saw a huge bird flying away, or what I thought was a bird. Part of its wing was on fire."

He leaned closer as if he wanted to absorb every word of her story. "Do you think this bird got too close to the flames?"

"Yes. In fact, I believed it caused the fire."

He cocked an eyebrow. "Caused the fire? What do you mean?"

Needing the fortification, she polished off the rest of her wine. "I know you'll think I'm crazy, or say that I was just an imaginative twelve-year old, but I swear the bird, or rather the animal, was a dragon."

"A dragon?" he whispered. "Are you sure it wasn't a hawk? They can have a five foot wingspan."

She held up a hand to stop him. "I know you think I was traumatized at seeing my house burn. I might have been, but at the time, I didn't know my parents were inside. They should have been teaching an evening class, only they weren't. Even though I was young, I knew this animal was a lot bigger than any hawk. Its wingspan had to be thirty or forty feet across."

"That's huge. Did anyone else report seeing this fire breathing *dragon*?"

"No. I told the policeman what I'd seen, but he just patted my shoulder and then ignored me. But I have proof."

"Proof? You mean that picture from the Internet?"

"No, it's something else." It was time to come clean. "When I saw the flames, I didn't know what to do. The sirens were drawing nearer, and because I didn't want to be in the way, I looked around for someplace safe to hide. That's when I noticed something smoldering on the ground."

"What was it?"

"A talon."

"Like one that belongs to a bear?" he asked.

"No, like one that came from a dragon. I would have taken a picture of it, but I didn't own a camera, so I picked it up. The claw was bloody and had a few scales attached. I'm not quite sure I understood the significance of it at the time, but I put it in my pocket. I still have it with me. I can show you when we get back."

Connor sat back as if stunned. "So that's why you've spent your life trying to find a dragon. You want to prove that this animal set your house on fire."

"Yes. The one who did the damage fourteen years ago is probably long gone, but it's why I believe his kind exists. I want to know that I'm not crazy."

"Why would this animal set your house on fire? He'd be taking a big chance of being spotted."

Her pulse soared. Connor actually sounded as if he believed her. "I wish I knew, but the night before the fire, my parents were arguing about hearing the flapping of wings outside their house. My mom was afraid, but Dad said it was nothing. He claimed it was probably just a gust of wind."

"Flapping of wings? As in loud enough to be a dragon?"

"I'm not sure, but that's my guess."

"Did you ask them about it?"

She pressed her lips together. "Yes, but they clammed up tight. My parents had always believed that shifters existed, or something akin to shifters, so it had to have been something far scarier to them. My mom thought shifters were creatures who were humans during the day and animals at night."

"That sounds like she believed in vampires."

"It does, but she never used that word, possibly to shield me. However, she never even hinted that these animals meant to harm anyone."

When Connor looked down at his plate, she dug into her sautéed fish, which was lightly breaded and covered in a wonderful lemon caper sauce. One bite of the tasty meal made her groan, almost forgetting about that fateful day.

"Good?" he asked with a quick smile.

"More than good. Yours?"

Connor cut into his meat and took another bite. "Mine's outstanding. Let me ask you. Did the police ever determine the cause of the fire?"

"They said it was arson."

"So it might not have been set by this animal then?"

"Possibly, but I'm not convinced. While they did find an accelerant, the report said that something more than a match was involved—something like a flame thrower to be exact. That had to be true because my parents were in their office at the time of the attack. They would have smelled the smoke and been able to get out if it had been an ordinary fire."

"What's your theory?" he asked.

"I wish I had a plausible one besides believing the dragon did it."

"Could someone have broken in, incapacitated them, and then set your house on fire?"

EmmaLee winced at that horrible possibility. "If a blow torch was used—or if the flames came from an animal's mouth—the old wooden structure might have gone up so quickly that my parents wouldn't have had time to escape."

His mouth sagged, and his eyes turned a very dark brown. It was almost as if he was experiencing their pain. "Did you ever read the arson report?"

"Yes, but it was years ago."

"Was anyone arrested for the crime?" Connor asked.

She shook her head. "No suspects were identified either. What does that tell you?"

"That the arsonist was careful. I'd like to read that report. It might be time to reopen the case."

EmmaLee couldn't believe they were having this conversation. Throughout the discussion, Connor never once mocked her or thought her theory was stupid. "What good would it do now?"

"It might support your theory that some kind of dragon was responsible."

She studied him, trying to see if he was making fun of her, but he seemed sincere. "I'd like that, but if no one has come forward with any clues in fourteen years, I doubt there will be any proof now."

"If we look at it from a different perspective and a different knowledge base than what was around back then, we might make some progress. Don't you want to know why your parents were targeted?"

"Yes, more than anything. It wasn't like they were drug runners or anything. They were history professors, researching Lore and Legends. That's not a topic to scare many people unless they knew some of it was true."

"Your parents could have asked questions of the wrong person. Maybe he or she was a shifter and feared exposure."

"Like me, they just wanted to know the truth, though I'm not sure if they were committed to keeping what they learned secret. It was Vinea who explained that a lot of people would be hurt if I told the world about your kind."

A sad smile appeared on his face. "Just telling the world about us wouldn't do much more than make that person look a bit crazy, since people usually don't believe wild claims. One of us would have to shift in public to cause a stir."

"You have a point. No one believes me without proof."

Connor grimaced. "I admit I'm guilty, but I'm trying to be more open-minded."

She smiled. "It's all I can ask."

As if the topic were now closed, he went back to eating. A minute later, he pointed his fork at her. "Did you ever get the dragon claw checked out?" He acted so casual she would have thought they were discussing the weather.

"Eventually. As a kid, I believed they would take the talon as evidence and I'd never see it again, so I kept it hidden. When I enrolled at the University, I became friends with an ornithologist and showed it to him."

"Did he know what kind of animal it came from?" His tone turned serious.

"No. He said he'd never seen anything like it."

Connor finished his wine. "I trust that you asked if it could belong to a dragon?"

She nodded. "Being an expert in birds, he sent me to someone who had studied dinosaurs. While that person said the desiccated scale looked like it might have come from a Pterodactyl or a Pteranodon, he was quick to note that those flying animals weren't actually dinosaurs."

"Don't tell me he thought they were dragons."

"He never claimed that. Since both types are extinct, he had no way of knowing what kind of animal this talon belonged to."

"Interesting. I can see why you wanted to stay in Billard to meet this expert."

EmmaLee leaned back and blew out a breath. "Thank you for believing me."

Connor studied her. "I'm a cut and dry type of guy. I don't buy into new theories often, but yours has me intrigued."

"Yet you yourself are of a different sort, so to speak."

"I guess you could say I'm a walking contradiction." He smiled, and his eyes lightened.

She liked that he was able to loosen up at times. "You are indeed."

The corner of Connor's lips tipped upward. He turned back to her and rested his arms on the table. "Listen, I know I've been distant with you from the moment we met, and I'm sorry."

Whoa. Where had that comment come from? "Why was that?" *Please don't say it was because I was just a crazy lady.*

"When I'm in protection mode, I can't afford to lose my focus."

"I can buy that." It didn't mean she had to like it though.

"You might not believe me, but I'm really curious what makes you tick. You fascinate me."

Her heart pounded. "Me?"

"Yes. Why would a young, vibrant woman devote her life to something so unorthodox? Now I know."

"That you do." His words almost made her giddy. "Turnabout is fair play."

The sparkle in his eyes returned. "Fair enough. What would you like to know?"

Really? He was giving her carte blanche to ask him questions? She had a ton of them, but she'd bet she probably wouldn't want to know the answers to many of them. "What's the best thing about being the type of…ah…*person* you are?"

He glanced around. "You mean being a wolf?" He mouthed the last few words.

"Yes."

"That's easy. Fighting is a lot quicker and easier in my *other* form. Plus, I have a great sense of smell and excellent eyesight. That comes in handy at night."

"I bet."

He tapped the table. "There's one more thing. I heal quickly, or rather something inside can heal me."

Her thoughts shot to Slater. Once he'd cut his finger, and a day later it had healed. But he was no werewolf that was for sure. Or had he failed to tell her? "What else?"

"I can't help but go into protective mode. It's what makes my kind good bodyguards."

She loved all those attributes. As much as EmmaLee wanted to question him about shifters in general—especially concerning mating—someone might overhear. Besides, she didn't just want to know about his shifter side. She was interested in him as a man. "What's your favorite desert?"

He laughed. "Really? I let you ask me anything and this is what you want to know?"

Was he actually flirting with her? Heat raced up her face. "Yes."

"Fair enough. It's pecan pie."

She hadn't seen that coming. "Why?"

"It's sweet and kind of salty at the same time. My mom makes the best."

"Perhaps that's why you like it. It reminds you of the good times growing up."

He stared at her. "You might be right. I need to add intuitive to your list of traits. Are you sure there is no Wendayan blood in you?"

That made her laugh. "No."

"Speaking of family," he said, "what was it like growing up with your aunt and uncle?"

Her heart dropped to her stomach. "I never mentioned that I grew up with them." Oh shit. Connor ran an investigative firm. She tried to swallow her anger, but she couldn't help but ball her hands into fists. "You checked into my past?"

Connor inhaled deeply, his chest expanding, and the lines around his eyes deepened. "I needed to find out if there was something in your background that made Slater target you."

He said it with such confidence that it might be the truth. "What do you mean target me? I didn't get the sense that Slater set out to harm me. He just lost his temper at times."

Connor stabbed a hand through his hair. "I'm wondering if he dated you because he wanted something."

She widened her eyes. "Oh, is that what men do? Date a woman because they want something?"

"Shit, EmmaLee, nothing is coming out the way I intended it to. The truth is that I wanted to learn why you ended up with someone as scummy as Slater Coghill. Please don't take this the wrong way, but women who are abused often have been abused before. Did that happen to you?"

Her teen years flashed before her eyes—the pushing, the slapping, and the confinement in her room for the smallest infraction. "Maybe a little, but one doesn't really have to do with the other. Slater would have acted that way with any woman."

"You're right. I'm sorry the abuse happened in both cases."

She would have told him to fuck off, but he really sounded sincere. EmmaLee pushed her plate away. "I'm not hungry anymore."

"I didn't mean to ruin our date, I swear, but we can go if you like." He raised his hand and motioned the waiter. By the time the man arrived, Connor had his credit card out. "Our bill, please."

They'd been having such a great time before she found out about his investigation. She was most likely overreacting, but the rush of bad memories had upset her. EmmaLee slid out of the booth and slipped on her coat just as he finished signing his name. He stood and placed a hand on her back, but she wanted nothing to do with him at the moment.

Walking fast to get away from him, she shot out through the front door of the restaurant with Connor right behind her. The lights flashed on his car, signaling he'd unlocked the door. Not waiting for him to do his bodyguard thing, she hopped in. If she didn't live so far away, she would have walked home.

He got in and then jammed the key into the ignition. She turned to stare out the passenger window.

"EmmaLee, look at me please." She turned, connecting her gaze to his. Connor touched the side of her face, then tucked a stray hair behind her ear. "I'm sorry."

I'm sorry, I'm sorry. Like she hadn't heard that phrase often enough before. A tear slid down her cheek. Was she being too harsh? Probably. He was an investigator by trade, and it came naturally to him to find out as much as he could about the person he was asked to protect. She wasn't sure how he'd learned that she'd lived with her aunt and uncle. There was a reason why he hadn't wanted him to know. It was bad enough when people looked at her when she remained with Slater after he hit her the first time. If they knew how unpleasant it had been with her aunt and uncle, people would wonder why she wasn't smart enough to avoid abuse the second time around.

In order to cover her embarrassment, she allowed her anger to take over, but she needed to know what else he knew about her past.

"When you investigated me, did you uncover any other skeletons?" Perhaps he'd learned something about her parents she hadn't been aware of.

"Just that your parents were history professors, but you already confirmed that. Were they searching for proof of dragon shifters like you?" Thankfully, his words weren't laced with skepticism.

Her anger dissipated. "I don't think so. As I said, they were more into normal animal shifters. Maybe that was why my mom was kind of scared when she heard the beating of wings."

Connor said nothing more as he drove home. When they reached the guesthouse, he killed the engine and jumped out. She didn't need him walking her to the door, but when he pulled open her car door, it would have been rude to tell him to go away. Despite his prying, and the emotions it stirred up for her, EmmaLee couldn't deny her attraction to Connor. She liked him, a lot.

Ugh, it was all so confusing right now. She just needed some time to process everything they'd talked about tonight. It was possible that he truly had been researching her for her own good. If only she had been sure of his motives, she might not have reacted so badly.

EmmaLee rushed up to the door and tried to open it, but the key wouldn't go in.

A second later, his hands wrapped around her fingers. "Let me. The door can be temperamental."

EmmaLee moved out of the way and couldn't deny how caring

he'd become recently.

"There you go," he said, motioning her in.

She spun around and blocked the entrance. "Thank you for dinner."

"I'm coming in, EmmaLee. I want to make sure no one is here."

Her heart pounded. "You said Slater was in New York." He opened his mouth, and she held up a hand. "I know, I know. You're just doing your job." She stepped aside.

"It's more than a job, EmmaLee. I want you to be safe." Connor flicked on the light by the door and then proceeded to do a thorough check of the whole house. He then returned to the entryway. "Everything looks good," he said.

"Thank you." As he searched the house, she'd had some time to think. She had been rash in believing he had gone behind her back. He was only trying to help.

"Can we talk for a minute?" he asked. "I know I hurt you somehow by investigating your past, but I believed it would help me find Slater."

"I realize that now. I'm the one who's sorry for reacting so strongly. Would you like something to drink?"

Connor raised eyebrow and the sexy grin on his face caught her body on fire. With a purposeful look, he stalked toward her. Her pulse soared.

When he reached her, he cupped her face, and her heart zinged. "What I'd really like is to drink *you* in."

Chapter Twelve

C ONNOR KNEW THIS was a mistake, but he couldn't help himself. All through dinner he'd been battling his urges. Being with EmmaLee in a casual setting made all the difference in the world. When she wasn't looking over her shoulder, waiting for Coghill to arrive, EmmaLee was delightful, charming, and exciting.

Once he learned where her desire to prove that dragon shifters existed came from, the more he was able to put aside his prejudice and see her for who she really was—someone resilient and focused. She had every trait he wanted in a woman and damn that attitude turned him on. The way she had looked when she tried to block him from entering her house had his wolf clawing at him and his cock practically breaking through his zipper.

EmmaLee stepped backward until she bumped into the kitchen counter. As he neared, she gripped the edge. "Care to explain your comment?" she asked.

"I think it's obvious. I want you EmmaLee. Plain and simple."

Her eyes narrowed. "Since when?"

"I have from the moment I laid eyes on you." *And ever since your scent invaded my body.*

She laughed. "You are full of shit. You couldn't stand me."

He slipped off his jacket and tossed it on the counter. "That was what I wanted you to believe." He undid his cuffs and rolled up the sleeves of his shirt.

"You did a good acting job then." She turned her face away.

Talking about his desires was uncomfortable for both of them, but he had to make her see that they were meant to be together. Connor touched her chin and turned her face toward him. "Would you like me to show you that what I'm saying is the truth?"

When her cheeks turned a pretty shade of pink, his inner wolf gave a lusty growl.

Be patient, he warned. *Or we will end up shifting.*

Mate, his wolf chuffed out.

His wolf was hanging on by a thread, and so was Connor. He inhaled deeply, trying to gain a semblance of calm for both of their sakes.

"Show me how?" she asked.

Connor smiled, and because his canines had already sharpened, her eyes widened in recognition of what was to come. "By doing this."

Connor wrapped his arms around her waist and pulled her into his body as he leaned his head toward hers. He might have stopped had EmmaLee not closed her eyes and tilted her head upward to meet his, giving him full permission to proceed. That act alone unleashed an intensely powerful urge to ravage her, but he had to be careful. He didn't want to scare her or push her too fast. She was the one—his mate—and he would do anything to protect her and make her happy.

Slowly, he pressed his lips to hers, keeping alert to any hesitancy on her part. When he found none, Connor deepened the kiss. She inhaled and gripped the front of his shirt as she pressed her breasts tighter against his chest.

He delved deeper, and when she stroked her tongue against his more forcefully and let out a small moan, he couldn't control his wolf any longer. Oh, shit, oh, shit.

He broke the kiss and stepped back just as his bones cracked and his vision blurred. His shirt ripped as the hair sprouted on his body. A second later, he was on all fours.

Damn it to hell! I told you to control yourself. Now look what you've done, Connor shouted at his wolf.

His wolf whimpered and whined. *I'm sorry. Please, we need our mate.*

Sorry my ass. She will probably run away now, he warned.

A beautiful face dropped in front of him. "Hi," EmmaLee said with a wide grin.

Thank goodness she didn't race down the hallway screaming. She might be fascinated with shifters, but she'd never seen anyone turn into an animal before.

She stroked his head. He hoped she didn't expect him to answer. To show her he understood her, he nudged his head against her hand.

She giggled. "You are so cute!"

He wasn't cute! He was a ferocious animal capable of tearing a man apart. She dragged her hand down his snout, and Connor almost jerked away. The last time anyone had tried to pet him was when he was a young cub. And that had been his mother. As much as his first instinct was to move away, he didn't. EmmaLee seemed too delighted with seeing him in his animal form. If he was honest, both Connor and his wolf were enjoying her soothing hands.

"Can you understand me?" she asked.

Connor let out a small howl and then licked her cheek to show he understood and that he wouldn't hurt her. Big mistake. Her scent from the kiss had been enough to turn him into a wolf. Tasting her took his need to a whole new level.

Changing back into his human form, however, had its pitfalls—namely he'd be naked. Connor might not be embarrassed about being undressed, but EmmaLee probably would. While he had a spare set of clothes in his car, she'd still see him in all his glory. At some point he'd have to chance it though.

"Why did you change? Was it the kiss?" she asked with too much satisfaction in her tone. She must have figured out why he'd lost control.

While he didn't want to give her the upper hand, after realizing how he'd invaded her privacy without asking, it was only fair to grovel a bit. Connor looked up into her eyes. As he lay down at her feet, he whined then placed his head on his front paws.

EmmaLee played with his ears while she sat on the floor next to him. "So now what? How long do you have to stay in your wolf form?"

So she didn't know all of the lore behind shifters. He could change anytime he wanted. Connor returned to all fours and slowly backed away from her, all the while panting. His sister always told him that when his mouth was open, he had a natural smile in his wolf form. He hoped that was true.

Connor then turned and trotted down the hallway toward the bathroom.

"Where are you going?" she called after him.

If he could have answered, he would have said to cover himself. After ducking into the bathroom, he nudged the door closed then quickly changed back into his human form. He immediately snatched a towel off the rack and wrapped it around his waist.

A soft knock sounded on the slightly opened door. "Are you okay?"

He chuckled. "I'm good."

Connor pulled open the door, and EmmaLee's eyes widened. "Um, you're almost naked."

"My clothes are ruined, but I have an extra set in the car." He placed a hand on her shoulder. "Excuse me while I grab my jacket so I can get them."

"Connor, what just happened?" The cheer in her eyes disappeared. In its place was concern.

"I'll be happy to explain, but I think you'd feel more comfortable if I'm dressed." He returned to the kitchen with EmmaLee right behind him

She moved in front as if to block his exit, and when she ran her gaze up and down his body, a trail of fire followed.

"I don't want you to get your clothes."

She wants us, his wolf said. *Kiss her again. Make her ours.*

Connor had to agree with his wolf this time. That kiss they'd shared had altered something inside him. Her eyes were shining and there was a glow about her that implied she'd been hot and bothered by what just happened, but he didn't want to assume anything. "What are you saying, EmmaLee?"

"Isn't it obvious? I want what you want." She glanced down at the towel, and when he followed her gaze, sure enough his cock had lifted the fabric.

Connor carefully moved closer, letting her decide just how far she was willing to take things. The moment she ran a finger down his chest, his body went haywire. "Take it easy on me. You saw what happened the last time."

Once more, her eyes widened, and she clamped a hand over her mouth. "My kiss really caused that?" She seemed delighted.

"Yes. Why else do you think it happened?"

"Uh, I'm not sure. At first, I thought you wanted to stop kissing me, and that was a rather subtle way of doing it."

Connor cracked up. "Seriously?" She nodded. "The truth is, if you tempt a shifter too much, he often can't control his urges. I've wanted to kiss you from the moment I met you. When I finally did, it was too much for my wolf to handle."

She dragged her thumb across the tucked in part of the towel. "Is that so?"

He swallowed. "That's so."

"How about I kiss you again and see if I get the same reaction?"

"I won't let my wolf get the upper hand a second time."

You have to promise to behave, he chastised his wolf who no doubt was grinning.

She looked up at his face and smiled, stealing the breath from his body. "I liked your wolf."

Connor wrapped his arms around EmmaLee. She lifted her hands to his face and drew him near until their lips met—lips that were soft and kissable. After a long taste, he let up on the pressure and drew her bottom lip between his teeth. Her groan made his cock even harder, and he wasn't sure how long he could last. His wolf clawed at him, and Connor fought for control as he pushed him back. Finally, his wolf backed down and let him have control—for now.

EmmaLee lowered her hands and latched onto his towel. *Take it off*, he silently pleaded. Someday, they'd be mated, and he could convey all of his thoughts to her using only his mind.

As if she could read his already, she slipped one end of the towel from his waist and let it drop to the ground. He watched EmmaLee's eyes widen, and he couldn't help but smile. He wasn't a small guy by any means.

For weeks he'd imagined what he would do if she had been eager. Take her against the wall? Take her with her legs over his shoulders with him pounding into her? Or would he have EmmaLee sit on him, smiling and clawing at his chest while he held on for dear life?

The position didn't matter. All he wanted was to be inside her now. While the human part of him understood the art of seduction, he wasn't sure he was capable of taking his time. Without a word, Connor reached out and lifted off her sweater. His breath caught. "Pink looks good on you," he said.

She smiled. "I wore it with you in mind."

A lump clogged his throat. Had she really expected to end up in bed with him? If so, he needed to work on reading her signals better. In all honesty, he'd expected her to tell him to leave after that gaffe he'd made, or say that she wasn't ready to be with anyone, but fortunately, he'd been wrong.

Right now, all Connor could think of was touching her and bringing her a bit of joy. Dragging a finger along the top of her perky breasts, her soft skin ignited his soul. "So beautiful."

EmmaLee reached out and stroked his cock, short-circuiting his brain.

Standing in the kitchen wasn't the place for their first encounter, but he wasn't sure he could make it as far as the bedroom so he walked her backward into the living room until they were in front of the couch. As EmmaLee toed off her boots, he undid the button on her jeans. With one hard tug, he drew them and her panties down until blonde curls bounced out. Connor had to close his eyes to keep from tossing her on the sofa and making love with her without any prelude. His senses were exploding, and he wanted to kiss her, eat her, and fuck her all at the same time.

Willing himself to go slow, Connor straightened and reached around her back to undo the bra clasp. When she sucked in her bottom lip, he smiled. He loved her sultry look, though he doubted she understood what it was doing to him.

Once he lowered the straps and tossed the bra aside, Connor turned back toward those beautiful exposed breasts. While he'd dated some gorgeous women, none of them had been his mate. Now he understood that they had merely been a diversion until EmmaLee came along.

"What are you waiting for?" she asked. This time she seemed less sure of herself, and that cut him to the core.

"I want to absorb everything about you. You're incredible." His eyes partially closed as he stared at two perfectly round brown nipples that begged to be sucked. Only then did Connor realize he needed a condom. "Hold on a sec."

She grabbed his arm. "What's wrong?"

"I need some protection."

"I'm on the pill. I'd rather experience all of you."

He grinned. "Then all of me you will get. Go ahead and sit on the sofa arm."

EmmaLee sat down, and Connor dropped to his knees in front her. He then drew her closer in order to reach her breasts. Cupping one, he toyed with her nipple as he sucked the other into his mouth. The moment he tugged on the tip, EmmaLee drew in a breath and groaned. His wolf scratched and clawed.

If you appear again, I'll never forgive you, he warned his horny animal.

Once was bad enough, but twice would ruin everything. Emma-Lee dragged her hands through his hair, and the power of her touch set off every desire in his body. Connor lifted his gaze and peered into her eyes. He groaned as he released her nipple with a pop. "What you do to me, EmmaLee Donovan."

She stared back at him with a sexy smirk. "I could do a lot more, ya know."

Where had this sassy woman come from? He stood then flipped her over, bending her upper body over the arm while leaving that gorgeous ass exposed. Connor pressed up against her, and then reached around to cup her breasts, which filled his palms perfectly. As he lightly pinched the tips, he aligned his cock at her entrance. Damn. He'd never taken the time to taste her. That pleasure would be delayed until the next time.

Wanting to take it slow for EmmaLee's sake, he eased in an inch and then waited, in part because she was so damned tight. When his nails grew, he had to make sure he didn't scratch her. Connor lowered his head, and when he kissed the tender spot between her chin and neck, images of sinking his teeth into her surfaced.

Bite her, his wolf urged.

Not now. Someday, he'd claim her as his.

He rocked his hips back and forth slowly, each forward motion allowing him a bit more access.

When EmmaLee arched up on her hands and pressed her hips back, Connor's wolf took over. He scraped his sharpened teeth lightly across the shell of her ear and fully entered her.

"Oh my god! That feels so good," she panted and then lowered her head, exposing her neck once more.

Connor had no idea how much she knew about mating, but he wouldn't bite her—not yet anyway. They had to talk about that first. As if his cock had a life of its own, he withdrew and then plowed right back in, finding the place where he belonged. His vision blurred as his fingers found a sensual rhythm kneading her breasts and toying with her nipples.

Her groans increased with each foray, edging him closer to his climax. Determined to wait until she was satisfied, Connor dragged his forehead to the back of her head and inhaled deeply, memorizing her scent for all time. He slid his hand from her breast to her pussy, sliding his finger through her outer folds until he found her clit and began stroking and gently pulling at it.

"Yes, Connor, yes!" Each word escalated as he drove into her deeper and harder.

When he plunged into her again, she yelled his name as her climax claimed her. A second later he expelled his hot seed. Out of breath from the intensity, both of their bodies sagged and he wrapped his arms around her. When their ragged breaths finally slowed, he withdrew.

Connor ducked into the kitchen and came back with a warm wet cloth he used to clean them both up. He tossed it on top of the discarded clothes then reached down and scooped her up. Without a word, he leaned over and kissed her softly as he lay down on the couch with her in his arms.

Facing him, she pressed her breasts against his chest and kissed him back. She opened her mouth and invited him in. Never had he skipped so many steps before while making love, but his mate had royally messed with his head.

His heart still refused to slow down. Finally, he had to break the kiss or take her again. "Thank you," he said.

"Hmm, you are very welcome, but I think I should be the one thanking you."

Connor rubbed his nose against hers. "Whatever for?"

She stole another kiss from him. "For making sure you got yourself into the house. I wasn't going to invite you in."

He laughed. "I was well aware of that." He fingered a strand of hair and tucked it away from her face. "I truly am sorry about how things ended at the restaurant."

"I know that now."

Connor smiled. "Do you want me to carry you into the bedroom?"

EmmaLee snuggled closer to him. "I'm comfortable here, unless you need to go. I know you have to work in the morning."

Connor grabbed the afghan off the back of the couch he had seen earlier and pulled it over them. "I'll have to go home eventually, but right now, there is no place else I'd rather be than here with you."

Chapter Thirteen

CONNOR PROBABLY SHOULD have spent the entire night with EmmaLee. After all, they'd just had the most amazing, life-altering sex of his life, but the longer he stayed, the harder it became not to mate with her. If they did, he worried it would affect his concentration at work. Becoming distracted in his job wasn't an option. It could put EmmaLee at risk, and it certainly wouldn't help him find Slater Coghill.

Before heading in the next morning, Connor decided to stop by the guesthouse to make sure EmmaLee was okay. If she had any regrets about last night, he wanted to address them. Connor had to knock twice before she opened the door. Most likely it was because he'd told her to look through the peephole before opening up.

As soon as he saw her, his wolf begged for release. EmmaLee was wearing a robe with a coffee cup in her hand, and the image of seeing her like this for more mornings to come raced through his mind.

Connor smiled. "Good morning!"

EmmaLee's face lit up. "Hey, I thought you would be on your way to work already."

"I'm heading there now, but I wanted to see how you were doing first? Did you sleep okay?"

"Some." She motioned him in and lifted her drink. "Can I get you a cup? It's already made."

"Sure."

He followed her into the tiny kitchen. "I stopped by to see if you had any regrets with what we did."

She spun to face him, her eyes wide. "Regrets? No. Did you?"

Way to go, you idiot. You have to stop messing up, his wolf chided.

She does that to me.

"No! It was the most amazing moment of my life."

Then hug her. And kiss her, his wolf urged. *You need to make it up to her.*

Then I wouldn't make it into work until noon.

So? his wolf shot back.

A pink blush rushed up her cheeks. EmmaLee moved closer and his wolf cheered. "For me too. You did things to me that I'd never experienced before."

Connor almost lost control once more. Here he thought that if they had sex once, his intense yearning would lessen. Wrong! It was worse, if that was possible.

Instead of returning to the table, they remained in the kitchen drinking their strong morning brew. The longer he watched her, the more he needed to be with her. Being away from her for another day wasn't an option. "I thought you might want to come into work with me today. I know the Internet here isn't the best," he said.

As if he'd pumped her full of energy, her eyes brightened. "I'd love that, but I don't want to be a bother."

"No bother. I think Ronan and Jackson would be upset if you didn't come."

"You think?" He nodded. "Okay. I'll need a sec to change." She set down her cup and immediately winced.

"What's wrong?"

She rubbed her back. "That stupid back injury. I thought it was getting better, but I must have slept on it wrong or something."

EmmaLee blushed again, and he knew what she was thinking. He couldn't resist teasing her a bit. "Well, you were pretty bendy, leaning over that sofa arm." He took a sip of coffee while looking at her over the rim, wiggling his eyebrows at her. She chuckled even though her blush deepened. "Seriously though, do you want me to call Blair for you? I am sure she can fit you in."

"That's okay. If it doesn't improve in a few days, I'll contact her. Let me change so we can get going."

She eased down the hallway before he had the opportunity to get in a kiss. Damn. With the way her bathrobe was trailing behind her, he could picture what was underneath.

A few minutes later, she returned wearing jeans and a long sleeve bright pink shirt, looking way too cute.

A large purse was slung over her shoulder that probably contained her laptop. "I'm ready," she said.

Once she locked up, he called his dad to tell him that once more EmmaLee would be with him.

"How's that working out?"

Now wasn't the time or place to discuss it. "Great. We'll touch base later."

"You can't talk. I get it. Call if you need anything."

Connor disconnected. "What are you going to research today?" he asked EmmaLee as he held open the car door.

"I'm not sure, but I'll find something of interest." She twisted toward him. "Actually, there is something I'd like to do. I'd love to speak to Zane."

"Zane? Why?"

"He's from Cargonia. Maybe there are dragons in his realm."

Connor had never thought to ask him about any of that. Zane was still new to Silver Lake, and he hadn't spent a lot of time with him yet. "I'll see when he's free."

She placed a hand on his arm. "Thank you."

That one touch jacked up his hormones once more. Connor would have to ask his brother how he handled being mated while doing his job. As much as he wanted to keep his relationship with EmmaLee a secret for now, sooner or later, Rye, as well as the rest of his team, would be able to tell.

He parked in front of their office and escorted her inside. As usual, Lexi was at her desk. When she looked up and saw them, she smiled. "I see you have a new chauffeur!"

"Connor stopped by and offered me a ride. I couldn't say no."

"Let me know if you need help with anything," Lexi said.

Connor was happy EmmaLee was making friends. If he had any hope of her wanting to stay in Silver Lake, the key might be in having friends. If he were lucky, she'd want to stay because of him. "Are you okay to work in the break room again?" he asked her.

"Absolutely."

Once she was settled, he hurried to his office. As much as he wanted to kiss her, once he started, he might not be able to stop. Thankfully, Ronan was staying in the room downstairs preventing Connor from taking her there. And although it elicited a hot image and an even hotter response, EmmaLee certainly deserved more than sex on his office desk. Maybe one day, after they were mated, he could convince her to have an afternoon delight in his office, but not now. His cock twitched at that thought.

Geezus, he needed to get his mind back on business. He adjusted himself then quickly settled down to do some work. Today, he needed to help Ronan with his case, gather more information on Coghill, and handle the day-to-day operations of running the firm.

Before he had the chance to do any of those things, someone knocked on his door. It wasn't EmmaLee; that much he could sense.

"Come in."

It was Ronan. He pulled up a chair and sat. "I think I should fly up to New York and nab Slater."

Connor appreciated his proactive behavior. "As much as I want that ass in jail, we need to be sure he's there first. Ask Jackson to reach out to our informant again. He is the one who's seen him. Our man in New York might even know where he's staying."

Ronan stood. "Thanks. I'll get right on it."

"While you're with Jackson, ask him if he has any information on your Delahart man. Last I heard, Jackson was monitoring his spending habits."

"Sounds great."

As soon as Ronan left, Connor did a search for the arson report on EmmaLee's parents. After a few phone calls, the detective handling cold cases said he'd email it. "If you come up with anything," the detective said. "I'd appreciate a heads up."

"I will." Unless it really was a dragon, then no.

Fourteen years was a long time, but Connor wanted to see if the cops in her hometown had missed anything. His email notification dinged, indicating he had mail. It was the arson report. He downloaded it and read it a few times. Because it used some technical terms he wasn't familiar with, he needed some help deciphering it. Drake Manson, who happened to be a shifter, was the arson investigator in Silver Lake. He'd be able to help. At least Connor could be honest with him.

He pushed back his chair, looking forward to a brisk walk to the fire station. Since Zane worked there as their janitor, perhaps EmmaLee would like to go with him.

When he returned to the break room, his body went crazy.

Really? I am just going to ask her to go for a walk not jump her in the break room, he told his horny wolf.

I can't help it. Now that I've had a taste, I want more, his wolf whined.

Enough! He mentally pushed him back. Crap, it was hard enough controlling himself around EmmaLee, never mind now that his wolf wanted to hump her at every opportunity.

"EmmaLee?" Connor called, partly to shut out his wolf. She was sitting in her chair, head down into her research.

She spun around and smiled. "Hey."

"I received the arson report from your parents' fire, but I don't understand all of it, so I thought I'd ask the arson investigator to help. Would you like to come with me? You might be able to speak with Zane, your Cargonian man." She jumped up so fast the chair tumbled backward. He laughed and then righted it. "I take it that's a yes."

"Definitely a yes."

"Be aware that he might not be willing to speak with you. From what Rye has told me, Zane keeps a low profile."

"That's okay, but I need to ask."

He adored her positive attitude. "Let's go then."

EMMALEE WAS NERVOUS. Connor was off speaking with the arson investigator while she stood next to the fire truck waiting for some huge man to speak with her—a man, or rather a werebear who wasn't even from this realm! If only her mom were alive, she would have loved to learn about him too.

"Excuse me," said the deepest voice she'd ever heard.

Refocusing on the giant before her, she was unable to form words. He wore a tight black T-shirt that outlined his huge arms, with the fire department's logo blazoned across the front. Thankfully, he had a kind face. "Hi, you must be Zane."

"Yes, and you must be EmmaLee."

"I am."

He looked around. "Care to come into the back where we can talk? Not many people beside Rye know my history."

"I can understand why."

Ohmigod. He was really going to speak with her regarding another realm. How cool was that? She had her phone with her, but tape recording him might be a bit too much. If she'd been from another realm, she wouldn't want the world to know either. The questions would be endless.

When he opened a storage closet full of cleaning supplies, she hesitated. If Rye and Connor hadn't vouched for him, she might have turned around.

"Sorry we have to meet like this, but I put my life on the line every time someone learns about me."

"Not a problem. I totally get it."

"Connor told me you are researching shifters and such. What do you want to know?"

"You're from Cargonia, right?" He nodded. "Are there dragon shifters there?"

He studied her, but she couldn't tell if he was debating whether to answer her honestly, or if he thought she was plum crazy. "Dragon shifters, you say?"

Why was that a hard question? "Yes."

"I've never run into one."

Her muscles tightened up. "Are you sure?"

Zane smiled. "There are no humans on Cargonia either, so there is no reason to hide our identity. Wolves, bears, tigers, and such run around in their animal form all the time, but I've never seen a dragon."

"But could one exist?"

He crossed his arms. "I suppose so, why?"

"Did Connor tell you what I saw when I was younger?"

"No."

She gave him a brief rundown on what happened.

"If that had occurred on Cargonia, I would have said a demon was responsible. They can shoot fire out of their hands—or at least some are able to."

Maybe demons were descendants from dragons. "Thank you for speaking with me."

His eyes widened. "You don't want to know about the portal or what life is like there?"

"All of that sounds exciting, but I don't want to get sidetracked. If you're open to it, I might ask you other questions later."

"It would be my pleasure."

Zane escorted her back to the main area where Connor was speaking with another man who looked a lot like him. He glanced over at her and smiled. "Come here and meet my brother."

She shook Zane's hand and then stepped over to the McKinnon brothers.

"This is Rye, my oldest brother."

"Nice to meet you," she said.

"Did Zane help you with your questions?" Rye asked.

"He did."

Connor wrapped an arm around her waist and faced his brother. "Thank Drake again for taking the time to look over the report."

"Will do." Rye turned and headed back to work.

As soon as they were outside, she looked up at him. "Did you learn anything?"

"You first. What did Zane say?"

"He said he'd never met a dragon shifter, but he added that it was possible one existed."

"I'm sorry, Em."

She liked how he shortened her name. "It's not your fault. What did you find out?"

They crossed the street and then headed north. "The report was incomplete or else the fire marshal in your hometown wasn't thorough."

"What do you mean?"

"While there was accelerant found, most was poured along the perimeter."

"So?"

"The fire didn't start at the bottom of the house."

She tried to picture it but failed. "I'm not sure I understand."

"Drake says from the burn pattern, the intense heat came from flames about six feet off the ground."

Her mind spun. "So a dragon could have been responsible!"

He placed a hand on her back and led her across Maple Avenue. "He wasn't able to say, other than it appeared as if a flame thrower had been used."

"Has he ever known an arsonist to use a flame thrower?"

Connor smiled. "No, never."

"Then it's possible I wasn't imagining things."

"I think your next step is to have someone identify that talon."

They crossed one more street to reach the McKinnon and Associates' parking lot. "The dinosaur researcher is scheduled to begin his month long class next week, but he's giving an introductory seminar this Saturday in Billard. What do you say to a road trip?" Her heart pounded awaiting his answer.

Chapter Fourteen

C ONNOR COULDN'T BELIEVE he'd let EmmaLee talk him into
driving her back to Georgia. Once EmmaLee's thesis advisor
confirmed that Dr. Wilmer Crenely, the expert in dinosaurs, had
arrived in Billard two days ago, Connor could hardly say no to her.

He wouldn't have agreed to it had Ronan not flown up to New
York, and then told him he'd spotted Slater Coghill in the hotel. By
tonight, Ronan should have him in custody and EmmaLee would be
safe for good.

Be careful, his wolf growled.

Connor didn't need the warning. He understood the chance he
was taking by driving her to her hometown. If Ronan called and said
Slater had been arrested, EmmaLee might decide to stay. While she
didn't have a job lined up at the college, he bet she could secure a
place there as soon as she finished her thesis.

I will take care. I'll make sure she wants to return home with us.

As he neared Billard, Connor glanced over at her. "When do you
plan to show your talon to this expert?" She'd shown him what she'd
found on the ground the day of the fire, and he had to agree that it
wasn't from any ordinary bird. Even an eagle's talon wasn't that thick
and long. It had to have come from the animal EmmaLee had seen
flying away from her house.

"I imagine he'll have a line of grad students waiting to speak with
him before the lecture. I might have a better chance of getting some
quality time with him if I make an appointment with him after-

ward."

"Sounds good." That would keep them there for two more days, but this was important to her, and Connor seemed incapable of not giving her what she wanted.

It was close to two in the afternoon before they pulled in front of her apartment.

"Home sweet home," she said.

Connor was surprised at the bit of sadness. "Miss your friends?"

"Yes, but it's more than that. Billard represents my freedom. It's been a long uphill battle to work full time in order to pay for school, attend classes, and study. It didn't leave a lot of time for fun."

He'd been lucky. His folks had paid for his education. "You are an ambitious woman."

She looked over at him and smiled. "Thank you."

As much as he wanted to ask about how Slater had fit into her life, he kept quiet. Why bring up a sore topic?

He cut the engine and EmmaLee pushed open the car door before he had the chance to open it for her.

"Let's hope I didn't leave some food in the fridge and the place stinks," she said. "We did leave in a hurry."

"You didn't ask anyone to check on your place?"

"I saw no need. I don't have any plants or animals that needed care, and I forwarded my mail to your office address like you asked."

He opened the back of the car and dragged out their suitcases. "After you."

Shoulders straight, she dug her hand into her purse for her key as she walked to the front. As soon as she unlocked the door and opened it, she froze. "Ohmigod."

The fear in her voice sliced through him. Connor placed his hands on her shoulders. "Let me see." He didn't sense anyone, but he wanted to be sure no human was there. "Wait here."

Connor stepped inside and was immediately stunned at the level of destruction. The pillows on the sofa were slashed, chairs were tipped over, and books and other knickknacks were strewn all over the place. He whipped out his cell.

EmmaLee placed a hand on his arm. "Who are you calling?"

"The cops. We have to report the break-in."

"I want to check one thing first."

He faced her. Her chin, as well as her hands, was trembling, but from the determined look on her face, she really needed to do this search. He had the sense it had something to do with her research. "I'm coming with you."

"Fine."

EmmaLee made a beeline to her bedroom. At the mess, a whimper escaped. Instead of crying or whining over the loss though, she raced over to the bed and dropped down on her knees to pull out a box. She then dumped the contents on the floor and pawed through her things. "It's gone."

The hurt in her voice twisted his insides. "What's gone?"

"That photo of the dragon I showed you."

That didn't seem so bad. "If you found it on the Internet, maybe you can locate it again."

She sniffled. "Maybe."

The violation from the break-in probably caused her to overreact to this particular loss. He glanced around. The bed was the only thing undisturbed. "Can you tell if anything else was taken?"

She dropped down onto her butt. "I don't know, but I bet whoever did this was looking for my dragon's talon."

"Who knew you had it?"

She looked back over her shoulder. "Only Slater."

"He's in New York. Ronan spotted him yesterday."

"Who's to say this happened recently?"

She had a point. "Let's sit in the car and wait for the police. You can tell them what you suspect."

He helped her up. "I'm not discussing a stolen picture of a dragon or an artifact I found fourteen years ago. The cops would dismiss the case in a heartbeat. The best thing is to say I don't know what the thief was looking for. Other than the backup copy of my thesis, there's nothing here." Her shoulders sagged. "Oh shit."

"You think he took that?"

"Maybe." EmmaLee rushed over to a dresser and pulled out the bottom drawer. She pawed through the contents. "Son of a bitch."

His heart broke for her. "So he took the copy?"

"Yes."

"We'll have the cops dust for prints. They'll find whoever did this."

She looked up at him with the saddest eyes. "They'll find mine, yours, and Slater's fingerprints. If he didn't do it, I bet the intruder wore gloves."

That almost made him smile. "I may ask you to work for me."

She straightened and punched him lightly in the arm then pressed her face against his chest. Connor wrapped his arms around her, wanting and needing to protect her from all future hurt.

She leaned back. "Guess you better make that call."

FIFTEEN MINUTES LATER, a police car arrived. EmmaLee told Connor she didn't want to go into the house again.

"I don't think they want you in there anyway," Connor said as he pushed open the car door. "It's a crime scene. We can speak with the cops outside."

EmmaLee slipped out. She recognized the officer as he often came into the diner. "Hey, Rod," she said without her usual enthusiasm.

"Hi, EmmaLee." Rod checked out Connor then looked back at her. "How are you doing?"

He'd asked her out a couple of times, but she'd turned him down, saying she was dating Slater. With a new man by her side, he'd feel slighted, but that couldn't be helped. "Before I came back here, I was doing well."

Connor straightened his shoulders and moved next to her. "We arrived only a minute before we called. When we went inside, we found the place trashed."

Rod pulled out a pad of paper. "What did they take?" he asked her.

Saying the thief stole a copy of her nearly completed master's thesis wouldn't make her look bad, but it would send Rod on a wild goose chase. Unfortunately, she couldn't point a finger at Slater since she had no proof.

"I didn't notice anything missing, but I didn't spend a lot of time inside."

"We'll check it out. Where are you staying?"

"Not here."

Connor wrapped an arm around her waist. "We'll stay at a hotel in town."

"Try the Billard Motel. It's the nicest one we have."

It was a nice motel, but EmmaLee wasn't sure she could enjoy it. She was too upset.

"We need to let him get to work," Connor said. He then handed Rod a card. "Call if you learn anything."

"Will do."

She slipped back into her car. As soon as Connor was seated, he reached out and took her hand. "Don't worry. We can replace the furniture."

That was the least of her problems. "The place came furnished, but I don't need others reading my thesis. What if Slater reveals to the world that shifters exist?"

He brought her hand to his lips. "I don't think he will."

"Why's that?"

"I didn't want to mention it before because it didn't seem relevant, but Slater is a shifter."

She jerked her hand back. "No way! How do you know? You've never met him."

"Vinea told me."

Vinea? "That little traitor. I need to have a talk with her."

"I imagine she was only trying to protect you. If you'd known

Slater was a shifter, you might never have left him."

Technically, she hadn't left him. After the assault, he had a price on his head and had scrammed. "You might be right."

Connor started the engine. "Where's this hotel?"

"Turn right and I'll show you."

EMMALEE DIDN'T REALLY have the energy to sit through a two-hour lecture, but she had to go. It was a once in a lifetime event to hear the renowned archaeologist, Dr. Crenely. Plus, she needed to make an appointment to see if he could identify her talon.

"Ready?" Connor asked.

He'd been so kind with this whole robbery thing, never even suggesting they head back to Silver Lake. The fact Connor was willing to hear a talk on dinosaurs when he had no interest in the topic proved he was an amazing man, though she'd figured that out a while ago.

And then there was the motel. While the Billard Motel was really nice, she worried about paying for it. It didn't matter that Connor insisted his company pick up the tab. She believed in pulling her weight.

"EmmaLee?"

She adjusted her seatbelt and looked at him. Twice, Connor had apparently asked her a question, and twice EmmaLee had been so distracted she hadn't answered. "Yes?"

"You sure you want to go to this talk?" he asked.

"I admit, I can't help but see those slashed pillows and everything on my shelves carelessly strewn on the floor, but I truly believe this man is my last chance at resolving the issue of whether dragons exist."

"Do you think he'll say that they're around today?"

That caused her to smile. "Not at all. I doubt the man has any idea shifters even exist. No, if a dragon ever existed, it was millions of years ago. A shifter is a different story."

"Good to know."

When they arrived at the college auditorium, the parking lot was packed. "Wow. It seems I'm not the only one interested in this topic," EmmaLee said.

"I'm glad," he said.

Just as Connor cut the engine, his cell rang, and he looked at the screen. "I'm sorry. I need to take this. It's Ronan." He placed the phone to his ear. "Did you get him? Hold on and slow down. I'm going to put you on speaker so EmmaLee can hear."

Her heart dropped to her stomach.

"Your informant had his facts right," Ronan said. "Coghill was at the Excelsior Hotel."

The Excelsior? "I've stayed there once," EmmaLee blurted. "It's right next to the Natural History Museum in New York."

"Yes," Ronan said. "I thought I had the perfect plan to draw him out and find out if he had any intention of harming you, but I failed."

"You didn't arrest him?" she asked. Her heart fluttered awaiting the answer.

"Not yet, but I will when I locate him. Remember that even if he's in jail, he'll be out in a few years. I wanted to learn more about him to know what we're up against."

"What happened?" Connor said with a sharp tone.

"I didn't want Coghill to know I was after him, so I came up with an idea. I took the photo of EmmaLee you gave me and showed it to random people in the lobby. I mentioned, rather loudly, that I was researching dinosaurs that might have become dragons."

"Coghill was in the lobby I take it?" Connor asked.

"Yes. In fact, he edged closer to me, so I walked over to him and gave him the same spiel. I told him that a few days ago, my new girlfriend, EmmaLee Donovan, stole my research."

She almost hyperventilated. "Did he believe you?"

"Hard to say. I waved your picture at him, asking if he'd seen you. I said that you were staying in this hotel and that you planned to leak my research to someone from the Natural History museum."

"That's quite inventive," Connor said.

"Thanks. Unfortunately, he said he'd never seen her before, but he was clearly lying. I could almost smell his fear."

"Then what happened?" Connor asked.

"He walked out of the lobby. I swear I was only a few steps behind him when he disappeared."

"Disappeared?" she asked.

Connor pounded a fist against the steering wheel. "You told me you could track him by his scent."

"That's the thing. His scent is very different than any other shifter. It was the strangest thing I'd ever experienced."

EmmaLee didn't really understand what had happened, but Connor seemed to.

"How is that possible? Are you saying he's not a shifter?" Connor asked.

"He's a shifter all right, just different somehow."

"So now what?" Connor asked.

"I just got off the phone with Jackson to see if he could follow Coghill's whereabouts. I suggested he locate some footage at all the local airports and bus stations. If he's anywhere close to New York City, I'll find him."

As much as EmmaLee wanted to believe him, she had a feeling Slater was gone. She could only hope he hadn't gotten wind of where she was staying and decided to head to Silver Lake.

Chapter Fifteen

D R. CRENELY HAD yet to make an appearance, and the crowd was becoming restless. Connor leaned over to EmmaLee. "Had you heard that the man has a tendency to be late?"

"No, but if you look at my thesis advisor, he's checking his phone every few minutes. I don't think he knows where Dr. Crenely is either. Crenely should have called if he couldn't make it on time."

"What do you want to do?" Connor asked. "Stay or leave?"

He was being so nice. The Connor of old would have demanded they get out of there. This man seemed to understand how important this talk was to her. "I say we wait until we learn something."

As if she were psychic, the side doors to the auditorium opened and two police officers walked in. The room buzzed louder than a disturbed beehive. Her thesis advisor rushed down the steps. The cops said something to him, but EmmaLee was too far back to read their lips. Damn.

Connor clutched her hand. When she looked up, his jaw was clenched, and his brow had furrowed. "What is it?" she asked.

"Let's go."

She leaned closer. "I'm not leaving until you tell me what happened."

Connor squeezed her hand and then let go. "Your professor isn't coming."

That made no sense. This talk had been planned for month. "What did they say?"

"Someone murdered him."

A band tightened about her chest, threatening to cut off her air. "What?"

Connor stood and edged his way toward the aisle, and EmmaLee was forced to follow on wobbly legs. Her mind whirred. Dead? Connor had to be wrong. Before they made it to the door, her thesis advisor stepped up to the podium and tapped the microphone. She stopped, and the audience quieted.

"I'm afraid Dr. Crenely's talk must be postponed."

Postponed? Hope surged through her. Maybe he'd only been injured and would recover. Connor glanced back at her and slightly shook his head, sending her down that dark tunnel once more.

"I can't give you the details now, but I will as soon as I'm able. I'm very sorry. Please check the message boards for further information," her advisor said.

The crowd erupted into chatter once more and then began the mass exodus. Because she and Connor were close to the door, they slipped out without being crushed. As soon as they made it outside, EmmaLee grabbed his arm. "What did you hear exactly?"

"The cops didn't give your advisor many details, other than to say his body was found in the woods near here." Connor grabbed her hand and led her to the car.

"That's horrible. I can't believe he's dead. So what are we going to do?" she asked.

"We pack and go back to Silver Lake."

She stopped. "Go back?"

His lips pressed together. "Your expert can't help you now. I also think staying here will put you in danger."

"You think Slater's behind this, don't you?"

"I can't say, but someone murdered your expert. I wish I knew how long Dr. Crenely has been dead."

"He arrived two days ago. Hasn't Slater been in New York the whole time?"

"We can't know for sure. He somehow seems to have the ability to travel between cities unnoticed." Connor opened the car door, and she slipped in. "We'll find answers. It just might take time."

"Can you speak with the cops to find out what happened?" He'd say no, but the whole situation was too unreal.

"I'll see if Jackson can find out more."

"Before we leave, can we go back to my place?"

"Why?" Connor asked.

This was decision time. If she packed up her belongings, she would be saying goodbye to a town that had been good to her. She enjoyed the women she worked with and those who lived in the town—at least most of them—but her classes were complete, and that had been what had kept her here. Once she polished her thesis, all she had to do was email it in and then defend it. While it might have been nice to work in Billard, most likely she'd receive offers from a school out of state.

"I think it's time I say goodbye to this town. It has some good memories, but some bad ones too. That means I'll have to pack what hasn't been torn up."

Connor smiled then quickly sobered. "Are you sure?"

She loved that he really seemed to want her to move to Silver Lake. "Yes, but I'll have to get a place of my own. I can't stay at your parents' guesthouse forever."

His mouth opened as if he was about to say something, but he then quickly shut it. She didn't want to get her hopes up in thinking he'd suggest they move in together. Connor wasn't the impulsive type.

"Let me call the cops to see if the scene has been cleared," he said. "If it has been, you can pack. We'll figure out the rest later."

AS THRILLED AS Connor was that EmmaLee wanted to move to Silver Lake, he hoped it wasn't the bad memories that were driving her decision. He wanted her to be in his town because she wanted to be with him.

For most of the drive back to Tennessee, she remained quiet. As much as he wanted to console her, she probably just needed time to figure things out for herself. Her hopes of learning that dragons might exist had been dashed, and he bet her heart ached at the loss of the great man.

Around eight p.m., he pulled in front of the guesthouse. Connor was still worried she'd breakdown. "Are you sure you're okay?"

She shrugged. "Kind of. I feel…violated. And the worst part was that I trusted Slater." She shook her head. "I was such a fool."

"We all have done foolish things. What matters now is that you don't make the same mistake twice."

She looked over at him and attempted to smile. "I don't think I will."

His wolf rejoiced. "Glad to hear it." He picked up her hand. "I know no one wants to think they need help, but maybe seeing a therapist would do you some good."

She shook her head. "I'm okay."

Connor figured she'd say that. "It's your call, but from what I can tell, your childhood was traumatic. No one can come out of that unscathed, especially since your aunt and uncle weren't the supportive type."

Her chin trembled. "You're right. I always thought I had worked through my issues, but given I put up with Slater for so long, maybe it's time I face the fact that I might need some outside counseling."

Connor rubbed a thumb over her wrist. "You know I'll help you any way I can."

"Thank you."

He smiled. "Let's get you unpacked."

EmmaLee didn't have many possessions, and what clothes she had were stuffed into garbage bags. The rest fit into two boxes. Someday, he'd make sure she lived in a house that was full of love and had everything she ever needed and desired.

"Just set them in the bedroom," she said. "I'm not in the mood to unpack."

Connor had never seen her so listless, and that worried him. "Why don't you take a hot bath? That might perk you up."

Her eyes shone. "That sounds wonderful, but what about you?"

"I'll clean up later. I'll watch TV or something while you soak in the tub."

EmmaLee stood on her tiptoes and kissed his cheek. "Thank you. I just wish this place had a tub built for two."

His wolf howled. "So do I," he said as he tapped her on the butt. "Go. I'll be waiting."

Connor grabbed a beer from the fridge and returned to the living room. He'd have to thank his mom for sneaking in and refreshing the drink supply. More than ever, he realized how lucky he had been to grow up with such loving parents.

He sank down onto the sofa and enjoyed listening to EmmaLee run the water, imagining doing this for years to come. As much as he wanted to sneak in and watch her, she needed this time. She had a lot to process: first the break-in and then the death of the one man who could have helped her understand what she'd seen the day her parents died.

These next few weeks would be critical for her. He'd ask his dad for suggestions for a good shifter therapist, and then try to convince EmmaLee to go. Hopefully, Slater Coghill would be found and brought to justice, and the Billard police would have some answers as to who might have broken into EmmaLee's house. He doubted the cops would figure out who killed Dr. Crenely in that time, but he could hope.

While he waited for EmmaLee to finish her bath, he watched a little television, but the show held little interest, so he called his father. Even when his dad stayed home, he seemed to know things.

"How was your trip?" his father asked.

"It was cut short." Connor explained about the break in and the death of the man EmmaLee wanted to speak with.

"I'm sorry. Any ideas on either event?"

"EmmaLee said the only person she'd shown the talon to, other than me, was her ex-boyfriend."

"I thought he was in New York City."

"He was, but we don't know when the break-in occurred. Hell, he could have been waiting for us to leave the first time and then broken in."

"That's depressing."

"As for whether he could be involved in Dr. Crenely's murder, I'm hoping I can get a hold of the autopsy report to see the time of death."

"Do you know how he died?"

"You mean was the good doctor shot to death, beaten, or attacked by an animal?"

"That covers the bases, yes, but if it had been the later, it would narrow down the suspect pool."

"Agreed." The soft padding of feet approached. "EmmaLee just finished her bath. I have to go, Dad." Darn. He'd have to ask his father for suggestions for a therapist later.

"I'll put out some feelers."

That was what he'd hoped his father would say. "Thanks."

Connor disconnected, and when he looked at EmmaLee, his body went wild. Her wet hair, freshly scrubbed face, and creamy skin excited his wolf too much. Wrapped in a soft pink bathrobe, he wanted to make love with her so badly he could taste it.

"Would you like to take a shower?" she asked. "My bath was divine."

Was that a hint that he needed to wash off the road dirt? He had a spare set of clothes in the car. "I'd like that if you don't mind waiting."

"Not at all."

Connor slipped out to his car and gathered the emergency set of clothes he kept there, which consisted of a pair of track pants and a t-shirt. Once inside, he headed into the bathroom. Not wanting EmmaLee to be by herself for long, he quickly showered. As he dried off, he debated walking out with just a towel around his waist like he had the last time but then decided she needed to rest. It didn't matter that he wasn't sure he could last another few days without making love to her. Connor couldn't afford to rush her. His future mate had a lot on her mind.

Once he dressed and returned to the living room, he found her stretched out on the sofa, sipping a glass of wine. "I couldn't wait," she said.

"No problem. I already had my beer."

Connor lifted her legs, sat down, and placed them on his lap. He wanted her to talk him. Her mind had to be spinning.

She set down her glass and sat up, curling her legs underneath her. "Thank you for everything," she said.

He hadn't expected that comment. "I didn't do much."

"You drove me to Billard when you were worried Slater might have been there."

"Ronan had spotted him in New York, remember?"

"I know, but still. I wouldn't put anything past that man."

Connor stroked her arm. "He can't hurt you—not when I'm here. I won't let him."

Her glance shot down to the side. "And I appreciate that."

"If you must know, I took you to Billard because meeting the archaeologist was important to you. I didn't want you to wonder whether what you'd seen that day was a dragon or something else."

"Now I'll never know."

Her pain tore at his heart. "I'm sorry. So what are your plans now?" He'd thought about asking James, their resident immortal, to look at the claw, but even if he knew what it was, he probably wouldn't tell. While Connor didn't interact with him and the goddess Naliana very often, he knew their philosophy regarding humans and shifters. They wanted those on Earth to figure out their own problems and would only interfere if someone were in serious danger.

"I plan to finish my thesis, but this time I'll be omitting all of the dragon parts. I need to move on. I have to accept that I might never know if they exist."

He dragged a knuckle down her cheek. "I'm glad. Personally, I don't want to meet one."

That got a smile out of her. "Me neither—at least not up close and personal." She yawned.

"You've had a long and stressful day. Why don't you head to bed?" he suggested.

"I will if you join me."

If he joined her, they'd be making love, and he didn't know if she was emotionally ready for that. "Are you sure?"

"More than sure." She picked up his hand. "I came back to Silver Lake to be with you. Even if Slater is tossed in jail and they throw away the key, there isn't anything in Billard for me now."

Connor couldn't help but smile. "That's the best news I've heard all day."

Chapter Sixteen

EMMALEE COULDN'T BELIEVE she'd blurted out her feelings, but she was tired of being afraid and timid. Yes, the theft at her house had her reeling, but Dr. Crenely's death had hit her ten times harder. She kept telling herself that maybe it was for the best that she never find out what she'd seen in the sky the evening of the fire, but somehow it was hard to convince herself of that. As for getting help with her tormented past, she didn't have the energy to think through her issues right now. For Connor's sake, she would soon.

And while she could spend hours discussing who might have killed the good doctor and who had motive to ransack her house that discussion would have to wait too. Right now, she wanted to lose herself in the man she was falling in love with. He was a good person, one that she could trust. She eased herself up from the sofa and held out her hand. "Why don't you come with me?"

Connor grabbed her hand and stood. "Lead the way."

She loved when his eyes turned amber and the growth on his face darkened right before her eyes. "You won't shift on me, will you?"

That had been really scary but super cool at the same time. Sure Vinea had told her how some people could transform from human to animal in a few seconds, but never in a million years did she think she'd actually witness it.

"That all depends on how much you tease me." His eyes twinkled.

VELLA DAY

She chuckled. "So it's my fault you shifted the last time?"

He grinned. "It was definitely your fault. If you hadn't enticed me so much, my wolf wouldn't have appeared."

"You normally don't have the urge to change into your animal form?" EmmaLee had so many questions, but she'd ask them later.

"I do, but I decide when to shift. The other night, I had no control over my wolf. He wanted you too badly."

She grinned. "I like your wolf."

Connor swooped her up into his arms. "Keep that up and you might see him again all too soon."

"I'll be good."

EmmaLee hugged him. Connor was warm and strong and oh so sexy. As soon as he entered the bedroom he set her down. "Don't move," he commanded.

"Why?"

"Because I said so."

The bedside lamp was off, but the ambient light from the hallway filtered in enough for her to see his outline and some of his features. He stepped behind her. If this had been Slater, she might have been afraid, but with Connor she wasn't.

He leaned closer. She could smell the minty zest of his soap and feel his breath on her neck. "Close your eyes."

His whisper set her body on fire, and EmmaLee did as he asked. "What are you going to do?"

Connor swiped her hair to one side and then nuzzled her neck. "I'm going to make love to you until you can think of nothing else."

EmmaLee instantly closed her eyes and locked her knees, fearing she might swoon at his romantic words. "I would really like that."

Connor pressed his chest against her back and ran a tongue along the shell of her ear, igniting her insides once more. He wrapped his hands around her waist and deftly undid the bathrobe tie. As soon as the belt dropped to the ground, cool air rushed in, puckering her nipples. Wearing nothing underneath her robe had been chancy, but it had paid off.

140

"Christ Em, what you do to the beast in me." He growled out his words.

"Mmm, tell me."

"You've made me feel alive for the first time in my life."

She smiled. No man had ever said anything so wonderful.

She reached back and gave his erection a squeeze through his pants. "I bet I can really make you feel alive if you let me. She tucked her fingers into his waistband and tried to cop a better feel.

He lightly swatted her butt. "You'll have to wait your turn." Connor dragged the chenille over her shoulders, and the robe joined her belt on the floor.

When his hands found her breasts, he gently massaged them. Even though she wasn't supposed to move, she wiggled her hips and rubbed her ass against his crotch.

He spun her around, and she opened her eyes. "Just what do you think you are doing, missy? Didn't I say not to move?" EmmaLee could tell by his teasing tone he wasn't upset.

When she giggled, he gave her a fake frown. While it was too dark to see the true color of his eyes, she'd bet they were a deeper amber by now.

EmmaLee dragged a finger down his chest. "Since I've upset you, let me make it up to you." Before he could protest, she undid the drawstring on his track pants, and when she started to pull them over his erection, he stepped back.

"Let me. You're taking too long."

EmmaLee swallowed a laugh. Faster than he could shift, Connor dropped his pants, whipped off the t-shirt, and then tossed them next to her robe on the floor.

Connor grinned at her. "Now where were we?"

Wow. He was such a magnificent man. EmmaLee moved forward and grabbed his thick shaft then pumped her fist up and down his length. "I was about to do that."

Connor groaned. "Fuck Em, that feels so good but you have to stop."

"Do I? What are you going to do if I don't?"

"This." Next thing EmmaLee knew, Connor pulled her hand away and then ducked his shoulder, lifting her in a fireman's hold. EmmaLee squealed in delight at his he-man antics. She reached down to give his ass a squeeze and then ran her finger in the crack of his ass. A second later, she went flying, landing on the bed with a huge bounce. EmmaLee laughed so hard, tears fell.

Connor straddled her and then tickled her. "You think that's funny?"

She grabbed his hands. "No, not funny." Yes, it totally was.

"Let's see if you laugh when I do this."

He spread her legs wide and crawled between them. Anticipation soared. When Connor leaned over and swiped his tongue across her wet slit, all thoughts of laughter disappeared, replaced by pure ecstasy. Her man had the ability to take her from amusement to total lust in one second flat. She grasped the sheets and held on as he sucked and licked, forcing all other thoughts from her mind just as he'd promised.

Needing to touch him, she reached out and clamped a hand on his head. He in turn reached up and teased her nipple, but the combination proved to be too much. She wanted more. Wanted him. In her. Plunging. Pounding. Loving.

"Connor, please!"

Ignoring her request, he raised his right hand and massaged her left breast while he flicked her clit back and forth with his tongue. EmmaLee bucked her hips to signal she needed his cock.

He grunted and huffed, as if he too were clawing for control. When she opened her mouth and gulped in air, he must have sensed how close she was to a climax because he crawled on top and kissed her deeply. Their tongues entwined as their breathing turned ragged. She could taste a hint of herself but mostly the flavor was all Connor. She loved how he seemed to need her to breathe.

As much as she was thrilled with the way he was loving her, it was only fair she return the favor. EmmaLee broke the kiss. "I need to taste you too."

"Hmm, all right," he said with slight hesitancy.

His giving her control was a true sign of respect. "Get on your back," she ordered as politely as she could, considering her heart was pounding against her ribs.

Once Connor obliged, she rose to her knees and slipped between his legs. She bent over and ran her tongue up the full length of his cock and then gave a little flick under the head.

Connor groaned. "Be careful, dragon lady; you're playing with fire."

EmmaLee chuckled. "Don't worry—I'm not aiming for an explosion just yet." Then she gave him a saucy wink.

Connor gathered her hair and held it in one hand. EmmaLee drew him deep into her mouth and marveled at his thickness. She swirled her tongue around his thick shaft then sucked just on the head.

"Easy there," he said with a grunt.

It was fun to be with a man who seemed to appreciate her every touch. Keeping his length upright, she nibbled her way around the tip of his cock. Connor growled then tugged on her hair.

When she sucked on him once more, a drop of cum surfaced. Not wanting him to go off too soon, she released him. Now for the real fun. Without asking permission, EmmaLee straddled him.

He reached up and clasped her hips. "Fuck Em, I'm so close, and my wolf is going crazy."

EmmaLee was super excited too, and she wasn't sure she could control herself either once she began. Connor drew her in like no one she'd ever known had. While she'd never read about male sirens, he seemed to be one—reeling her in hard and fast.

Taking a hold of him, she placed the tip at her entrance. Even though they'd made love before, this time he seemed bigger and thicker. Widening her knees, she dropped down but was forced to stop halfway. As if he understood what had prevented her from taking in all of him, Connor pulled himself up into a near sitting position and placed a hand on her back. When he leaned in to suck on a nipple, explosions of need slammed into her. He then reached down and rubbed her clit while encouraging her to rock against him.

With all the different sensations happening to her body at once, along with the change in angle, it didn't take long for EmmaLee to scream out in ecstasy. With her orgasm cresting, he was able to fill her to the hilt. Holy hell. Sparks of desire shot up her spine, and her body went wild.

"Be mine," he whispered.

Those words resonated deep within her, bringing her joy and love. Needing to experience all of him, she swooped down and kissed him. His teeth had sharpened, forcing her to use caution with her tongue at all times. Even though his feral control excited her, she wanted to test the boundaries. Not that she desired him to shift, but she was curious how far she could push him.

She dragged her hands up his face and pressed her breasts against his chest. Pumping her hips up and down, EmmaLee soared higher and higher. Connor was everything she wanted in a man—or rather a shifter-man. He worked hard all day long to protect others, yet he managed to love even harder.

Connor broke the kiss and grabbed her ass, making her feel totally feminine and truly desired. He then dragged his lips down to her neck and her breath caught, thinking he might sink his teeth into her.

A trickle of fear shot through her—not at the pain that might occur—but at what this would mean to her future. Vinea gave her the lowdown, but could a formerly dark goddess be trusted? He kissed her throat and then flipped them over, managing to stay deep inside her.

"I want you so much," Connor said as he closed his eyes and pummeled into her once more.

EmmaLee hung on for the ride of her life. She arched her back and pressed her head against the pillow. Stars burst on the back of her lids as heat ripped up her body, wrapping her in total bliss.

When Connor changed the angle of entry again, another climax took hold. She dug her nails into his shoulders and hung on tight, enjoying the sensual ride to erotic bliss as her inner walls gripped his cock hard. It was an orgasm that eclipsed all others.

When Connor lifted his head and opened his mouth, what sounded like a howl escaped. The next moment his hot cum exploded and seared her insides, causing her vision to flicker.

Exhausted, her body seemed to float away as her muscles weakened. Gathering her in his arms, Connor kissed her forehead, her nose, and then her lips, but she couldn't even muster a pucker.

They lay in an embrace for a few minutes before Connor slipped out. "Be right back."

He returned with a warm washcloth to clean her. "Do you want something to wear to bed?" he asked.

His concern thrilled her. "That depends. Will you stay with me tonight?"

"Just try and keep me out of your bed." Connor winked at her.

EmmaLee smiled. "Then no, I don't want anything around me but you."

Connor gathered her into his embrace, and EmmaLee snuggled into his chest, feeling more content than ever.

"SO WHAT THE hell happened?" Connor worked hard not to yell at Ronan, who was sitting in his office with his elbows on his knees. The man looked like shit. If his slumped shoulders and dark circles under his eyes were any indication, he'd already beaten himself up over his failure to bring in Coghill.

"Like I said on the phone, as soon as I spotted him in the hotel lobby, I went from person to person showing them the picture of EmmaLee. I was trying to establish my cover as an angry boyfriend with a thief for a girlfriend."

"That sounds all good and well. Do you think he saw through your ploy?"

Ronan shook his head. "No. When Coghill stepped up to the desk to ask the clerk something, I spoke rather loudly to someone a few feet away. I clearly stated EmmaLee's name. Trust me; that got his attention."

"I bet. Then what?"

"When he'd finished with the clerk, I walked up to him and asked if he'd seen EmmaLee at the hotel. His eyes turned dark, and the tension in his jaw and shoulders was clearly visible."

"And he said he'd never seen her in his life?

"Yes."

"That doesn't surprise me." Connor tapped the pen he'd been holding on the table, but quickly stopped, the noise even irritating him today. "Did he ask why you wanted to know?"

"No, but that was because when I spoke to the man right before Coghill, I said that EmmaLee had stolen some of my research."

Ronan had been smart and careful. "So what went wrong? Why not arrest him for skipping bail?"

Ronan sat up straighter and stabbed a hand through his hair. "I should have taken the man in when I had the chance, but the guy was huge. Fighting in the lobby wouldn't have done anyone any good. Hell, I was so angry I feared my wolf might have escaped."

Connor nodded. "I understand. I take it you followed him?"

"I tried. I wanted to get Coghill to a quieter location before I cuffed him. You can imagine how hard that is in New York City. Here's the thing. Five seconds after Coghill walked out of the lobby, he disappeared. I asked the doorman if he'd hailed a cab, but he hadn't."

Connor's pulse shot up. "I thought you could track his scent."

Biting down on his bottom lip, he shook his head. "I did for a while, but it was as if he'd vanished into thin air and took his scent with him."

Was that just an excuse to explain his failure? "I don't understand."

"Hell, neither do I."

This wasn't making any sense. Pounding a fist or yelling wouldn't get them anywhere. "Then what did you do? Did you wait for him back at the hotel?"

"Yes, but he never returned. I asked the desk clerk, and he said he hadn't checked out."

"So you lost sight of him for a day?"

"Try two days. When he didn't show, I flew back here. I swear the next time I see him, I'll arrest his ass—assuming I can take him down."

"The next time, I'll send Sam with you. Not only can he bend a person's mind, he's military. Coghill won't be a problem with the two of you."

Ronan stood. "I don't need help. I won't let Coghill go the next time. Until we find him, I'll stay here. What can I do to help?"

As long as he was paying Ronan, he might as well be of use. "Can you drive down to Billard, Georgia and check out a few things for me there?"

"Can do."

Chapter Seventeen

A T NOON, EMMALEE'S burner phone rang. Thankfully, Connor had given her a cell and programmed his number into it. "Hey there," she said, happy to connect with him again.

"Hey yourself. I was wondering if you wanted to grab some lunch."

That took her by surprise. While Connor had shown her a more caring and considerate side, she understood his obsession to his job. "Do you have time?"

"Sam is picking up some pizza for everyone, and I thought you might be hungry."

"I am, thanks." That sounded more like him, but she sensed an ulterior motive for wanting her close by. "What's the occasion?"

"No occasion. Can't a man just want to see his woman?"

Her heart pulsed hard, and EmmaLee had to grab the kitchen counter. *His woman?* "Of course. I'm always happy to take advantage of your faster-than-light Internet."

"That's all?"

Connor actually sounded disappointed. "No silly. I want to see you too, but be forewarned that I might try to tease the wolf out of you."

"You better not, dragon lady."

She loved that nickname. "Are you going to pick me up?" He'd promised that when Slater was in jail, he'd have someone drive her car to Silver Lake.

"Dad called and said he was stopping into work, so I asked him to pick you up. But don't worry. As soon as two of my guys have finished their regular cases, I'll have them bring back your car. Ronan is in Billard now, but he can't drive two cars at once."

"I'd appreciate it. I'll be on the lookout for your dad."

As soon as EmmaLee disconnected, she rushed to the bedroom to put on a cuter top, since she wanted to take advantage of her time with Connor. Just as she changed her shirt, a knock sounded on the door.

"Coming!" She grabbed her purse. Since it was often cold in the office, she took a sweater with her. EmmaLee hadn't met Connor's dad yet, so she was a little nervous. When she opened up, she was quite taken aback by the similarity between the two men.

Mr. McKinnon smiled and held out his hand. "I'm Connor's dad."

"So nice to meet you, Mr. McKinnon."

"Same here, but please call me Cameron, or Cam. Everyone does."

"Cam it is."

"Ready?" he asked.

"Yes." EmmaLee locked up, and he escorted her to his Cadillac.

Mr. McKinnon, or rather Cam, was about an inch shorter than Connor, but he stood straight and held his head high. He might be retired from running the Clan, but he had an air of confidence and authority she found appealing.

He held open the door and she slid in. Once he took off, he glanced over at her. "Connor tells me you had a few setbacks in Billard. I'm sorry for your losses."

"Thank you. I'm trying to put it behind me and move on."

"Smart. So what are your plans now?" he asked.

"Plans?" She could see where Connor learned his bluntness.

"My son said you've relocated here. He told me you're getting your master's degree in Lore and Legends. That's very commendable."

"Thank you." She didn't know how else to respond.

"The dean of the college is a personal friend of mine. If you're planning to pursue a career in teaching, I can put in a good word for you."

EmmaLee was shocked. No one, except for Vinea and Connor, had ever tried to help her. Since the age of twelve, she'd basically been on her own. Her aunt and uncle certainly never did much—other than berate her for not doing a better job of helping them.

"I'd like to try on my own first, but I appreciate the offer."

He grinned, and her blood pressure dropped. That must have been the right answer.

Instead of parking in front of the office like Connor did, Mr. McKinnon drove around to the back and parked underground. She hadn't been aware this garage existed, and she wondered why Connor didn't use this space. After all, he ran the company.

Once inside, they found Connor in the kitchen, the area attached to the break room where she'd been doing her Internet work. As soon as he spotted her, he rushed over and lightly kissed her on the lips. Heat raced up her face at the public show of affection.

His dad cleared his throat. "So where's this pizza you promised?"

Connor looked up at him and smiled. "It's in the oven; just keeping it warm until you two arrived." He took out the food and set it on the table.

Chatter filled the hallway and grew louder as a group of men entered the area. Jackson and Ronan were the only two she recognized. As soon as the other two men spotted her, the group quieted.

"EmmaLee, meet my team." Connor told her about Sam Pompley, soldier and Wendayan extraordinaire, and Kip Landry, who was their non-shifter of the group but who could manipulate electricity. "You know Jackson and Ronan."

Connor asked Kip to demonstrate his talent, and she was delighted at the way he could turn the lights on and off with a wave of a hand.

"I can do a bit more, but Connor would be pissed if I set anything on fire." He winked.

These men were so extraordinary. "I'd love to see a demonstration of what Sam can do."

"Later perhaps. Connor would kill me if I scared you."

"Later then." She so enjoyed their sense of humor.

Pizza was served, and for the next few minutes, EmmaLee forgot about the robbery and the murder. When they finished, she pushed back her chair and grabbed a few of the empty paper plates.

Jackson held up a hand. "We clean up after ourselves. Besides, I want to show you something that I think will fascinate you."

She glanced over at Connor who just shrugged. Maybe it was some dragon sighting or perhaps more information on Zane's home realm. Coming to Silver Lake had been the best thing in the world—for many reasons.

Once she dumped her plate in the trash, Jackson escorted her to a conference room. "It's easier to share a screen in here," he said.

"What do you have?" She took a seat and waited for him to boot up.

"Mind you, it might be hooey, but it's right up your alley of Lore and Legends."

She was almost giddy. "Does Connor know what you found?"

He lowered his chin. "Connor doesn't buy into anything that can't be proven. He has this need to see things for himself. He is willing to admit that Zane came from another realm, but that's all. If his brother's mate, Vinea, hadn't appeared and then disappeared right in front of him, he'd deny she was a goddess."

She chuckled. "That sounds like him." Jackson was definitely different.

He clicked on a saved link. "I'll preface this by saying that this could totally be a figment of the author's imagination."

"I'd like to read it anyway."

"Okay then. This article claims there is a realm—different from the one Zane came from—called Tarradon."

"Tarradon sounds intriguing," she said. Learning about new legends always made her imagination flow. "But I thought there was only one realm."

"Me too. Like I said, this might be the author's imagination."

She could understand that. "It still sounds interesting."

"What's noteworthy is not its existence, but the fact that Tarradon is full of dragons." He looked over at her and smiled.

Butterflies beat against her belly. "Dragons? Are you kidding me?"

"As I said, there is no proof any of this is real."

She leaned closer. It was a thirty-page PDF file. It would take a while to read. "Can you summarize it for me? I'll study it later."

"It contains the history of how the realm evolved. What to hear it?"

"Absolutely."

He sat up straighter and cleared his throat, acting as if he would be delivering a great speech. "Once upon a time, the daughter of the King fell in love with one of the palace guards."

"Aw."

"Princess Rhiannon might have been happy about this new relationship, but her parents were not. They told her to stop seeing this lowly guard since he was a commoner. Like most women, she didn't listen." Jackson ran a finger along the screen and skipped the parts he must have thought were too boring. "Needless to say, they were furious that their precious daughter would even consider dating outside of their royal circle. It was forbidden, you see. To stop this unwelcome union, they requested their resident black lighter—a witch to us—put a spell on Rhiannon's lover. They told this black lighter to turn his heart so black that he'd reject their daughter."

"That's terrible. Can witches, or rather black lighters on Earth do something like that?"

"I've not heard of it, but maybe."

She believed him. "Go on."

"Once the spell was cast, the parents thought they'd won. They were so joyous at the change of event that they told Rhiannon that all was forgiven. She and her lover were even welcome at the castle once more."

EmmaLee loved Jackson's story telling. "I hope the daughter saw through their lie."

"Yes. Why is that you might ask? Apparently, when the black lighter cast her spell on the lover to turn his heart black, the spell landed on the daughter too."

"How sad!"

"Wait, it gets better. Vowing revenge on her family for what her parents did to them, the two fled to the mountains, all too aware that their bodies were starting to betray them. Not wanting this darkness to consume them, they sought out a white lighter witch who claimed she could reverse the spell. All that was needed were a few items— one of which was the heart of a dragon."

"I don't care if this is real or not, it's a great tale."

"I agree," Jackson said.

"Then what?"

He scrolled down. "The rest of this tale is about the two lovers searching for these hard-to-find items. They had to sneak back into the castle grounds, fight off a few dragons, and perform other dangerous deeds."

"This would make a great movie."

"A movie you say? You don't believe this tale?"

She lowered her chin. "Do you?"

Jackson lifted one shoulder. "Maybe not."

"I'll try to keep an open mind. Were they successful?"

"Yes and no. When they retrieved these items, they took everything to the white lighter, but she failed to reverse the spell. She blamed it on the fact that they brought her the wrong kind of heart."

"What kind did she need?"

"It had to be a royal heart," he whispered, his eyes widening.

"So they had to kill one of Rhiannon's family members?"

"Apparently so, but remember neither Rhiannon nor her lover

had any affection for them."

She could understand that. "So who did they kill?"

"They took her mother's heart because she was the one against them in the first place."

"And was the spell reversed?"

"Yes," he said. "But they did commit murder, so they had to live with that forever." He held up a finger. "But there's more. In the process, this new spell set the evil witch on fire to ensure she could no longer harm anyone."

The image made her shiver. "I'm glad."

"But..." Jackson chuckled. "The black lighter managed to fool them all. As she was dying, she cast a spell over the entire realm: all future royalty would succeed in eliminating the weak—the weak being those of non-royal blood. Not only that, she prophesized that this royalty would be the leaders over all of the other realms."

"Other realms as in Earth and Cargonia?"

"It doesn't say," Jackson said. "The black lighter died a fiery death, but some say her spirit rose from the ashes and became even more powerful."

"Like the story of the Phoenix, rising from its ashes."

"Indeed, but here's the main difference—during certain times of the month, it is said she can emerge in her spirit form and inhabit a person's body."

"So her evil ways will always live on?"

"Apparently. She can make these poor souls do unspeakable things, all as a way to help the royal dragons conquer the worlds."

"I didn't see that coming."

"Me neither." Jackson smiled. "It has a happy ending though. The *loving* couple vowed that their children, and all of their children's children after them, would fight the evil royalty until they were all vanquished. They called themselves the Guardians of Tarradon."

EmmaLee clapped. "While I can't use that tale in my thesis, I thank you for sharing it with me."

"My pleasure."

The conference room door opened, and Connor stepped in. His eyes were dark, and his lips thinned. "EmmaLee."

Oh, shit. "What is it?"

He handed her an envelope. "This came for you in the mail."

Why would he be upset about mail? When she spotted the return address, she understood his reaction. "It's from my aunt."

"The one who raised you, right?"

"Yes."

Jackson pushed back his chair and gathered his computer. "I'll leave you two alone. Thanks for letting me share my story about the beginnings of Tarradon."

That brought a smile to her lips. "I loved it. Anytime you want to share, I'm all ears."

Once he left, EmmaLee fingered the envelope, not really wanting to know what was inside. It couldn't be good.

"Aren't you going to open it?" Connor asked.

She inhaled. "I guess I should."

Her fingers shook so much that Connor slipped it from her grasp. "Let me."

He had it opened in a second and extracted two items: a note and a key. Picking up the slightly rusted key, he twisted it around. "Do you know what this belongs to?"

She shook her head. "I don't have the faintest idea. Hopefully, the note will tell me." Since she didn't want to keep any secrets from Connor, she read the letter out loud. "Dear EmmaLee. I hope this finds you well. I'm writing to let you know that your Uncle Robert passed away this past weekend."

Connor placed a hand on her arm. "I'm sorry."

To her surprise, she wasn't. "He was a bastard."

"I'm still sorry."

She nodded. "I know Uncle Robert was a difficult man," her aunt wrote. "He loved your father very much, and as you know, he didn't think your mother was good enough for him."

"He doesn't sound like a pleasant man," Connor said.

"That's an understatement, though why she decided to rub it in, I don't know." As much as EmmaLee didn't want to relive her past, if she had any hope of staying with Connor, he should be aware of what her life was like growing up. EmmaLee leaned back, not bothering to finish reading the letter. "Uncle Robert controlled everything in the house, including his wife. Aunt Kathy was no saint—mostly because she let Uncle Robert treat me badly. In retrospect, I think she was just as abused."

Connor took her hand. "You couldn't leave?"

"I was twelve."

"Right."

"Don't get me wrong. I dreamed of running away, but I had no other relatives that I knew of. I always felt a little like Cinderella, except that I had no other cousins or siblings around. I tried really hard to please my uncle, but it was as if he thought I was my mother."

"He transferred his anger to you."

She nodded. "My dad had a scholarship to a big university and was a pre-med major, but he had to settle for the local college when he got my mom pregnant."

"That's tough."

"My dad didn't care. He loved my mother and wanted a child. It was my Uncle Robert who had lofty plans for Dad, wanting the two of them to open a medical practice together. It was because of my mom that Dad became interested in Lore and Legends."

"I can see why your uncle would be upset, but to take it out on you was unconscionable."

She thought so too. "Thank you."

Connor said nothing for a minute, as she let some of the bad moments race through her head. He then pointed to the letter. "What else did she say?"

Chapter Eighteen

E MMALEE PICKED UP her aunt's letter again and continued reading. "Your uncle will be buried this Saturday, May 12th. I don't expect you'll want to come, but I wish you would. I feel terrible about the way he treated you, and I am sorry if it looked as if I allowed it, but there would have been consequences if I had." EmmaLee lowered her head, and a tear streaked down her cheek. She sniffled and wiped it away. "I'd always wondered why she didn't defend me. Now I know that he was even worse to her."

"I can't imagine what it would be like to grow up without love," Connor said, sounding wistful.

EmmaLee appreciated that he didn't tell her she should have been grateful they had taken her in the first place, but he was mistaken about one thing. "Oh, I had plenty of love. It just wasn't from them. My parents loved me unconditionally."

"I'm glad." He nodded to the letter. "Did she say what the key was for?"

"Let me see." EmmaLee found where she'd left off reading. "Enclosed is a key that belonged to your parents. Your dad left it with your uncle in case of his death." She rolled her eyes then looked over at Connor. "And it took him almost fourteen years to give it to me?"

"Well, we have established the man was an asshole," Connor said.

"Yeah. He obviously didn't want me to have anything of my

father's. I told you he hated me."

"Does she say what the key goes to?"

EmmaLee checked the rest of the letter. "It's to a storage locker in Dunlap Gorge."

"Do you know what's in the locker?" he asked.

"I didn't even know a locker existed." EmmaLee ran a finger down the page. "She doesn't say, but she gave me the address to the storage facility."

"Maybe she doesn't know."

EmmaLee was about to say that was a crock, but in reality her aunt probably had never asked. "Then I guess I'll have to go there and find out."

"Sounds good to me. We can go now if you want. Jackson can take care of anything that crops up here."

"If Ronan is in Billard, is he there to find Slater?"

"That's one of his chores. Don't worry. When Coghill pops up, we'll get him."

"Let's hope that place isn't Silver Lake."

He cupped her face. "I promise I won't let him near you."

"If he does, will you shift into a wolf and tear him limb from limb?" She was kind of making light of the situation, but Connor stiffened nonetheless.

"Let's hope he's a wolf. While I pride myself on my fighting skills, if he's a bear or a tiger, let's just say the odds don't usually fall in a wolf's favor."

"You really can't sense what he is?" she asked.

"I believe I mentioned I couldn't." Connor pushed back his chair and stood. "Let's focus on something else, like finding out what's in that storage unit. It might help solve the crime of who killed your folks."

She stood, and when she hugged him, his delicious scent teased her nostrils. "Thank you. You are the best."

He lifted her chin. "I try to be."

CONNOR WAS AFRAID that EmmaLee would either be disappointed there was nothing of value in the storage unit, or she'd find something that ruined her whole image of her parents. Either way, digging up skeletons probably wasn't smart, but he couldn't say no to her.

The only consolation to driving more than three hours to Dunlap Gorge was that there was a low likelihood of Coghill finding them there. No proof existed that he was planning to seek her out again anyway. However, Connor had the distinct impression that she had learned something Coghill didn't want the world to know. What that was, Connor didn't know.

"Turn here," she said two blocks before the light.

"When was the last time you were in your hometown?" he asked.

She glanced downward. "I haven't been since I was almost seventeen."

"That was pretty young to leave the nest."

"A very uncomfortable nest, mind you. I worked really hard in school to get ahead so I could graduate a year early. Nothing was going to stop me from getting out from under Uncle Robert's watchful eye."

"Good for you." He turned into the entrance of U-Storage and parked. "Are you sure you're ready to look through your parents' possessions?"

"More than ready."

"Then let's do this."

After signing in, they located the unit. As soon as Connor lifted the garage door, he stilled and studied the contents. The place was stacked with boxes in a not-so-neat order. "What do you think?"

"It's a mess," EmmaLee said as she stepped inside. She ran her fingers over the dusty boxes. "It looks like they are dated at least."

"How does that help?"

She shrugged. "I'm not sure, but I'm thinking the answer to their deaths would be found in the more recent boxes."

He liked her logic. "I agree."

She twisted her ponytail in an absent-minded way. "One thing's for sure. We can't fit all of these into your SUV."

He figured she'd want to go through each one. "We could stay at a hotel for a day or two and look through them all, taking a few boxes each day."

EmmaLee smiled and his wolf went crazy. She wiped her palms down her pants and stepped close. Even in the moldy smelling interior, her scent excited him. When she wrapped her arms around his neck, he wanted to taste her, so without hesitation, he kissed her.

Close the door, and let's enjoy our mate, his wolf yipped with too much cheer.

Christ, you have a one-track mind. I am not making love to our mate in a mildew infested storage unit.

His animal huffed and whined, but Connor blocked out his complaint. Instead, he enjoyed her sweet mouth.

Hearing voices outside, Connor broke off the kiss and cleared his throat. "I guess we should put as many as we can in the car and then find a hotel."

"Works for me. Thank you," she said.

For the next few minutes they stacked the boxes in the back and on the seats. "Do you know where a hotel is located?" he asked.

"There used to be one on Elkart Avenue, but I can't say if it's nice anymore or even if it's still there. It's been a long time since I left."

"We'll give it a try." Connor programmed his GPS then took off. "I just realized the storage unit person didn't say the payments were in arrears. Do you think your uncle paid for the unit all these years?"

"I doubt it. Uncle Robert was such a tightwad."

"Maybe he believed his brother's research was valuable, and he wanted to make sure the information was preserved."

"My uncle probably never took the time to listen to my father's ideas. Every time Uncle Robert talked about dad's vocation, it was with scorn."

"Then who would have kept up the payment?"

"Perhaps my aunt did though I'm not sure why. I don't see my father paying in advance either—certainly not for fourteen years."

"I'll check with the manager the next time we come," Connor said.

The hotel wasn't far, for which he was thankful. While Connor didn't think the place was very nice—at least on the outside—EmmaLee didn't bat an eye. They ended up taking what the clerk claimed was their nicest room. The best part was that they could park in front of the room, making lugging in all of the boxes less of a chore.

"So how do you want to do this?" Connor asked once they placed the boxes in a neat arrangement on the floor.

"If a secret caused my parents' death, we should start with the newest box."

That made sense, but he feared if her parents had discovered something, they might not have had time or enough warning to hide it. "I'll let you decide what you want me to sort through."

EmmaLee pointed to a box. "You take that one. I'll do the most recent one."

Just because Connor was used to this kind of research didn't mean he liked it. Jackson was the one with the patience to dig and dig until he found that one small nugget of truth. For EmmaLee though, he'd do his best.

His box contained notebooks of their findings, a yearly calendar, and a lot of interviews. While he wasn't sure what any of it meant, Connor would do his damnedest to figure out what the killer was so afraid would be exposed.

For the next two hours, they pored over the files, jotting down notes, and occasionally EmmaLee would read him something that they would then discuss. Potential clues went in one pile, unimportant items in another.

Around dinnertime, EmmaLee stilled. "I think I have something. Listen to this. A man promising them an exclusive interview about seeing a dragon was supposed to fly in on Thursday, October 16th to the Atlanta Airport. My parents noted that while the plane arrived on time, their man was not on the flight."

"So? People miss flights all the time."

Her shoulders slumped. "I know, but later that night, Mom wrote in her journal that she thought she heard wings flapping overhead and that they came close to the window. The next day their house burned down."

"What does one have to do with the other?"

"Maybe nothing."

Connor didn't like seeing her so dejected. "The guy who supposedly saw the dragon might have been trying to make sure no one followed him, so he missed the plane on purpose. Does it say in her journal if he called your folks later that evening to explain what happened?"

"No."

Connor told her how Coghill had booked a few flights but he never arrived on any of them.

"Yes, but Slater was a wanted man," she said. It makes sense he'd do that to keep the cops busy while he took the train or a bus."

Connor liked the way she thought. He saw no reason to mention that a bus or train wouldn't have allowed Coghill to arrive in New Orleans three hours later. "It's reasonable to think this guy believed he was being followed. Did your parents mention the man's name? My team might be able to do a little investigating."

"No. They just called him *Mr. F.* I find it odd that he was anxious to tell them about what he'd seen but then never showed up. That combined with the flapping of wings caught my attention."

"Your mom might have been upset that he didn't show. She probably had dragons on her mind."

EmmaLee nodded. "You're probably right. Aargh. This is so frustrating."

"Remember, it's a cold case. It will take time and patience to find something that helps. We need to learn the man's name so my team can figure out why he never showed."

Her mouth opened. "Are you thinking someone killed him?"

"It's possible."

For the next half hour, they read through the letters and note-books, but he came up empty. She closed her book. "Nothing. How do you do this day after day?" she asked.

Connor was pleased she was beginning to understand what he did for a living. Once they were mated—assuming she was willing—EmmaLee would have far less difficulty adjusting to his long hours if she could relate to what he did. "I'm determined to find justice."

"Is it because your father was the Clan's Alpha and ran the busi-ness before you?"

He smiled. "Someone has been doing her homework."

She returned his smile. "I've also met your dad. He's sharp and seems driven to do his best."

Her insight impressed him. "I'm surprised you could see through his facade. Sometimes he acts like he just stumbles into uncovering things, but in truth, he works all the time."

"Well, I like him."

"I'm glad. What do you say we make another trip to the locker and sort through the rest of the boxes? We can return any we've already searched through to make room in here."

"Sounds good."

They took back more than half of the boxes. When they re-turned to the office to sign in, the clerk's eyes widened. "Ms. Donovan, your brother was just here. You missed him by five minutes." He chuckled. "Why, your parents' locker hasn't seen this much activity in years."

"My brother?"

It had to be Coghill. "What did he look like?" Connor asked.

The clerk's mouth gaped open. He looked at EmmaLee. "I don't understand."

"I don't have a brother. Did he have identification?"

"Yes. A driver's license."

"What was the name on it?" she asked, the tension in her voice escalating.

"Let me check the log." He twisted the pad of paper around and tapped it. "Slater Donovan."

Well damn. Connor's protective nature shot into high gear. He had to have followed them there, not giving a damn if they found out. If was almost as if he wanted them to know he was one step ahead of them.

"He's not my brother; he's a thief."

"A thief? I...I'm so sorry. I didn't know."

"It's not your fault," Connor said. "The man had identification. Can you tell me if the rent is up-to-date?" he asked the clerk.

His hands shook. "Let me look." He clicked the keys on his computer then dragged his fingers across the screen. "Yes. The unit has never been in arrears."

"Who has been paying for it?" asked EmmaLee.

"A Kathleen Donovan."

EmmaLee grabbed Connor's hand. "Why would Aunt Kathy pay for the unit? She rarely mentioned my father."

Connor ran a hand down her arm. "You read her letter. She probably felt guilty for the way your uncle treated you. Maybe by keeping the storage locker fees up-to-date, she hoped it would help bring you closure."

She blew out a breath. "I wish I'd known how she felt when I lived with her."

"At least you do now."

The clerk cleared his throat. "What should I do if this guy shows up again?"

"Call the police, but I don't think he'll return," Connor said, his mind swirling.

EmmaLee's hands tightened into fists. Wanting to avoid a scene, he led her outside.

As soon as they were clear, she faced him. "Can you believe Slater? He must have followed us."

That was what worried Connor the most. "If he did, he was damned good. Did he say if he was in the military?"

"He never mentioned it."

That made him even more dangerous. He possibly worked in special ops.

In silence, they drove over to her father's storage unit. When they arrived, Connor made EmmaLee stay in the car until he'd thoroughly checked out the area. He didn't detect any shifter signatures, but Ronan said Coghill's scent was faint.

As soon as Connor stepped up to the unit, he noticed the lock had been broken. "Son of a bitch."

Even though he was convinced Coghill was long gone, Connor looked around once more—even checking the unit rooftops, half expecting Slater to be there with an assault rifle in his hands. What the hell was so valuable about the Donovan's research that at least two people had to die?

Connor lifted off the latch, and when he opened the door, his heart cracked. Oh, shit.

Chapter Nineteen

A S SOON AS EmmaLee peered inside the storage unit, her stomach tumbled, the violation making her want to vomit. Assuming it had been Slater and not someone using his name, the thief had emptied out everything. This gave her more proof that her parents had stumbled on some important discovery—only what had it been?

She and Connor returned to the car. "I'm sorry, EmmaLee. What do you want to do now? Put the boxes we have back in the storage unit or take them to Silver Lake? We'll have to buy another lock if you go with the first option."

Connor was being so supportive. If she weren't so mad right now, she'd say that the intense emotion coursing through her was love. Hell, if she hadn't already decided to stay in Silver Lake with Connor, she would have agreed all over again. "Let's take the boxes back. I can get a storage unit in Silver Lake."

"My parents have room in their garage. A paid storage unit might not be safe, even in Silver Lake. I don't trust the thief not to try again."

Merely calling the man a thief implied Connor thought the robber might be someone other than Slater. "You don't think it's my ex?"

"He is definitely my number one suspect, but I'd like to know his motive for wanting the boxes before I point a finger at him."

"So do I."

When they returned to the hotel, EmmaLee was curious what he planned to do about the incident. "Are you going to involve the police?"

"I'm not sure what they can do, but we need to report it," Connor said. "The problem is we can't even tell them what was in the stolen boxes."

"I figure they contained more of what we have—only older. Let's hope the thief left prints or some trace elements."

Connor gave her a half smile. "You've been watching too much TV. I'll make the call."

Connor was so matter-of-fact on the phone. When he finished, he disconnected.

"Well?" she asked.

"They told us to stay put so they can ask questions."

Damn. Questions they didn't have answers to. As much as she just wanted to grab their luggage and drive back to Silver Lake tonight, they couldn't. No doubt the cops would ask a ton of questions that would dredge up more bad memories—but it couldn't be helped.

When the officer arrived, EmmaLee mentioned that her parents' house had been burned down fourteen years ago, and that she thought there might be a connection to the theft. The officer in charge said he didn't see how the two were related. She sure as hell wasn't about to say anything about shifters and dragons.

Around eight, the officer said they were free to go and promised to be in contact should they find the thief, but EmmaLee was less than hopeful. If the cops located him, it would be due to Connor's efforts, not the Dunlap Gorge Police Force.

As soon as the officer left, Connor closed the hotel room door. Circles had begun to form under his eyes, implying the strain of this trip had taken a toll on him too.

"You up for some food?" he asked.

Her stomach was too upset to eat, but Connor seemed to want something. "Sure, but nothing too big."

"Works for me."

They stopped at an all-night diner, and to her delight the menu held a ton of appealing choices. EmmaLee ordered a chocolate chip waffle and a glass of sweet tea.

She planted her elbows on the table. "With Dr. Crenely dead and the rest of the files gone, I'll never know why my parents were targeted."

Connor reached out and squeezed her hand. "Sometimes not knowing can be for the best."

"Perhaps. And Slater? What happens to him?"

"Ronan wants him for the bounty money. At the moment, we have no evidence he has any interest in you," Connor said.

"Maybe not me, but he knows I have that talon."

Connor smiled. "That's my dragon lady. Always on the case."

She looked up at him. "What do you mean?"

"What it sounds like. I don't think you'll ever give up trying to find the truth, whatever it might be."

The waitress delivered her drink and EmmaLee took a sip. "You're probably right."

"I know I'm right."

After a delicious meal that she was unable to finish, they returned to the hotel.

"I'll carry the boxes in," Connor said. "I don't want this person to break into my car."

That thought gave her the chills. "Smart thinking, though I doubt there's anything of value in those boxes."

Connor stroked her cheek. "Not that we can tell, but whoever took the other half doesn't know that. How about you take a shower while I grab them?"

"You are too good to me."

Connor moved closer, and EmmaLee had the urge to drag him into the room and tell him to forget about the damn boxes. This lifelong journey of hers had basically come to an end, and what better way to say goodbye than to indulge in the splendor of loving him?

He tapped her nose. "I know that look in your eyes, but I need to move these first. You'd feel terrible if someone stole them while we were enjoying ourselves."

"Why do you always have to be so practical?"

"I just want to keep you safe." He winked.

"Fine." She was dusty, and a shower would feel good.

While Connor moved the boxes, she went in to clean up. She'd just shampooed her hair when the bathroom door opened and the shower curtain eased back.

She twisted around, joy spearing through her at the sight of his naked body and his raging hard on. "What are you doing?" she asked, acting as if she couldn't figure it out.

"What does it look like? I'm going to take a shower."

Delight filled her. "Let me rinse my hair first and then you can have it."

Connor moved closer, his eyes turning a beautiful amber color. "No need to rush. I'll just enjoy the view."

She smiled and then dipped her head back to rinse her hair. A second later, Connor's mouth was on her right breast, and she squealed. "Don't get me too excited," she said. "This tub is way too small to have sex in here."

He lifted off her tit. "Who said anything about sex?"

"Connor McKinnon, I know you."

"I hope that's true," he said before moving to the other side. "Don't pay me any mind."

EmmaLee laughed. "I can't ignore you. You've kind of attached yourself to me." As he nibbled on one breast, he slipped a finger into her opening, causing her to clamp down. The intense pleasure made her moan.

"You have no idea how hard it is to keep away from you," he said, his voice sounding strained as if he was working to keep his wolf in check.

"I'm not very patient," she said, letting the water hit her shoulders.

He stood up. "I can see that."

"You're not immune either. Your eyes are practically yellow, your beard looks like you haven't shaved in two days, and your teeth have sharpened." She ran her hand down his furrier-than-usual chest.

"That always happens when I'm near you—more so now than ever."

He was too sweet. "I repeat. No sex in the small tub."

He laughed. "I'm just warming you up. Once I get you to the bed, I'll be getting you really hot and bothered."

EmmaLee laughed. "I'm always hot and bothered when I'm around you."

"Mmm, good to know."

"I need to rinse." It took her ten times longer than usual, mostly because she was enjoying herself too much. Testing his resolve however could be even more fun. "I'm done. You're turn."

They stepped around each other, and when Connor faced the wall and ducked his head under the water, EmmaLee reached around him and grabbed his cock. Instantly, his hand was on her wrist. "None of that."

"Why not? You played with me. Turnabout is fair play, right?"

"Not when one of us is a human and the other is a shifter."

EmmaLee loved the power she seemed to have over him. "Okay, we'll do it your way."

He set down the shampoo he'd just picked up and faced her. "This isn't about my way or your way."

Yikes, she'd only been teasing him. "I know! Now hurry up. Someone will be naked in bed when you finish."

EmmaLee stepped from the shower tub and grabbed two towels. After wrapping her head in one, she dried off with the other. Just as she draped her two towels over the shower curtain rod, Connor stepped out, looking sexier than hell. He sure had been fast.

"I hope you're ready for some hot loving," he said as he locked his gaze on her face.

"I am very ready." He stepped closer and hugged her. "Ew. You're all wet," she teasingly complained.

Connor's grin dimpled his cheeks. "Maybe you could lick the water off me."

EmmaLee laughed. Life with Connor would never be boring. Even though tragedy seemed to follow her, he was the one bright shining light in her life. "Let's go into the bedroom where I can begin."

"I can't wait."

Her heart swelled. Hand in hand they crossed the room to the bed. EmmaLee sat down and held out her hands. "Stay right there."

"I'll get the carpet wet."

"It's better than sleeping in a wet bed. Let me help you dry off first. After all, it was your suggestion." She leaned over, drew his cock toward her, and sucked him into her mouth.

He clutched a handful of her wet hair. "Dear goddess, your mouth is heaven."

The first taste had her reeling, and she wanted more—much more. EmmaLee had spent her life searching for something. Today, she realized what that something was—Connor McKinnon. He was a man who was protective, kind, caring, super hot, and a beast in bed. Sure he worked a lot, but he'd never hit her or take advantage of her.

One minute she was pumping her hand up and down his thick shaft and the next, she was on her back with her legs over his shoulders.

"My turn," he growled.

Connor was the best lover. Not only did he genuinely want to please her, he knew exactly what she liked. And as much as she loved his cock, his tongue could twist her insides until she wasn't able to think. Given all that had happened recently, that was a good thing. The first swipe across her clit had her letting out a growl of her own.

"You're like a racecar," he said.

"Huh?"

"You can go from zero to sixty in three seconds."

"And whose fault is that?" she asked, failing to contain another smile.

"Oh, it's definitely mine."

It most certainly was. On the next lick, she clawed the bedspread and lifted her hips for more. His thumbs pried open her lower lips, and when he sucked hard on her little nub, she almost came right then and there.

"Please, Connor."

He looked up at her. "Please what?"

"I need your cock."

"You'll get it." As if she hadn't asked, he continued flicking his tongue while he reached up and pressed on both nipples.

The quick shot of pain morphed into an incredibly strong erotic pulse. She'd barely reached his shoulders when her orgasm overtook her. EmmaLee's chest heaved as sparks of need tripped up her spine.

"I can't wait any longer," Connor said. "If I don't make love with you right now, my wolf might take over and make an appearance."

"Then take me now." Even though she thought his wolf was one sexy animal, there was no place for him in the bedroom.

With her legs still slung over his shoulders, Connor crawled forward until his cock was pressed against her opening. She drew his head toward her and locked lips. The kiss spoke of eternity. A second later, he plunged in, and she soared. Their breaths mingled as he pumped into her, over and over again, while keeping a rhythm she tried to match. Stars flitted across her vision as blood pounded hard in her ears. They devoured each other, needing each other and loving each other hard.

Breasts pressed against his rock hard chest, EmmaLee had never felt so complete in her life. Connor broke the kiss and trailed his mouth down her chin and across her throat.

"I love you." He whispered it so softly she had to repeat it in her head to make sure she'd heard it right.

"I love you too."

Connor stilled, and when he lifted his head, she thought she'd ruined everything. But then he grinned, and his sharpened teeth told her she'd just given him the keys to the kingdom.

"Then you will be mine," he announced.

Joy slammed into EmmaLee, nearly robbing her of much-needed oxygen. While they hadn't talked about her being his mate, everything pointed to it being true. She expected him to sink his teeth into her neck right then and there, but instead he slipped her legs off his shoulders, and hugged her tight.

The tender motion made her love swell even more. "Come for me again," he said.

"Yes." It was all she could manage to say.

Connor eased in and out, creating a slower build up this time, until she finally had to grab his hips and lift up to make him go faster.

"You want it hard, dragon lady?"

"Give me all you got."

What happened after that was a total blur. Connor went after her with the fury and force of a tsunami. Who came first she didn't know, but he certainly transported her to a different place and time for those few moments. When they were both spent, they lay in each other's arms. Exhausted, they fell asleep.

Sometime later, EmmaLee roused to the sound of running water. Connor returned with a washcloth to clean her up.

"I think it's a little late for that," she said. "I'm not sure we can salvage these sheets."

"They're hotel sheets. They must be used to it."

She chuckled. "You're probably right."

Chapter Twenty

EMMALEE WAS WORKING away in the office break room, and Connor was with Ronan in his office discussing their plan for finding Slater Coghill, when Jackson stepped into the office. "I've got something."

They both looked up. "I could use some good news. Tell us," Connor said.

"Timothy Delahart made a mistake. He used his debit card at an ATM in Chattanooga."

Ronan sat up straighter. "When?"

"Less than fifteen minutes ago."

Ronan stood. "I need to go after him. Where was this ATM? He won't still be there when I arrive, but I might be able to pick up his scent."

Connor appreciated his new recruit's enthusiasm, especially after the fiasco with Slater Coghill.

Jackson flipped through his phone. "Bank of Chattanooga."

"Do you know where he's staying?" Ronan asked.

"As a matter of fact, I do. Delahart is at the Train Station Inn Motel."

Ronan looked at Connor. "I won't ask how you know that, but thank you." He turned back to Connor. "This might be my only chance to nab him. I hope you weren't counting on my help with Slater just yet."

"Not at all, but this seems too easy to me. It's almost as if Delahart wants you to find him so he can take you down first," Connor said.

"What else is new? Bounty hunters often become the hunted."

Connor closed his laptop. "If you're determined to go, I'm coming with you."

"What about EmmaLee?" Jackson interjected.

"She's in the break room doing more research."

Jackson nodded. "I can watch her if you want."

"I'm not sure I can handle you two being in the same room for that long. You'll fill her head with all sorts of crazy stuff." Actually, Connor thought it was cute that they had so much in common.

Jackson grinned. "I'll be good. I promise."

"Actually, I was hoping you'd volunteer. We might not be back before five, so can you do me a favor?"

"Sure."

"So she doesn't feel like a prisoner, can you drive her back to the guesthouse when you're ready to leave and watch her there? You can ask my dad to help if you need to leave."

"Can do." Jackson looked over at Ronan. "If you need any more information, let me know."

"Do you know what kind of vehicle Delahart is driving?" Ronan asked. "I wouldn't put it past him to swap out his Jeep."

Jackson grinned. "I do."

As soon as Jackson had given them the rest of the information, Ronan left to gather his gear, and Connor called Rye to fill him in on the latest news regarding Slater Coghill. Since Rye was an excellent sounding board, he told him of the possible connection with the theft of EmmaLee's parents' belongings. Connor then told his brother he needed to leave town for the day. "She'll be in Jackson's capable hands."

Rye chuckled. "She seems special—more special that just someone to keep safe. Is there something you need to tell me?"

From his tone, their father must have leaked the good news. "I can tell you've figured it out, so yes, EmmaLee is my mate."

"Well, it's about time. Does she know?"

"No, and I'll tell her when the time is right."

"I understand. I can take a sweep around the old homestead to make sure everything remains calm."

"I appreciate it. I've been meaning to ask, have you spoken with Finn lately?" Connor asked.

"As a matter of fact, I stopped by the bar yesterday. Zane challenged me to a game of pool."

He'd heard the man from Cargonia was quite good. "And?"

"He cleaned my clock."

Connor laughed. "I meant did you speak with Finn? Although, I am thrilled that someone finally kicked your ass at pool."

"Oh, piss off. He obviously has some super pool playing powers from the other realm. I did speak to Finn afterward, and you were right. He looks like death warmed over. He told me the same story you did. Our baby brother is convinced his dream girl is real somehow. Not that he's delusional enough to think she's in his room at night, but there's something about her that calls to him. I'm not sure what to make of it."

"Maybe you could ask James what it might mean." As the Alpha of the Clan, Rye had quick access to the resident immortal.

"I might have better luck with Ophelia, though the old lady can be a bit mysterious in her explanations."

Connor chuckled. "So I've heard. I hope that Finn decides to get some help before it kills him."

"Amen."

"I'll call you when I return," Connor said.

"I have your back, little brother."

CONNOR WAS WITH Ronan, across the street from the hotel where Timothy Delahart was staying. Both of them were more than ready to nab the son of a bitch. Ever since Connor had heard what a scumbag he was, he wanted the satisfaction of taking him down. It didn't matter to him that Ronan would get all of the bounty money, Connor wanted to make sure the man never saw the light of day again.

"There he is," Ronan whispered.

Delahart had just walked out of his hotel onto the busy street and looked around, as if he were looking for someone. Tourists were crowding around a coffee shop next door to the hotel, making an arrest more difficult. Because Delahart might try to use someone as a hostage, they sat tight.

"What is he waiting for?" Ronan asked with impatience.

"A ride maybe?"

"Wait!" Ronan pointed to a black SUV that slowed and pulled to the curb.

"He's getting in," Connor said. "Let's go."

Faces averted, they sauntered to Connor's car and then waited for the SUV to get ahead by a block before taking off. As soon as Connor pulled into traffic, Ronan turned on the GPS and then planted a flag in their current location.

"Could you tell how many were in the car?" Ronan asked.

"Given that Delahart slipped into the backseat, I'd say at least two other men." If Ronan's Wendayan powers were to be believed, the two of them should be able to take down three shifters no problem.

"Agreed. Let's follow them."

Connor kept as far back as he could so as not to attract attention, but close enough not to lose them. When they left the main part of town, the traffic thinned, making it more difficult to keep out of sight.

"I wonder where they're going." Strain laced Ronan's voice.

"Beats me, but if he's as bad as you say, he could be doing a deal. Why else come halfway down the country unless it's for something big?"

"True."

Would it be drugs, gun running, or human trafficking? If he'd been sure something illegal was about to go down, Connor would have alerted the Chattanooga police.

"He's turning into that lot," Ronan announced.

When the black SUV stopped in front of a warehouse, Connor kept on driving. With one eye on the rearview mirror, he continued until it was safe to turn around. He didn't dare get too close to the warehouse for fear of being spotted.

"I'll park on this side street next to this store where we'll be out of sight."

"I wish I could walk up to his whole gang and say I was there to take him in, but that would cause quite a stir."

Now Connor wished he had asked Jackson to come with them and have Rye watch EmmaLee. Having a bear would have helped even the odds. More than ever, he wished Dalton Garner had decided to become an investigator instead of a sheriff's detective. A white tiger on their side would have assured them a win, assuming all of those inside were wolf shifters.

Keeping out of sight, he and Ronan made their way to the south side of the warehouse. The problem was that the building only had high windows, so there was no way to see in.

"We could shift and lie in wait until Delahart comes out, but if he exits with too many men, things could get deadly."

Connor didn't like the odds. "We could follow them back to the hotel and you could nab him there."

Before they could decide, the side door to the warehouse opened, and Delahart came out with two other men. He was carrying a briefcase—contents unknown. Most likely, it contained money—or drugs.

"They're all shifters," Ronan said. "I can smell their scent. What I'd really like to know is what kind of shifters and how many more are inside."

Before they could figure out the best plan to take them down, Ronan stepped from the parked car they were hiding behind. "Hey, fellows."

Well shit, Ronan.

Three sets of guns instantly appeared out of their holsters, but Ronan remained cool. He held up his hands. "Just want to talk."

"Drop your weapon." This came from the taller of the other two goons.

Crap. Even from where Connor was hiding, he could see their eyes change and their hair sprouting. *Be careful, Ronan.*

Ronan removed his sport jacket. Next he slid off his holster containing his weapon and placed it on the ground. Before any of them had a chance to react, Ronan shifted and charged.

Connor hadn't expected that move. Only someone as big as a tiger could handle three wolves at once. It didn't matter that Ronan had some special Wendayan talents.

As fast as he could, Connor shifted too.

Claws scratching the cement, Connor charged. He leaped into the air and tore at the belly of the man closest to him. Ronan, in the meantime, was busy alternating attacks between Delahart and his goon—and winning. The stench of blood, along with a few blood-curdling screams, filled the air.

Even though Connor wanted a piece of Delahart, Ronan had tracked him this far and deserved to take him down. Connor should have asked if there was a dead or alive bounty on the man's head, but at the moment, Ronan probably didn't care.

The man Connor had attacked shifted and came at him. The first swipe slashed Connor's side, but the cut was superficial. He growled, and the smaller tan wolf backed up, long enough to crouch down and spring forward again, but Connor was ready for him. Mouth open, Connor clamped down on the wolf's neck. He would have torn out his throat had the animal not grabbed a hold of Connor's under belly with his sharp claws and tugged hard. The sudden blast of pain caused him to gasp for air. Those few seconds gave his prey a chance to escape. The tan wolf stumbled backward and wheezed. He was down but not out.

Blood poured from his opponent's throat, giving Connor a

minute to regroup. He turned his attention to Ronan to see if he needed help. The first man Ronan had attacked was bloodied but still managing to fight. Somehow, Timothy Delahart was nowhere to be seen. What the hell?

A car engine revved up, and the same black SUV that had driven the men there shot to life. Delahart! Connor debated shifting and taking off after him when the door to the warehouse opened and two more men exited.

Ronan quickly finished off his shifter just as the wolf Connor had been battling regained some of his strength. It took a moment for Connor to sense these two men with the duffle bag in tow were not shifters. Finally, they had a break.

Their eyes widened, and Connor bared his teeth.

"Nice wolf," the beefier of the two said.

The tan wolf scrambled across the pavement toward Connor making enough noise to alert him. Nose down, Connor opened his mouth and lifted a paw.

Sorry fellow. It's not your day.

Ronan was chasing off the two humans while Connor delivered the final and fatal blow to his wolf.

In less than a minute, both foes had died and had returned to their human form. Connor sat on the ground for a minute to heal while Ronan trotted back. Before Connor had fully recovered, Ronan had shifted. "I'll meet you at the car. We need to go after Delahart."

Naked, Ronan grabbed his holster and took off for the side street.

If he could speak, Connor would have mentioned the man was long gone. Hopefully, Ronan had injured him enough to cause some problems. Because Ronan was chomping at the bit to go after Delahart, Connor shifted then followed.

Once they both reached the SUV, they grabbed their spare set of clothes from the back and donned them. Ronan's arm was sliced open, as was his hip, but he didn't wince when he pulled on his spare jeans.

Ronan slammed the back closed. "I can't believe that fucker got away."

"What happened?" Connor slid into the front seat and fired up the engine.

Ronan climbed in. "I wish I knew. I only had to battle two of them. I thought I'd landed quite a blow to Delahart when I gouged out his cheek and part of his eye. His wolf had even dropped to the ground. Just as I was about to finish him off the other guy came at me. He was good too. I'm sorry."

"Sorry? It wasn't your fault. You did great."

"Delahart escaped."

Connor understood. He often beat himself up, but that kind of attitude never helped. "I say we return to Silver Lake. If Jackson found your man once, he can find him again."

"How about we swing by the hotel to see if that black SUV is there?"

Even if the man was stupid enough to return, neither of them was in any shape to tackle Delahart. However, Ronan wouldn't be able to keep his mind on the game until he knew. "Sure."

When they arrived, the SUV wasn't there.

"Well damn," Ronan said. "It's an hour's drive back to Silver Lake, right?" Connor nodded. "Do you mind if we find a drive-thru here?" He was leaning slightly forward in the seat, as if he was trying to hide how much he was really hurting.

"No problem."

After they chowed down a quick meal, Connor suggested that Ronan should shift and rest in the back. Then when he regained his strength, Ronan could switch places with Connor. If EmmaLee saw him in this state, she'd freak out.

WHEN JACKSON'S CELL rang, he pulled it from his shirt pocket and smiled at EmmaLee. "Your man is calling."

She let out a long breath. Connor had told her that he and Ronan needed to drive to Chattanooga and arrest some man, promising it would be easy. If that were true, why had he been gone for four hours already?

"Where are you?" Jackson asked. He listened for a bit and then nodded. "Okay. No problem. I've enjoyed hanging out with EmmaLee. She is amazingly knowledgeable about all sorts of things. Sure." He disconnected. Standing, he pocketed his cell. "Connor's next door at his dad's house. He'll be right over." Jackson stood and gathered his computer. "I appreciate you putting up with my crazy theories."

She smiled. "They weren't crazy." At least most of them weren't. "It was my pleasure."

As soon as Jackson left, EmmaLee dashed to the bathroom to comb her hair. Before she'd taken one stroke, someone knocked. She smiled. Connor must have forgotten his key. She rushed down the hallway and then pulled open the door.

Her heart stopped. "Slater?"

Chapter Twenty-One

"ANYTHING YOU CAN find out about this guy or what Timothy Delahart was doing in the warehouse would be greatly appreciated," Connor said to his dad.

"I'll ask around." His father nodded to the dried bloodstains on his shirt and pants. "Shouldn't you change before you see EmmaLee? She seems like the type to fuss."

Connor smiled. "Yes, it would be better. I'll dash home before I see her. Speaking of leaving, I need to go."

"All right, son."

Connor jumped in his car and was home in a minute. His body had mostly healed on the drive home since he was able to shift when Ronan took the wheel. After a quick swipe of a wet cloth and a change of clothes, he looked presentable.

A minute later, he pulled in front of the guesthouse. The front room light was on, making it look cozy, and Connor's wolf growled.

Hurry, his wolf said with an urgency he hadn't heard before.

I know. I want her tonight too.

As Connor neared the front door, he vaguely sensed a shifter presence, and it didn't belong to Jackson even though he'd just driven away.

Adrenaline pumping through his system, Connor charged toward the door, and when he twisted the knob, it was locked. Connor pounded. "EmmaLee open up."

He fumbled in his pocket for the door key, but by the time he found the it and jammed it into the lock, EmmaLee opened up, seemingly unhurt.

"Connor!" She flew into his arms.

Fear sliced through him. "What happened?"

"Slater was here."

His mind couldn't comprehend the words. "What do you mean he was here?" He half walked, half carried her back into the house, searching for any evidence of him.

"Once he heard your SUV coming, he ran away."

She wasn't making any sense. "Ran? Ran where?"

EmmaLee was shaking so hard, he wasn't sure she could answer. She lifted an arm and pointed toward the bedroom. "He took off running in there."

"Stay here."

He dashed down the hallway, but when he burst through the bedroom door, Coghill had gone. The only evidence he had been there was the open window. Connor shut it and locked it. "Motherfucker."

As much as he wanted to go after him, he didn't trust Coghill not to have come with others. If he left to find him, Slater and his men could take EmmaLee and Connor couldn't chance that. He returned to the living room where he found his very pale mate leaning against the kitchen counter.

He gently clasped her shoulders and walked her over to the sofa. "Sit here while I get something to calm you." *And me.*

After making sure the front door was locked and the rest of the windows were secured, Connor poured them two glasses of wine and carried them over to the living room. If there'd been a bottle of Jack, he would have downed that. He handed her a glass and sat next to her. "Tell me what happened," he said.

"I forgot to look through the peephole because I thought it was you. Jackson had just spoken with you. He said you were at your dad's house and were on your way here, so he left."

"If I thought Coghill was coming after you, I never would have gone with Ronan in the first place. What happened after Jackson left?"

Her hands were still shaking, so Connor slipped the glass from her fingers.

"Jackson was gone no more than a minute when I heard a knock. I ran to open the door, and there was Slater."

"Did you try to slam the door in his face?" Acid burned in his gut.

"I tried, but he stuck his foot between the door and the frame. He is a lot stronger than me and just pushed his way through. I am so sorry, but I really did try to get it shut so I could lock him out."

He rubbed her arms. "It's okay, babe; I'm just glad you weren't hurt. Did he say what he wanted?" Connor had to work hard not to grind his teeth.

"The talon. When I said I didn't have it, he ordered me outside. Before I could tell him I wouldn't go with him, your car engine grumbled down the drive. That's when he ran to the bedroom."

"Damn, I was so careful driving back. I never saw a tail. The man is either the best at keeping a low profile or else he's a witch who can make himself invisible!"

"What do we do now?" she asked, her voice trembling.

He clasped her to his chest and held on tight. "I think it's time you switched places with Ronan."

She leaned her head back. "I don't understand."

"I want you to stay in the safe house and have Ronan come here."

She nodded and then sniffled. "I'd like that."

He kissed her forehead. "I know it's late, but I'd feel better if you pack up now."

"You really think he'll come back?" she asked. Poor EmmaLee. Her voice was strained, and her color had yet to improve.

"He wants the talon. Hell, he probably wants the boxes too."

"He won't get the talon. As for the boxes, there's nothing of value in them," she said.

"Coghill doesn't know that. And who's to say we didn't miss something?"

Her respiration increased. "You're right."

Her dejected tone caused more acid to fester in his gut. "How about you pack, and I'll ask Ronan to do the same."

He stood, and when he helped her up, Connor drew her close and held her, never wanting to let her go. He kissed her forehead. "This will be over soon. I promise."

She looked up at him. "How can you be so sure?"

"Because Coghill is up to something, and he seems to be escalating. I promise I won't leave your side again."

She wrapped her arms around him again and inhaled deeply. "Thank you."

"Do you need me to help with the packing?" he asked.

She looked up, and a bit of the old EmmaLee emerged. "No, I'm good. Really."

She stepped back and headed to the bedroom. While he waited, he called Ronan and explained the situation.

"Sure, I have no problem staying at the guesthouse. In fact, I'd welcome the asshole coming back. I lost him the first time, and I won't make that mistake again."

"Thanks. See you soon."

EMMALEE PLANTED HER elbows on the front of Connor's desk and balanced her chin on her palms. She'd moved into the office safe room a week ago and had barely left the premises. It was getting old.

He looked up from his computer and smiled. "Now what?"

Connor was being very patient with her. "I'm bored and a little tired."

He leaned back in his chair. "We just came back from lunch. Do you want to take a nap?"

"If you'll join me!"

Connor chuckled. "We have work to do, or rather I have work

to do. I'm determined to find Slater."

"Fine, so why don't we set a trap for him?"

"You sound like Lexi when she had a stalker after her. You know I won't use you as bait."

"I figured as much, but I had to ask."

Connor picked up his pencil and tapped it on the table, his tell for when he was thinking hard. "I have to admit I thought that after a week, he'd have made his move already."

"What is he waiting for?" Of course, he didn't know the answer any more than she did, but EmmaLee was tired and frustrated. She wanted him caught.

"I wish I knew."

Voices sounded outside Connor's door and then it burst open. A younger version of Connor filled the frame. He had dark circles under his eyes, and his mouth was pinched tight.

Connor jumped up from his seat. "Finn? What's wrong?"

"I need your help."

EmmaLee stood. "I can leave."

Connor held out a hand. "No stay. You might be able to help."

Help? What could she do? Connor dragged another chair over from the corner and placed it next to EmmaLee's. "Sit down and tell me what happened."

Finn sat and scrubbed a hand down his unshaven jaw. He looked over at her. "You must be EmmaLee. Sorry. I'm Finn, Connor's brother." They shook hands.

"I figured," she said.

Connor had mentioned that Finn was having a hard time sleeping because of some strange dreams. The haggard look confirmed it.

"Tell me what's gong on," Connor said.

Finn glanced between them. "Most of the dreams have been the same—sensual and light."

His face turned a light shade of pink as if he didn't want to talk about his erotic dreams in front of her. EmmaLee looked at Connor, but he held out a hand, implying she needed to remain.

"I take it something changed?" Connor asked. EmmaLee admired how Connor could remain so calm when his brother was clearly distraught.

"Yes, last night was different. Kaleena said she was in trouble."

"Kaleena is her name?" he asked.

"Yes. She told me she was in danger, and that she needed my help. Then I heard these gut-wrenching pleas that sounded like she was off in the distance."

Connor studied his distraught brother. "What can I do?"

"I don't know." He clenched his fists. "I don't know. I know this sounds crazy, but she said she lives on some realm called Tarradon, wherever that is, and that I have to find a portal to reach her."

"Tarradon?" EmmaLee's heart beat too fast.

"Yes, do you know of it?"

She explained what Jackson had told her.

"Well, shit."

"Ophelia might be able to help," Connor said.

"Ophelia?"

EmmaLee placed a hand on Finn's arm. "Kaleena's your mate, isn't she?"

"EmmaLee?" Connor asked. "What do you know about mates?"

Oh, crap. Even though she was almost positive she and Connor were destined for each other, she figured he'd tell her when the time was right. "A lot. Remember, I had a good tutor—Vinea."

"Who, by the way is a goddess, not a shifter." He lowered his chin and looked up at her, but he almost seemed delighted that she was so knowledgeable.

"EmmaLee's right," Finn said. "While I've only touched Kaleena in my mind and smelled her scent the same way, I'm convinced she and I are mates and belong together—forever."

Connor huffed out a breath. "You're totally serious?"

"Yes, but I can't prove anything."

"Finn, have you spoken with Zane? He's knowledgeable about realms and portals. Perhaps something Kaleena told you will resonate with him," EmmaLee said.

"She has a point, Finn."

"He was willing to discuss it when I spoke to him," she added. "And Zane's good with keeping a secret."

Finn pressed his lips together. "Hell, I'll talk to anyone. I'm so fucking scared for Kaleena. If she is some kind of witch I'm unfamiliar with, it might explain how she can talk to me mentally even though we haven't mated."

"Or she's a goddess," Connor said. "I'll call Rye and see if he can set up a meeting with Zane." He pressed a few buttons on his phone. "Hey."

Connor explained how the plea from Finn's dream woman had him rattled. "Could we bother Zane again? Oh, okay. We could do that too, thanks." He placed the phone back in his pocket.

"What did he say?" Finn asked.

"Zane has the day off, and yes we can ask him. Turns out Rye spoke with James regarding your situation."

"When did you speak with him?"

Connor huffed. "We've discussed your situation a few times. Your appearance, together with the lack of sleep has us both worried."

"I'd be worried too," he huffed.

"That's why Rye contacted him."

"Who's James?" EmmaLee asked.

"He's Naliana's husband," Finn said.

"Ah, yes," EmmaLee said. "I remember now. Vinea mentioned him. How can he help?"

"James has helped many of our Clan. He seems to know a lot," Connor said.

"Perhaps it's because his wife is a goddess," EmmaLee added.

"Yes. He has some powers of his own that no one, not even Rye or our dad, understand."

What she wouldn't give to pick his brain. "Do you think he would know anything about the origin of my talon?" Her pulse picked up speed.

"He might, but I doubt he'll tell you." Connor explained how he and Naliana worked. "If we are able to see him, take it with you. If the topic comes up, then you can show him."

That was all she could ask for. "Perfect."

"I'm up for any help," Finn said. "I can't go on like this. I know I'm not some surveillance expert and protector, but I need to so something for this woman or die trying."

"Let's hope it doesn't come to that." Connor stood. "EmmaLee, why don't you get that talon, and I'll call Zane to see if we can visit him?"

Happy to have a task, she rushed out. While she was sorry for the reason for the visit, she was looking forward to hearing what Zane had to say about Finn's situation.

Chapter Twenty-Two

"I WISH I could have been of more help," Zane said, "but I don't know what to tell you. Like your shifters here on Earth, we only have telepathy after we've mated." He faced Finn. "You're sure you've never met her?"

"I'm pretty sure, and I'm positive I've never bitten her. We were taught how to mate from a young age."

Poor Finn. Zane hadn't provided the answers he was hoping for. "Kaleena told me she's from Tarradon, if that helps." Finn said.

Zane stilled. "She's from Tarradon?"

"Yes. Do you know of it?" Finn asked, excitement coloring his tone.

"Just that it supposedly exists, though I've never been there. If it is real, it's possible the two realms interact regularly now. A lot can happen in one-hundred years."

Her heart beat hard. "I can't believe it might be real." That would imply dragon shifters could exist! EmmaLee wasn't ready to admit that the chance of them being here was slim to none.

Zane nodded. "I merely said I believe it does."

Finn's face had gone pale. "It has to. That means Kaleena was telling the truth," he whispered. "Kaleena and I have not mated—obviously—yet we do communicate when we sleep."

"You can dream walk?" Zane asked, his mouth opening slightly.

EmmaLee had never heard of that term. "What's that?"

"It's when a strong witch enters into a person's mind during their dream state, and the two communicate, but only if the recipient also possesses the ability," Zane said.

Finn dropped his head back and let out a breath. "Well, fuck. I'm no witch."

Connor sat up straighter. "You might be."

Everyone turned toward him. "What are you saying?" Finn asked.

"Our great grandmother on Mom's side was said to have witch abilities."

Shock registered on his face. "So we're part Wendayan? You're crazy. We have no magical abilities."

"No one in the family seems to, so maybe only you inherited some of her talents," Connor said. "We need to ask Mom."

"Why wasn't I told before?" Finn asked. He was becoming more agitated and EmmaLee felt sorry for him.

"I have no idea."

Zane tapped a finger on his lips. "If this Kaleena is a witch who is able to initiate this dream link with you," Zane said, "the only way to be sure you are communicating with a real person is to find a powerful witch here to help you. She will be far more qualified to know about these things than some lowly bear like myself."

He was hardly lowly.

Finn jumped up. "Then I definitely need to speak to Ophelia." He faced Zane and held out his hand. "Thank you."

"I didn't do much."

"You helped more than you realize."

"Any time."

EmmaLee had more questions, but Finn's eagerness to leave prevented her. Once they stepped outside of Zane's place—or rather Missy's house—Finn placed a hand on Connor's shoulder to stop him. "I need to ask Izzy if she can contact Ophelia for me, but I was thinking of speaking with James too. I know he's only an immortal, but if he's married to a goddess, he might know something—or at the least be able to find out more about portals, Tarradon, and dream walking."

Connor shrugged. "It can't hurt. I say let's give it a try."

"Do we need to call him first?" Finn asked.

"Rye already mentioned your situation to him, so I suspect he's waiting for us. I get the sense he doesn't need to be contacted."

The three piled into Connor's SUV. EmmaLee hadn't been this excited since she'd learned about this other realm. The road to the immortal's house was in the same compound where Connor lived. "Connor, have you been to his house before?" she asked.

"Once, but it was a long time ago. One doesn't just drop in for a visit—unless we're expected that is."

Vinea had told her the same thing. EmmaLee twisted around in her seat. "Have you met him, Finn?"

"Nope. I've never needed him before."

"Just so you know," Connor said, "I've been told he talks in circles, so we're to keep our questions to a minimum. The man can read minds, so don't be freaked out when he asks you something you didn't even mention."

"That's scary and quite unsettling," she said.

It only took him a few minutes to reach the imposing stone home.

"It's been said that his house looks the same as it did a hundred years ago," Connor said.

EmmaLee studied the rather ancient villa. "I don't see a car, and there doesn't appear to be a garage."

"Maybe he keeps his vehicle in back." Connor cut the engine. "Let's see if he's in."

The three of them marched up to the immortal's home. Connor knocked once and was immediately greeted by a handsome man with gray hair. For some reason she thought that an immortal wouldn't look old. His face however was fairly unlined.

"Welcome, Connor. Come in. I thought you'd stop by."

Impressive. EmmaLee wasn't sure if she should introduce herself, but before she could stick out her hand, James turned to her and held out his. "And you must be EmmaLee. I'm sorry for everything that has happened to you before and since you arrived in Silver Lake.

The air rushed out of her lungs. She was going to ask how he knew, but then remembered Naliana was his wife. "Thank you."

She glanced at Connor. Had it not been for the slight rise in his brow, she would have guessed that he'd already told Rye everything, who would have then relayed the information to James.

"You're Finn I take it." James smiled.

"Yes." They shook hands.

"Please sit. Can I get anyone some of my homemade ale?" he asked. James acted as if this was a social call, but he must know they were there for something far more important.

EmmaLee shook her head, but Connor and Finn said they'd take a glass. James smiled and then disappeared down a long hallway.

Finn looked between them. "How much did Rye tell him?" he whispered.

"I don't think much, but he might have," Connor said. "I don't know why he'd tell James EmmaLee's history though."

"Maybe he really is a god but tells everyone he's immortal," Finn said.

"Could be," Connor answered.

"Here we are," James announced as he carried in a tray containing four glasses, three filled with dark brown ale and one with water. On the tray sat a plate of what smelled like ginger cookies. "Tell me what you need."

Connor nodded at Finn. "I've been having these dreams." Finn explained the erotic nature of them. "Three days ago, this woman—who calls herself Kaleena—told me she was in some kind of danger. She sounded really afraid."

"And you want to help her," James announced.

"Yes, even though I've never met her, I have this need to. She told me she's from a place called Tarradon, in the province of Avonbelle. She said I needed to find a portal in order to reach her, only I don't know how."

"Why do you feel so compelled to help?" James munched on a cookie then washed it down with some ale.

"Whenever she comes to me in my dreams, my body reacts intensely. I feel as if she's my mate."

"Do you dream walk with her?"

EmmaLee stilled, and both brothers did too.

"Yes," Finn said. "What do you know about that?"

"Very little. Did she tell you want kind of shifter she was?"

"No," Finn answered, "but in my mind's eye, I can see flecks of pink and purple. I'm not sure what it all means."

James sipped his ale. "If she is from another realm, she might be able to telepath her thoughts."

"To just anyone?"

"That I don't know," James said. "The only way to be sure would be to ask her."

"But how? Do you know how to access the portal?"

"No, but Ophelia might, especially since magic is involved. I wish I could tell you more."

EmmaLee butted in. "Surely Naliana knows. I've never met her, but I'm a good friend of her sister."

"Ah, yes. You helped Vinea after she was cleansed. My wife told me to tell you thank you."

That wasn't the response she expected or was looking for. "You're welcome."

James stood, and Connor rose too. He speared his brother a look that said to ask nothing more. "Thank you for your time."

"Anytime."

EmmaLee wanted to pull out the talon and ask if he had any idea what kind of animal it came from, but Connor was right. James wouldn't tell her. A life was not on the line.

As soon as they stepped outside, Finn grabbed Connor by the arm. "He knew more than he was saying."

"Yes, but according to Rye, he lives by some code that we are to follow our own life's path, and he will only help when it's a matter of life and death."

"It is a matter of life and death—Kaleena's."

Finn's desperation cut her deeply. Her mind spun. "Do you think Zane could help you find this portal? After all, he came to Earth through one."

"Or Vinea," Connor said. "Apparently, she transported to the dark realm through one all the time."

Finn huffed out a breath. "All portals might not be the same. I'd hate to end up in the wrong spot and not know how to get back."

"Then you need to ask Kaleena," his brother said.

"I would if I could contact her."

When they arrived back at the office, Finn slipped out of the car. "Thanks for the help. I'll try to get a hold of Kaleena and ask for details. I'll also see if Ophelia can help."

Connor stepped next to his brother and wrapped an arm around his shoulder. "Perhaps you should take a few days off to get some perspective."

"You don't think I've tried that? Uncle Garth has been more than accommodating with my schedule, but I'm the manager of the bar. Besides, Kaleena needs me now!"

"By all means, do what you need to do. I'll help in any way I can."

Finn thanked him once more and then took off. Connor then escorted her toward the office entrance. With all that had happened, EmmaLee wasn't ready to sit inside and pore over articles. The day was too beautiful, and she yearned to breathe the fresh air and listen to the birds sing—anything to help her come to grips with this new information.

She stopped before they reached the entrance to his building and planted a seductive hand on his chest. "You know what I'd like?" she asked.

Connor fingered her hair. "What would you like?"

"What do you think if we have a little picnic near the caves?"

Connor chuckled. "I see right through you, dragon lady. You

want to search for the portal Zane came through."

Damn. He knew her too well. "His goes to Cargonia, but don't you want to know what one looks like? It's not like I want to enter it."

"What do you say we ask Missy if she's ever seen one? After all, she's spent quite a lot of time searching in and around the caves."

EmmaLee lowered her hand to his waistline, her thumb tapping lower. "I'm sure if she'd found anything, Rye would have heard and mentioned it to us." She moved closer. "What I was thinking was that after our picnic, I could have my wicked way with you."

He laughed. "You are worse than my wolf. You're starting to have a one-track mind."

"Am I? Are you saying your human side doesn't agree with your wolf about wanting to get frisky?"

"All my sides agree with that and letting you have your wicked way." He smiled and clasped her hand, lifting it away from his crotch. "Since you have been patient and remained inside for the last week, I'll agree to take you out—but just this one time."

EmmaLee clapped. "Thank you!"

"We'll stop at the store and pick up some wine, bread, and cheese."

She smiled. "No grapes? I was hoping you'd be willing to drop them into my mouth one at a time."

"I'll put more than grapes in your mouth, young lady." Connor growled as his eyes turned a lovely shade of amber. "Come on, let's get going." He grabbed her hand and tugged. "I'm not sure I can keep my wolf contained if we keep up this conversation."

"Take an extra set of clothes in case you get too excited and shift again." EmmaLee giggled.

"Keep talking like that and we won't make it to the car."

Chapter Twenty-Three

EMMALEE COULDN'T BELIEVE how beautiful the view was from on top of the ridge overlooking Silver Lake.

Connor leaned close and pointed. "Look to the right of the lake. See that clump of trees at four o'clock?"

"Yes."

"My parents' house is about a half mile southwest of there."

EmmaLee tried to find the brick structure, but the blooming leaves blocked her view. "What a great place to grow up." She sighed. "It's so peaceful up here. I could sit for hours and watch the world go by."

Connor turned her around to face him. "My wolf isn't experiencing any peace right now."

She grinned. "Do you want me to calm the beast?"

"EmmaLee." He grabbed her hand. "How about we let the beast lie for a bit longer and take a look in the caves. Then we can have our celebration of life." He winked.

"You're so romantic."

Connor grinned. "Only when I'm around you."

Hand in hand they walked along the ridge until they came to the imposing hillside. The surface was mostly granite but there was the occasional pine tree interspersed with some scrub.

"Where's the cave entrance?" she asked.

"The cave where Zane emerged is over here."

They walked across a grassy area, shaded by oaks and pines. "I love it here," she said looking around.

"Me too. Let's check inside for this portal first, and then we can sit under these trees and relax."

"You want to have the picnic outside, in the open?" she asked, trying not to show she was uncomfortable with that. "The cave would offer more privacy for our *dessert*." Then again, the caves were probably full of spiders and crawly things.

"No one comes here."

"Missy did, remember?"

He smiled. "True. Let's explore then decide where we want to eat."

"Good idea."

Connor entered through a three-foot wide slit, and she followed. He then extracted two flashlights from his backpack and handed her one. "Stay close to me."

She had no intention of leaving his side. While she'd explored caves as a kid, this one seemed more sinister for some reason. "Vinea mentioned there would be distinct air currents indicating the portal, but I can barely see where I'm walking, let alone detect a shift in air."

"Do you want to quit?"

Maybe. "No. Keep going for a bit. Maybe Vinea was wrong, and there'll be some physical marking to show the portal."

"Don't get your hopes up," he said. "We should have asked Zane what his portal looked like."

"True."

After ten minutes of searching, EmmaLee had to admit they wouldn't be coming across a flashing red arrow that pointed to a lit sign saying, *Portal this way*.

He lifted her chin, and all thoughts of finding other realms disappeared. "Had enough?"

"Yes, I'm ready for our picnic."

"So am I."

Once they made it outside, she had to squint at the bright light. The fresh air and whoosh of the wind blowing through the trees were a welcome relief. "How about we set up over there?" EmmaLee said, pointing to a flat grassy area under a large oak.

"Perfect."

Connor placed the blanket on the ground while she pulled out their bottle of wine, two plastic glasses, and the food from the pack.

Once Connor poured their drinks, he held up his glass, and she tapped his. "What should we toast to?" she asked.

"To us being mates?" Connor's chest expanded. It was almost as if he was holding his breath, waiting for her response.

She smiled, thrilled that he'd acknowledged what she'd suspected all along. "To us being mates."

His eyes widened. "You're okay with the idea?"

EmmaLee tucked in her chin. "I've suspected for a while now that we are, especially with the way your body changes when you're with me."

"Why didn't you say something?"

EmmaLee lifted one shoulder. "It wasn't my place to bring it up. Vinea explained the signs, and you exhibited them all."

"You have a choice, you know. If you don't want me, I'll understand."

He must not have believed her when she'd told him she loved him. "How can you even say that? I love you, Connor McKinnon. You are everything I want. You're kind, protective, caring, and yes—you're hot."

He set her glass down on the blanket and drew her close. "You've changed my world, EmmaLee and made me very happy."

"Oh, Connor, I feel the same way." As she leaned in to kiss him, someone clapped, and she stilled.

"Bravo, what a sweet moment. Sorry to have interrupted."

EmmaLee's heart dropped to her stomach. She jumped up and accidentally knocked over her glass of wine. "Slater? What are you doing here?"

"Putting an end to what I should have finished a long time ago."

Her throat closed up.

Connor rose and stepped toward him. "What are you doing here, Coghill?"

"Like I said, I need to finish something."

"What's that?" Connor's hands fisted.

"EmmaLee here is a bit too curious." Slater glared at her.

She was going to suggest that Connor shift and take him out, but then she remembered him saying that Slater was a shifter too. The question was what kind? Jackson was a bear and had once fought four wolves at the same time. What if Slater were a powerful bear too?

EmmaLee puffed out her chest and stepped next to Connor. He clasped her shoulder, probably afraid she'd move too close to her ex. "Curious about what?" she asked, trying to keep her voice from wavering.

"Dragons."

Her heart squeezed tight. "What about them? You never believed they existed."

He smiled, exposing his elongated eyeteeth. "Oh, I believe in them all right. I just didn't need you to know they existed and blab it to the world."

"So now you're a believer? Since when?"

"Since forever."

She shook her head, pretending as if she were brave. "You don't have to worry. I'd never tell. If I did, do you think anyone would believe me?"

"I couldn't take that chance. It was why I was sent here."

Connor squeezed her hand. "Sent here? From where?"

Slater looked at her. "I bet Em can guess, the little snoop. It was only a matter of time before she stumbled across my secret."

Her mind spun. Sent there? From where? Another realm? Surely he wasn't a dragon. No, he'd lost his mind and was trying to mess with her. "Don't tell me you're from Tarradon?"

Once more he clapped. "Give the lady a prize. Now you must see why I have to make sure you don't talk."

Her legs weakened. Connor must have sensed she was going to drop to the ground because he slipped his arm around her waist and held her up. "You'll have to kill a lot of people then," she said. "I've shown my evidence to many folks. They all know dragons exist." She prayed Slater didn't see through her lie.

"Evidence? Are you referring to that talon? The one I lost when I was fleeing the scene of your parents' fire? The one I hooked on a tree branch, and it came lose? That one?"

EmmaLee sagged against Connor. "That was yours? How? That was more than fourteen years ago."

"In human years, we age extremely slow. Dragons live to hundreds of years. Back then, I was just a juvenile dragon of one hundred."

One hundred? She couldn't fathom it. "Then you're not denying that you set the fire that killed my parents?" She was barely able to speak those painful words.

"No, I won't deny it. Just so you know, I had no choice. Your parents were going to meet with Mr. Fielding. He'd found out that my kind existed and wanted to announce it to the world. He felt that with your parents' stamp of approval, the world would believe him— and he was probably right."

"Why not just eliminate Mr. Fielding then? Why go after my parents?"

"Oh, I did eliminate him, but the asshole had already told your parents what he'd learned. I couldn't chance them talking."

Her chin trembled as tears ran down her cheeks. "All that time we were together, why didn't you kill me when you had the chance?" Her vision blurred, and she swayed. All of this was too much to take in.

"I've asked myself that question many times. Believe it or not, I cared for you. I really did, EmmaLee. I tried to make you stop your research, but you were too damn stubborn. I'd been instructed from the start to kill you; only I couldn't do it. But don't worry. I've seen the error of my ways."

She couldn't understand all of his words. It was as if he was talking in a different language. "Instructed? Who told you to kill me?"

"Why, the Royals did—our leaders in Tarradon."

Royals? Leaders? She couldn't listen to him anymore. Her blood pressure dropped from the overload of information. Slater was a killer! As if she'd been hit with a force field, her vision turned black for a moment as intense pain raced through her. Just as she tried to move, Slater seemed to disintegrate before her eyes. A second later, a large beast appeared where he'd been standing. Holy hell. He was a dragon—or was he merely a figment of her imagination?

He huffed and growled. No, he was real all right. She just hadn't expected a dragon to be so big or so black. The iris in each eye was a black slit, surrounded by a teal color. If he weren't such an evil person, she'd have to say his dragon was almost beautiful.

Connor stepped in front of her, and then he spun and shifted. No! Slater was a good fifteen feet in height, and Connor was a fraction of his size. The fight would be over in seconds.

Slater must have sensed his impending victory for he lifted his head and opened his mouth, looking like he was laughing at them. When he lowered his head again, a stream of fire shot out of his mouth and caught the grass in front of them on fire. Holy shit. Her heart stopped, and every one of her muscles locked.

Then Connor howled, freeing her from her frozen state.

Without thinking, EmmaLee rushed back to the oak, picked up the blanket, and tossed it on a portion of the flames. Slater opened his mouth again then shot out a few small puffs of flames, probably to keep her busy.

"Stop it!" she yelled, but the sound came out weak. She wasn't about to stand around and do nothing though. Slater scorched a different area, and she repeated her frantic moves, but no matter how fast she darted, she would never be able to keep up.

Realization hit. What if one of his flames hit them? They'd burn to a crisp just like the grass. Bile raced to her mouth as the vision of

Connor's death formed in her mind.

He howled once more and moved toward Slater. She couldn't let him sacrifice his life for her. Slater wanted her—not Connor. As a shifter, Connor might be trusted to keep his secret.

Slater had killed her parents and was about to do the same to the man she loved. Injustice and hatred filling her, she rushed the dragon, willing to sacrifice herself to save Connor's life.

When Slater sent a strong stream of fire straight at her, she held her breath, waiting for the horrible pain to consume her. During those two seconds, it was as if she were witnessing life in slow motion. The blazing hot light came at her, and then red and yellow flickering flames surrounded her, crawling up her legs then licking her face. Only she felt nothing. Blood pounded in her ears as fear and hopelessness coursed through her veins.

So this was what death felt like. She'd expected agony, but not even the intense heat affected her. EmmaLee lifted her arms to see the charred damage, but they were whole, encased in some kind of clear bubble.

She didn't understand what was happening at first since it felt as if she were in a dream.

Then Vinea's words came back to her. When EmmaLee had been lying in the hospital bed after Slater had attacked her, Vinea told her about the protective shield she'd given her. *If you become afraid, a bubble will protect you against Slater or against anyone who tries to harm you.*

A howl sounded behind her, jarring her back to the present. Connor charged the huge dragon. No! EmmaLee needed to stop him, needed to prevent Slater from harming him. Only she couldn't move. It was as if the bubble was glued to the ground.

Slater beat his forty-foot wide wings and hit Connor's wolf, sending him sprawling. But Connor's animal was not to be deterred. He jumped up, barred his teeth, and charged again.

She couldn't watch any longer. Closing her eyes, she tried to press her hands to her ears, but her arms still wouldn't move.

As if the world came to a halt, silence suddenly entombed her. She forced open her eyes, expecting the worst, but she was no longer peering through a haze. Her bubble had disappeared, and the only animal in front of her was Connor. He too looked around, probably as surprised as she that Slater was no longer there. Connor grunted and then shifted back to his human form.

"What happened?" she asked rushing up to him. "Where did Slater go?"

She didn't really care. All that mattered was that Connor was alive. She ran her hands down his body to make sure he wasn't a figment of her imagination.

"I don't know. I charged, but when I reached where he was, he just vanished."

"He disappeared? How? Are you sure he isn't hiding somewhere?" She looked around but saw nothing.

"I don't sense any shifter signature anymore. Ronan said the man didn't give off the same scent as we do, and now I know why. He was a dragon." He ran his hands down her shoulders. "Or did I imagine the big beast?"

"He was a dragon all right, but why would he threaten to kill me and then leave?" she asked.

"I don't know, but I don't intend to wait around and find out. We need to get out of here. Now."

"You're naked." That shouldn't have mattered when their lives were at stake, but she needed to focus on something she could understand.

"I have the shirt and pants in the backpack you suggested I carry in case I shifted prematurely."

"I remember now." But only vaguely. It seemed so long ago.

Connor didn't seem as rattled as she was. While he changed, she gathered his torn clothes. He then packed up the wine-soaked blanket and stuffed it into his backpack.

How she made it back to the car, she didn't know. EmmaLee had to work to even put one foot in front of the other as she tried to block out the image of Slater's dragon. All she could see in her mind's eye was his big fire-breathing head.

Her whole life she'd wanted to be convinced that what she'd seen the day her parents had died had been real. Even though she'd met the man who killed them, it hadn't given her the satisfaction she'd expected. It made her sick to think she'd liked him and had fallen for his lies.

Connor held open the car door and helped her in.

Once seated, her hands wouldn't stop shaking, and her heart refused to slow. The drive back to the safe room was a blur. Even after replaying what happened a hundred times, none of it made sense.

Connor parked. "How about you pack up your things?"

"Huh?"

"I want you to move in with me. We can't be sure that Slater won't return."

A hint of disappointment shot through her. "That's a horrible thought."

He rubbed her arm. "Even if Slater had died, it's time we share a life together. I want you EmmaLee. Forever."

The horror of the day seemed to disappear with his wonderful words. "I want that too, but I know Slater. He will return. He wants me dead."

"Fuck. Let's see if Ophelia can give us some guidance, assuming she's not with Finn."

For the first time since Slater appeared, she relaxed. "I'd like that, but how can she possibly know if Slater will come back?"

"Rye said she might."

"Rye? What does he know?"

"I called him on the way home. You must have been preoccupied when I spoke to him."

That she had been. "Okay."

This time Connor parked in the parking garage, probably not wanting anyone—meaning Slater—to see them. He pushed open his door, walked over to her side, and opened her door. "Go in and pack; I'll see if I can get in touch with her."

Right now, EmmaLee couldn't think clearly as the horror of him almost dying was too much to bear. "Why didn't he kill you when he had the chance?" Her voice sounded far away.

The slightest hint of a smile lifted his lips. "Don't tell me you wished he had?"

As if the fog in her brain disappeared, reality intruded. "No! Of course not—I just need to understand what happened back there near the cave."

"Come on. Pack up and then we'll get some answers."

Chapter Twenty-Four

"WHAT IS OPHELIA like?" EmmaLee asked as Connor pulled in front of a pretty yellow house where they were to meet this witch.

"She's old. And she talks in riddles like James does. Maybe more so."

"What could a witch know about dragons and Tarradon?"

Connor cut the engine before getting out and walking over to her side. His chivalry was something she'd come to love. He helped her out. "I don't know the details, but Ophelia is not some ordinary witch." He pointed to the copse of trees. "There she is now."

A small woman with a curved back slowly emerged. Connor placed a hand on EmmaLee's arm and led her closer. When they met, the witch studied both of them.

"I sense a lot of stress. I'm Ophelia, by the way." She shook each of their hands.

"EmmaLee Donovan, and this is—"

The old lady smiled. "Connor McKinnon. Always nice to see you. Finn just left. How can I help you?"

She wanted to ask if Ophelia had been able to help Connor's brother, but she'd have to be content to ask Finn. If Rye had called to contact Ophelia, she would have thought he'd have filled her in. EmmaLee looked up at Connor, but he nodded for her to tell the story.

EmmaLee began with how her parents had died in a fire fourteen years ago and how she'd seen a dragon fly overhead that day. "From that point forward, I've dedicated my life to learning if dragons exist."

"And now you know."

How did she do that? EmmaLee hadn't told her everything. "Yes, I do, but when Slater—that's the name of the man who used to be my boyfriend—turned out to be a dragon, I kind of freaked."

"I can understand why."

"Earlier this afternoon, he admitted that he killed my parents and wanted to kill me too. Before I could ask him all my questions, he shifted into his dragon form and shot fire at us. When Connor went on the attack, he disappeared."

Her eyes widened. "As in he vanished?"

Connor answered. "Yes. I was in mid air, ready to sink my teeth into his leg, and it was as if he was sucked away or became invisible."

Ophelia nodded. "Ah, yes. The four sisters of Fate must have interfered. They probably have been watching him all along."

The four sisters of Fate? EmmaLee's heart sputtered at Ophelia's intimate knowledge of the realm. "Have you been to Tarradon?"

She smiled. "I've been there many times. I'm surprised your friend Vinea didn't tell you."

"No. She said nothing." Perhaps she wanted EmmaLee to figure things out for herself when it came to dragons and this realm. A little hint would have been appreciated though. "What's it like?" EmmaLee asked, forgetting why she'd come in the first place.

"I believe you have more pressing questions than learning the details of this other realm."

"You're right, I'm sorry." Acid bubbled in her stomach at the reminder of their recent ordeal.

"Tell me why Slater said he wanted to harm you." Ophelia glanced between the two of them.

"On the night of the fire, I found a talon on the ground, and he feared I'd figure out what kind of animal it belonged to," EmmaLee said.

Connor leaned forward. "Coghill confessed that it was his."

"Interesting." Ophelia stuffed a hand into her pocket, turned around, and bowed her head. She said nothing for a full minute before facing them. She exhaled. "I can say with confidence that he's gone. For good."

EmmaLee wanted to believe her, but she needed to be sure. "Not to be rude, but how do you know that?"

"Killing you both would have raised too many questions. The manner of your death would have been hard to cover up. It seems that your young fellow got out of hand, and the sisters had to take him back."

"Who are these sisters?" she asked.

"Powerful beings."

"But how do you *know* he won't come back?" Connor asked. EmmaLee loved how he didn't shy away from getting proof Slater was gone for good.

"Because I just asked someone on Tarradon." Ophelia shoved her hand in her pocket again and pulled out what looked like a one-inch long scale. "This dragon scale is filled with magic. With it, I can communicate with Jamison Sinclair, the man who once ruled the Guardians. He told me that Slater had been dealt with. Now, if you'll excuse me."

Like Vinea used to do, this woman floated away and then disappeared into the woods.

Stunned, EmmaLee faced Connor. "What do you think?"

"In all the years our Clansmen and Wendayans have been coming to Ophelia for help, she's never steered them wrong. We need to believe her and move on, knowing that asshole won't ever harm you again."

She crossed her fingers. "Amen."

Connor hugged her tight, and she'd never felt more secure in her life. "How about we forget this terrible day and enjoy your new found freedom, huh?" He led her back to the SUV. "At least now you know that what you saw that day was real."

"True, but to think Slater killed my parents still freaks me out. They didn't have to die."

He ran a knuckle down her cheek. "No, they didn't. They were searching for the truth just like you. Only they got too close."

"I know." She looked up at him. "I've been thinking. It might be time for me to get the help I've needed for a long time."

He smiled. "I know just the doctor."

Connor helped her into the car and then drove over to his place. The exterior of the home had the same brick style as his parents, only his was one-story instead of two. The landscaping was rather minimal, but given how much Connor worked that didn't surprise her. He wouldn't have time to garden. If she stayed in his house with him, she would need to add some flowers along the entranceway path.

Before she had moved into the safe house, he'd taken her to his house once before, and while it could use a woman's touch, she loved how the light poured into the living room window.

He set down her two suitcases in the entranceway. "What do you feel like doing first?" he asked. "Rest, eat, or unpack?"

EmmaLee faced him. "I'm not sure. I still can't believe it's over."

Connor clasped her shoulders and drew her near. "It is. We can start living our lives. No more hiding."

She darted a look to the side. "I should feel elated to have my freedom, but something seems to be missing."

His eyes widened. "What's that?"

"I can't describe it. I have this sense of being incomplete. Maybe it's the fact that I know who killed my parents and why, so I don't know what to focus on now."

He smiled. "Ah, I understand. I've had cases that drove me day and night. When I finally caught the person, I also felt empty inside because the chase was over. My goal had been fulfilled."

Her pulse sped up. "Yes, it's just like that. So how did you handle it?"

"I focused on something else, like building the business. I

learned that attaining a goal though isn't nearly as rewarding as building relationships." He cupped her face, and her heart nearly burst. "Life is about love and being mated to the most wonderful and brave woman in the world, and not how many criminals I bring to justice. I'd give up my business if I had to in order to be with you."

She studied his face. "You talk of being mated, but so far I haven't seen any evidence of you making any kind of attempt to fulfill it." Of course, she was teasing.

"For that I am sorry. I was waiting until this mess with Slater was resolved before I claimed you for my own."

"I'd love to be your mate. Forever."

Connor picked her up in his arms and swung her around. "Then I say we get to it."

EmmaLee dropped back her head and laughed. "I could use a little less talk and a lot more action."

"Still as sassy as ever, I see."

She drew his head closer and sucked on his bottom lip. "You like my sassy mouth, don't you?"

"I love everything about you," he said.

Connor then proved just how much he loved it. They explored and tasted each other like never before. Knowing they were to be mated added extra zest to their already amazing sex life.

Connor set her down. "I think we're overdressed," he said, as he stepped out of his shoes.

"I couldn't agree more." She removed her sandals but then stopped. "Let me finish undressing you."

The hair on Connor's face thickened. "Don't take too long. Now that I have it in my head that we'll finally be mated, my wolf is clawing for release."

She held up her palms. "Please try to keep him hidden, at least until we're done. Afterward, I'd like to hold him and cuddle him."

"We'll see about that. My wolf is a warrior not a cuddler." He puffed out his chest.

She chuckled. "I think I could convince him to enjoy a snuggle or two."

"I think he would do anything you asked."

As she reached out to undo the button on his pants, Connor undid hers. It became a race to see who could undress whom first. He won, but that was only because he wouldn't lift his arms to let her take off his shirt.

By the time they were naked, her need to be with him nearly took her breath away. EmmaLee was nervous yet excited. "Will it hurt?" she asked.

"Not if I do it right. I'm hoping you'll be so lost in passion that you won't even notice I've pierced you."

"Then I'm ready." She inhaled and almost giggled.

She'd been waiting for this moment her whole life. Giving and receiving unconditional love had been something she'd lost after her parents died. Now, she could start her new life again. Reborn. Rekindled. Renewed.

"I can't wait," Connor said, his hooded lids hiding his sensual eyes.

His lips descended again, and when their tongues touched, heat exploded, licking its way up and down her body. As if they both had the same image in their mind, she wrapped her arms around his neck and jumped up, encasing his waist with her legs. Connor cupped her rear and lifted her up. He then kissed her with total abandon.

Pressing her breasts against his chest and wiggling her hips, she closed her eyes. EmmaLee blocked out everything but the love and joy rushing through her.

Connor broke the kiss. "Be careful."

She opened her eyes. "Of what?" she asked as innocently as possible.

"Of exciting my wolf too much." Connor nipped her chin and then her lips as he walked her down the hallway toward the bedroom. Once inside, they both dropped to the bed. "I don't think I'll ever get enough of you."

EmmaLee lifted up and kissed his nose. "I know I will never

have my fill of you either."

"I wish that were true. I can be cranky, overbearing, demanding, overprot—"

She placed a finger on his lips. "Shh. You're mine and that's all that matters."

"Show me." Connor dipped his face to her neck and kissed the tender skin under her jaw.

She'd be lying if she said she didn't hold her breath. It wasn't everyday a girl was bitten, enabling her to transform into a wolf. When Connor lifted his mouth from her neck, a wave of disappointment raced through her. It was quickly forgotten however when he ran his tongue around the tip of her nipple in a maddening circle.

"Yes, Connor. Harder, please."

He nipped and pulled, sending spikes of need straight to her core. With each tug, her climax built, but she needed more. Pressing the soles of her feet into the mattress, she reached between them.

Connor grabbed her wrist and chuckled. "You're always so impatient; just relax, Em. I got this."

As if a homing device was attached to the tip of his cock, he found her wet entrance. EmmaLee relaxed, letting him fill her completely. While her inner walls had to stretch to accommodate him, the slight pain pushed her closer to her ultimate bliss.

Connor dipped his head again and sucked one nipple then the next, his groans of pleasure increasing with each pull. Needing to touch him, she ran her fingers through his hair. Oh how she loved the course texture.

His sharpened teeth scraped her sensitive nipple, forcing her to suck in a breath. Connor stopped. "Did I hurt you?"

"A little."

"I'm sorry." He licked the swollen tip in a gentle, caring manner, and the tension in her body released.

"I'll forget about the ache if you move your cock."

Connor looked up and grinned. "Anxious are we?"

"Just horny and in love," she shot back.

He bared his sharpened teeth. "Me too."

Slipping his hands under her shoulders, Connor withdrew then drove right back into her, filling her to the hilt. Erotic bliss slammed into her as she held on for dear life. "Kiss me," she demanded.

"You don't have to ask," he said a second before devouring her lips.

Massive shots of excitement scurried over every inch of her body, and EmmaLee couldn't touch or kiss him fast enough. It was as if she'd been tossed underwater, and only Connor could provide her with enough oxygen.

He plowed into her once more, and EmmaLee rode every wave with him. He lowered his lips to her neck again, and she could tell by his sharpened nails, the growth on his face, that he too, was close to his climax. Anticipation filled her with joy as his teeth scraped the tender skin between her neck and collarbone.

As Connor continued to growl and huff, she sucked in more air. Just as his cock slammed into her back wall, his teeth sunk into her neck. Instead of the expected pain, euphoria filled her, sending her into a state of climactic oblivion. His cock pulsed and expanded as his hot seed shot into her.

Different colors swirled behind her lids like never before, and her body welcomed this new change. At that moment, EmmaLee had never felt more alive.

Holding on tight, they remained in some kind of suspension until her body sagged.

Connor withdrew and then cupped her face. "How do you feel?"

She smiled as much as her cheeks would allow. "Like I want to howl."

Chapter Twenty-Five

The evening of the white moon

"I'M NERVOUS," EMMALEE said as she ran her palms down her black pencil skirt.

Connor smiled down at her and skimmed a knuckle across her cheek. "There's nothing to be nervous about. Everyone already knows you're my mate. This is just an excuse to celebrate our union and to welcome you into the family."

"I know, but I'm not used to being in the spotlight."

"I'll be right by your side."

"Thanks." Knowing that made her feel much better. EmmaLee stepped back. "How do I look?"

She'd worn a skirt for a change, along with a moderately low cut white blouse. The striking addition to her outfit was the amethyst necklace Connor had given her. She fingered it now.

"You're beautiful," he said. "Let's go."

Because he hated to be late, she stopped fussing and grabbed a change of clothes for afterward—for when they celebrated her first shift.

Even though Connor lived close to his parents, he insisted on driving, fearing she might twist an ankle when walking in heels at night. She couldn't argue with that logic.

When they arrived, the party was already going strong. A rather large group was clustered in the kitchen, another bunch surrounded the dining room table that was full of hors d'oeuvres, and the rest were huddled in the living room listening to Rye tell them some story.

She knew most of those present, but a few faces were not familiar. She figured the woman speaking with Mrs. McKinnon was Chelsea, Connor's sister. Then again, she could be Elana, Jackson's brother's mate. Connor said his mom planned to invite the two main families—the McKinnons and the Murdochs—along with those who worked in his firm.

The one couple she was anxious to see was Vinea and Devon, but Connor hadn't been sure if they'd make it—something about a case Devon was working on.

As soon as they entered, Mrs. McKinnon rushed over and hugged them both. She turned to EmmaLee. "I can't tell you how happy I am that my son has finally mated. I thought I'd go to my grave first."

"Mom, please."

"I'm sorry. I always get excited when we add a member to our family. Come in. Drinks are on the counter and snacks on the table. Make sure you introduce your new mate to everyone."

"I know what to do."

A knock sounded on the front door and then it eased opened. EmmaLee spun around. "Vinea?"

EmmaLee squeezed Connor's hand and ran to her friend who looked the same as she had when she moved to Pittsburgh. So far, her baby bump wasn't showing.

They hugged. "Let me see you," Vinea said. "You're looking good. I can't wait for you to fill me in."

They'd spoken on the phone, but when she brought up the possibility that Slater had killed a professor and robbed her, Vinea became silent. Before they could talk, Connor hugged Devon, and the two of them started to chat.

Vinea touched her arm. "Let's sit. Now that I've had time to absorb what you told me about Slater possibly killing someone else, I need to know more."

Devon moved next to Vinea. "Can I get you some water?"

She smiled. "I'd love some."

She and Vinea found an empty spot on the sofa. "Did you really say that Slater was gone for good?" Vinea asked.

"Yes. Ophelia contacted someone in Tarradon who said so."

"Then it must be true. Tell me exactly what happened."

EmmaLee started with the picnic and how Slater just appeared out of nowhere. "When he shifted into a dragon, I freaked."

"I think I might have freaked too. What did you do?"

She explained about how when she ran toward Slater to save Connor, her bubble appeared and saved her. "I'd be dead if it hadn't been for you."

Vinea smiled. "I'm just happy it worked. I've never tried to give someone that kind of power before."

"You should have warned me it was a prototype."

"It worked, didn't it?" Vinea smiled.

"It did."

"I'm glad."

EmmaLee wanted to change the subject. "And you and Naliana? How's that going?" Vinea had said they'd met once during the last white moon.

"We've made up more or less. I don't think I'll be going up to the light realm any time soon—mostly because of the baby—but after our child is born, Naliana said it might be time to reunite with my parents."

"I'm so happy for you." EmmaLee hugged her again. "So you're really happy?"

"More than happy. It's like I've almost forgotten who the evil Vinea used to be. All I can think about is Devon and our child. Life is definitely good."

"That's so wonderful."

"So tonight is the night, huh?" Vinea asked.

It was why EmmaLee had been so nervous. "Yes, it's not every day a person shifts into an animal for the first time."

Vinea waved a hand. "I've seen a ton of humans do it. You'll do great."

"I hope so. Connor said he'll be by my side the whole time."

Jackson shouted out a hello, and EmmaLee turned toward the door. It was Blair. EmmaLee smiled. Blair had been her first friend in Silver Lake, followed by Lexi.

Vinea nodded to her. "Do I know her?"

"That's Jackson and Kalan's sister, Blair. When I wrenched my back, she helped me out."

"Pretty girl. Who is she speaking with?"

"Yes, she is. That's Ainsley. She and Blair went to school together and now work at the same physiotherapy business here in town."

"Ah, yes—Jackson's mate."

Connor and his brother came back over, and Connor handed EmmaLee a glass of red wine while Devon gave Vinea her water. "You two ladies catching up?" Connor asked.

"Yes. We need to visit Pittsburgh soon," EmmaLee told Connor. "I miss my friend."

"Absolutely. I can catch up with what is going on with Devon at that office."

Someone knocked on the front door, but unlike with the other visitors, this person didn't come in.

"I'll get it," Connor said.

EmmaLee returned her attention to Vinea. "I haven't been to a party this big in so long. I'm beginning to feel caged in."

Vinea laughed and rubbed EmmaLee's arm. "You'll get used to it. The McKinnons are a large family. Add in the Murdochs, who are like family, and it's never dull. For that reason alone, I miss Silver Lake."

"Do you think you'll ever move back?"

Vinea glanced at Devon. "I don't think so. Devon loves running the Pittsburgh office and the people there are really nice. His team and their mates are good people."

"I couldn't be happier for you."

Curious at who'd arrived, she turned around. "Oh good, Ronan made it."

"Who's Ronan?" Vinea asked.

"He's Lexi's brother. Didn't I tell you Connor asked him to come down from Vermont to help him take down Slater?"

"Ah, yes. Now I remember. So, now that Slater is gone, will Ronan return home?

"Connor offered him a permanent place in the firm."

"That's great," Vinea said. "I guess I kind of messed things up though. Once I became pregnant, Devon decided to stay home with me."

EmmaLee clasped her friend's hand. "I'm sure Connor is just fine with Devon running the other office."

Connor helped EmmaLee up. "Let's grab something to eat. You'll need your energy for later."

EmmaLee chuckled. "I am starving. You two coming, Vinea?"

She looked up at Devon. "I'd like to rest for a bit longer. We had a snack on the drive down here, and ever since I got pregnant, certain foods haven't settled well with me."

"Don't worry. I'll make up a plate for you when you're ready," Devon said as he sat next to her.

Now that Vinea was in good hands, EmmaLee and Connor meandered over to the buffet table. "Oh, my. It looks like your mom planned for a hundred guests. Do most shifters have such a healthy appetite?" she asked.

"I'm afraid so."

"Before we have kids, I guess I need to find a job to pay for food."

Connor laughed. "You just might."

While EmmaLee picked out her food, she couldn't help but watch Ronan who was openly staring at Blair. She nudged Connor. "What's up with him? He can't take his eyes off of Jackson's sister."

Connor shrugged. "He's single. She's single."

That was a lame answer. "I think it's more than that."

"Even if there is, it's none of our business."

Well darn. It was still fun to speculate. As they moved through the line, Connor introduced her to Elana and Kalan.

EmmaLee glanced from Kalan to Jackson. "I can see the family resemblance."

"Thank you. I'm just happy Blair takes after our mom. I wouldn't wish my unruly hair or big nose on any woman."

Everyone laughed. The clinking of glass sounded, and the crowed quieted.

Mr. and Mrs. McKinnon were standing by the unlit fireplace in the living room smiling. "Thank you all for coming—not that you had a choice," Mr. McKinnon said.

This time, EmmaLee laughed along with the crowd. Only Finn remained sober, poor guy. She wondered when he'd find peace.

"We are here today to celebrate our newest family member. EmmaLee Donovan. She and Connor have mated. While they were brought together because of a bad situation, love prevailed. Please welcome, EmmaLee." Everyone clapped.

"Thank you," she said when the crowd quieted. "It's a great honor to be part of the McKinnon family."

"Connor?" his dad said with a knowing nod.

Connor turned her toward him and wrapped his arms around her waist. "You've made me a happy man, Em. With your demons vanquished, may your life with me be filled with love and adventure." He lightly kissed her then looked at her as if she was expected to say something.

Wow. That was a hard act to follow. She inhaled then let out a big breath. "While our relationship started off on a rocky path—mostly because you were stubborn—I'm very glad you finally saw the light." That got a chuckle from everyone.

As much as she wanted to reference Connor's attempt to slay a dragon, the McKinnons felt it would be wiser to keep that story under wraps—except to Vinea.

The crowd chanted, "Kiss her, kiss her..."

And kiss her he did.

Don't forget to sign up for my newsletter to receive three free books, as well as up-to-date information on my stories. If you prefer to only receive notices regarding my releases, follow me on BookBub.

http://smarturl.it/o4cz93?IQid=MLite

bookbub.com/authors/vella-day

I hoped you enjoyed EmmaLee and Connor's story. Up next is the first book in a Silver Lake spin off series called HIDDEN REALMS OF SILVER LAKE, starring Finn McKinnon and Kaleena Sinclair—a dragon shifter from the realm of Tarradon. But don't worry, Ronan and Blair will have their story told.

Here's the first chapter from AWAKENED BY FLAMES.

FIRE SHOT THROUGH Kaleena Sinclair's body, and she stiffened as the poison coursed through her, stretching and then contracting her veins. Shooting arrows of pain aimed straight for her heart, and the inability to stop any of it made her pulse race faster than any dragon could fly.

To keep from falling off her bar stool, she gripped the shiny counter in front of her, all the while trying to make sense of what was happening. Sounds faded, and the bartender's face blurred. Her mouth turned sand dry. Then the sheer terror of possible death slammed into her.

"Are you okay?" the bartender asked. Or at least she thought that's what he said.

"I think so." Embarrassment made her lie. Because it would hopefully only take a minute for her dragon to heal her, she tried to relax, but her animal wasn't succeeding fast enough.

It's Seliarus, her dragon said. *This will take time. I'm sorry.*

Oh shit. This stuff was very rare, and if ground into a dust and ingested, it was extremely dangerous to a dragon. While it wouldn't kill her in an of itself, if she were lured into battle in her state of weakness, it would be deadly.

Had Christian slipped it into her drink? Or had the bartender laced her wine when she and Christian were on the dance floor?

Eyes wide, Kaleena looked around to see if anyone else was experiencing the same devastation. She'd come here with one of her coworkers, but Denise had received an emergency phone call and had to leave. Kaleena would have left with her, but this guy, Christian insisted she dance with him one time.

He'd excused himself a minute ago to use the facilities, so maybe he was ill too. Had she and Christian both been drugged, or had he been responsible for the burning acid wreaking havoc inside her? Kaleena didn't think she was that bad a judge of character.

Get us out of here! her dragon pleaded, snapping her focus back to getting away from the crowded bar.

Kaleena tried to push back her stool, but her muscles failed to cooperate.

Suddenly Christian appeared next to her, looking healthy. "Jeez, Kaleena. You don't look so good," Christian said, full of sympathy. "Let me help you."

The bartender placed a glass of water on the bar. "Drink this. It'll make you feel better."

She reached to take it, but then thought he might have been the one to lace her drink, so she let her hand return to gripping the counter. Before she was able to turn around, a wave of nausea made her almost fall off the stool, but Christian caught her.

"I'm taking you to the Emergency room," he said.

Kaleena was too disoriented to argue, but when he wrapped an arm around her waist to help her up, her mind snapped. Suddenly, she was convinced he was this evil warlock sent to harm her. Kaleena had been trained to fight, and she used what little strength she had left to swing a fist at his face. It was as if the air was made of clay though, and her delivery came out way too slow. No surprise, Christian was able to duck before she could connect.

Fight, dragon, fight, she pleaded.

"I'm trying to help you, Kaleena," Christian said.

Was he? So what if his support was all that was keeping her upright. "I'm okay."

"No you aren't. You can barely remain upright." Christian helped her off the stool and then managed to weave them through the crowd toward the back entrance. As soon as she stepped outside, her vision turned black and her knees buckled.

WHEN KALEENA AWOKE, her head was pounding something fierce. She slowly eased open her eyes to mostly darkness. Where the hell was she? Only scant light filled the small, disgustingly smelly space. From the stench, this wasn't a hospital. The drugs were still in her system and were definitely messing with her ability to focus well.

Pushing up on her elbows, she looked around, but she only remained upright for a moment. Weakness attacked her, and she fell back onto what felt like a cot resting on top of rocks. Even though cold dampness seeped into her body, she didn't have the energy to rub her arms to warm herself.

Don't move, her dragon warned.

No problem. I couldn't if I wanted to.

To help ease the ache stabbing her eyes, she palmed her lids and pressed inward. The pain eased slightly. Not only was her head throbbing, her stomach was threatening to revolt. This had to have been a mistake. If she lived long enough to tell her family what had happened, they would make certain the perpetrator would be punished for his indiscretion.

Sounds slowly filtered into her drugged mind. Something clanked, feet shuffled, and moans sounded, but she couldn't quite figure out her location. Pleading with her body to get rid of this devil potion inside her, she rolled onto her side and held in a moan. Kaleena blinked and focused on the small dirty white sink jutting out from a wall made from stone. Next to it sat a metal toilet. Cot, sink, toilet. Was she in some kind of jail cell? If so, why? It wasn't as if she'd committed a crime. And where was Christian? He was supposed to take her to the Emergency Room. Or was he being held captive too? Goddess this was such a nightmare.

When her vision finally cleared, her body turned even colder. Knives protruded at six-inch intervals from the walls. And not just a few knives, mind you—a whole shit ton of knives.

With a gargantuan effort, Kaleena managed to sit up and ease her feet to the floor. An ache stronger than the strength of ten dragon claws filled her, but she pushed aside the discomfort and glanced upward. Holy goddess. The eight-foot by eight-foot cell had daggers jutting down from the ceiling too. What kind of sick bastard had kidnapped her? At least the fourth wall was merely barred.

Drugged and imprisoned, but why? For money? Or did this person have a vendetta against her family? Perhaps her father or uncle had threatened to expose some deadly secret, and her kidnapper planned to use her as leverage to keep them quiet.

Think!

She was the head of public relations for SinCas Mining and Gems, but it wasn't as if she wielded a lot of power. Okay, that wasn't totally true. Her family was one of the most powerful and wealthy in all of Tarradon since they owned the two largest mines in the realm and employed a ton of the local shifters and humans. And yes, she possessed a level of magic the Royals wished they had.

Not only were the workers at SinCas always treated well, the Sinclairs and Caspians gave to many charities and supported those in need. She wracked her brain to think if she'd mention her last name to Christian. Even if she had, he didn't seem like the type to be after her for her money since he was a highly successful lawyer. Or had that been a lie?

Nothing made sense to her addled brain. At least if her captor demanded a ransom, her parents would find her. Whether she'd be alive was another matter.

Lay back down, her dragon said. *I need to heal you.*

Kaleena did as her dragon asked, and she closed her eyes once more to help center herself. The stench, which was a combination of unwashed bodies, mold, and stale air, pushed past acceptable, causing bile to rush up her throat. Forcing herself to reach the sink that was a mere two feet away in time, she bent over and vomited. Her knees weakened, and she dropped to the filthy floor. Jeez, she had to get out of there.

And she would too if only she could figure out how. Given all of the knives surrounding her, shifting was out of the question. Her nearly twenty-foot wings would be shredded in seconds. Only another dragon would be so cruel to think of that.

As Kaleena inhaled deeply, her body became wracked with a coughing fit. After she forced herself to calm, she rose to her feet but instantly dropped back down as a wave of dizziness assaulted her again. Damn drugs. No one was going to stop her from doing what she needed to do however. She was a Guardian, for goddess sake—imbued with magic and strength. She would escape.

With her lungs still on fire, Kaleena crawled back to the cot and dragged herself on top. One of her talents should enable her to escape. Only which one? She was strong and fast in the air, but shifting inside the cell wasn't possible. Cloaking only occurred in her shifted form too. Damn. If only she possessed the talent to teleport, she could get out of there right now.

Then an idea struck. There were hundreds of weapons surrounding her. All she had to do was extract one of the knives and wait for her captor to visit. If he was a dragon—which she suspected was the case—she'd stab him in the top part of the heart—the one vulnerable spot on his body. With the element of surprise on her side, she might be able to kill him.

Renewed by her fresh idea, she tried to stand once more. This time she succeeded. Focusing on keeping her balance, she made it to the sink and held on. Not wanting to slice up her hand when she tugged on the knife to remove it, she slipped off her lightweight jacket with the intention of wrapping it around the knife to pull it out.

To her great dismay, the moment the fabric came in contact with the metal, it jutted out from the wall another ten inches. Holy hell. If she merely brushed against the wall, the blade would impale her.

Strong footsteps sounded down the hallway. She quickly lowered her arm and slipped on her jacket then had to grab the bars to steady herself.

"Hello?" she called out.

A moment later, a man in a khaki uniform appeared. Unfortunately, the small logo on the pocket wasn't something she recognized, and the letters were too small to read. Damn. He handed her a metal cup but said nothing.

Not wanting to piss him off, she took his offering. "Thank you. Can you tell me why I'm here?"

As he stepped closer, his sour breath made her lean back. The man opened his mouth wide and laughed. Oh, dear god, he had no tongue. What kind of monster would do that to another person—especially to another dragon? Acid burned in her stomach at the injustice.

She stood as straight as she could without wincing to show him she wasn't afraid—even though she was. "I'm Kaleena Sinclair. Please ask my captor to come here and face me." She hoped her name would mean something to him.

The guard slammed his hand against her bars and leaned forward as if to give her some kind of warning. He glared at her and then grinned before shuffling back down the hallway. Well, that didn't go as well as she'd hoped.

The energy drain to remain upright overwhelmed her, and she returned to the cot. Kaleena needed to go over what had happened with Christian in order to figure out how she'd ended up there.

During the prelude to their three-minute dance, had he hinted at anything to indicate he was involved in some scheme to retaliate against her family? She didn't recall anything. While she'd never met him before tonight, he seemed like a nice guy.

Gaining strength slowly, she stood and paced, accessing the situation. So far, only one guard had stopped by, but she wasn't so naïve to believe there weren't more close by.

A whimper came from someone near, and Kaleena stilled.

"Hello?" Kaleena called out.

Silence. Even the small cry had stopped.

"Who are you?" Perhaps the caged person thought this was a trap. "I'm Kaleena Sinclair. Maybe we can help each other."

"Sinclair?" The woman whispered the name with reverence.

"Yes." Kaleena's pulse sped up.

"I'm Danita. Why are *you* here?" she asked.

That was a good question. "I'm not sure, but someone drugged me."

"Me too." The desperation in the woman's voice tore at her.

"Are you a white lighter?" Kaleena lowered her voice when she said the last word. It was the only logical explanation for why they'd both been taken.

"Um…yes." It was as if she was afraid to admit it in case a guard was near.

"When did they take you?"

"I think a week ago."

Kaleena's shoulders slumped. This was worse than she thought. As much as she wanted to speak with this woman, there was no telling if anyone was monitoring their conversation. She looked around the hallway, checking the area near the ceiling to locate any cameras, but she found none. "How many other captives are there here?"

"I don't know."

Kaleena returned to her pacing, careful not to walk too close to the walls. She stopped. "Are there knives sticking out of your walls?"

she asked the other captive, trying to see if every cell was equipped with such torture.

"Knives? No."

A heavy door opened, wheels squeaked, and then what sounded like metal trays were being slid across the floor. One scraping noise. Then two. And three. Finally, the same guard who'd handed her a drink appeared in front of her cage. He bent down and delivered a tray under her cell bars.

Without making eye contact, he left the same way he came, implying there were four prisoners. Were the others witches? And were any of the prisoners at the other end dragons?

She glanced down at her food. The porridge looked bland, but the bowl of vegetables was appealing. The problem was she didn't trust they wouldn't drug her again. For the time being, she'd go hungry.

Dropping onto her cot once more, she closed her eyes for a moment and allowed her mind to wander to Finn McKinnon—her safe haven each night. Even though she'd only connected with him in her dreams, he'd given her great solace. Finn, a werewolf, was from the Earth realm who she'd been dream-walking with for a while. He was her mate!

Over the last few weeks, their minds had grown into one, communicating and feeling so intensely, she almost felt as if they were in the same room. When she dream-walked with him, they'd been intimate too. For her, love had bloomed. But she'd been careful not to scare him. Telling him they were mates—or that she was a dragon—might have caused him to shut her out. And she couldn't chance that.

As much as she wanted to stay awake to figure out some kind of escape plan, her best hope might be to have Finn help her—a man who'd didn't know Tarradon existed. Hell, he'd questioned her many times whether she was real. Promising him that someday they'd meet didn't seem to be enough for him. Well, the time might be closer than he realized. To contact him, however, she needed to dream. That meant she had to fall asleep, and the damn lumpy cot wasn't going to make that chore easy.

FINN TOSSED AND turned. Normally when Kaleena came to him in his dreams, her brightness soothed his soul and excited his wolf. Not tonight though. Everything was different—darker, somber, and even frightening. While her face was always blurry and her long, red hair was swept behind her back, her body was in shadows this time.

"Finn?" Kaleena called as if she were very far away.

"What's wrong?" He'd become accustomed to her coy and flirtatious tone. She often shared some things about herself, while holding back at the same time, but this time was different.

"I need your help," she pleaded.

From the way her voice cracked, she wasn't used to asking for aid. In his dream world, Finn was invincible and capable of doing anything. *"What can I do?"*

"I'm being held prisoner. I need you to come to Tarradon."

He wondered why his imaginary woman had chosen this scenario to play out with him. *"Why of course. I'll ride in on a white steed and save you."*

"Finn, this is no joking matter. I'm real. You have to believe me. I need you."

Finn rolled over, his mind in a confused dream state. At times he wanted to believe that the woman in his head was alive, and that they'd even met at one time, but how could she be flesh and blood? Kaleena only appeared when he slept.

Because she sounded so desperate, he agreed to play along. *"Okay, I believe you. You said you live in Tarradon? Where is that exactly? And how can I reach you?"*

"Tarradon is a different realm from Earth. My best guess is that I'm still in Edendale, which is a town in the province of Avonbelle. Getting here will be tricky. You have to find a portal in order to come."

"A different realm? I don't even know how portals work."

"Someone must know. Ask a white lighter."

"A white lighter?" He could guess what she meant by the meaning, but he wanted to be sure.

"You call them witches."

The fact she used a name he wasn't familiar with gave credence to the fact she was real. *"I'll try."*

"If you don't help me, I might die."

PACK WARS (Paranormal)
Training Their Mate (book 1)
Claiming Their Mate (book 2)
Rescuing Their Virgin Mate (book 3)
Box Set (books 1-3)
Loving Their Vixen Mate (book 4)
Fighting For Their Mate (book 5)
Enticing Their Mate (book 6)

MONTANA PROMISES (Full length contemporary)
Promises of Mercy (book 1)
Foundations For Three (book 2)
Montana Fire (book 3)
Hart To Hart (book 4)
Burning Seduction (book 5)
Montana Promises Box Set (books 1-3)

ROCK HARD, MONTANA (contemporary novellas)
Montana Desire (book 1)
Awakening Passions (book 2)

HIDDEN HILLS SHIFTERS (Paranormal)
An Unexpected Diversion (book 1) – FREE
Bare Instincts (book 2)
Shifting Destinies (book 3)
Embracing Fate (book 4)
Promises Unbroken (book 5)

SOUTHERN SHIFTERS KINDLE WORLDS
Bear 'N Dirty

WERES & WITCHES OF SILVER LAKE
A Magical Shift (book 1)
Catching Her Bear (book 2)
A Surge of Magic (book 3)
The Bear's Forbidden Wolf (book 4)
Her Reluctant Bear (book 5)
Freeing His Tiger (book 6)
Protecting His Wolf (book 7)
Waking His Bear (book 8)
Melting Her Wolf's Heart (book 9)
Her Wolf's Guarded Heart (book 10)

A NASH MYSTERY (Contemporary)
Sidearms and Silk (book 1)
Black Ops and Lingerie (book 2)

Author Bio

Want 3 FREE books? Sign up for my newsletter.

COPY AND PASTE INTO YOUR BROWSER:
http://smarturl.it/o4cz93?IQid=MLite

Check out my latest interview on You Tube:
youtube.com/watch?v=sQo5pyyVMDI

Not only do I love to read, write, and dream, I'm an extrovert. I enjoy being around people and am always trying to understand what makes them tick. Not only must my books have a happily ever after, I need characters I can relate to. My men are wonderful, dynamic, smart, strong, and the best lovers in the world (of course).

I believe I am the luckiest woman. I do what I love and I have a wonderful, supportive husband, who happens to be hot!

Fun facts about me

(1) I'm a math nerd who loves spreadsheets. Give me numbers and I'll find a pattern.

(2) I just moved to Costa Rica and live on the beach!

(3) I also like to exercise. Yes, I know I'm odd.

I love hearing from readers either on FB or via email (hint, hint).

Social Media Sites

Website:
www.velladay.com

FB:
www.facebook.com/vella.day.90

Twitter:
@velladay4

Gmail:
velladayauthor@gmail.com

www.ingramcontent.com/pod-product-compliance
Lightning Source LLC
Chambersburg PA
CBHW022009170626
46808CB00001B/344